TWO BAD BOYS TRYING TO GO LEGIT...
ONE GOOD GIRL WHO COULD BE THEIR DOWNFALL.

Max and Jesse grew up on the streets of Philadelphia, working for the city's most successful crime boss before going straight. They're inseparable, their friendship honed by danger. They share everything, including a burning desire for the same woman. But an affair, while they're still untangling themselves from their past, could be dangerous, not only to their friendship but to their lives. And to hers.

Mary Alice has always walked the straight and narrow, but her secret craving for Max and Jesse is fast becoming an obsession. They don't fit into her safe little world of family, friends and work. That doesn't stop her from wanting these intensely sexual men who fascinate her. When fate hands her an opening, Mary Alice proposes an indecent arrangement guaranteed to rock their worlds.

Their powerfully erotic relationship is shattered in an instant. Jesse and Max stand united even though they're miserable without her. Mally is hurt and angry but she's not ready to give up on them. She has to make them understand that they're safer together. And that she's tougher than they realize.

AN INDECENT
ARRANGEMENT

AN INDECENT ARRANGEMENT

STEPHANIE JULIAN

MOONLIT NIGHT PUBLISHING

Don't miss updates about new books and sales. Join Stephanie's newsletter on her website at www. stephaniejulian.com.

Don't miss any of the books in the Indecent series:

An Indecent Proposition
An Indecent Affair
An Indecent Arrangement
An Indecent Longing
An Indecent Desire

1

"Seriously. You're stalking her? Buddy, you need a new hobby."

Max Burdanov stifled a sigh and refused to rise to his friend's bait.

"I'm seeing a movie. Is that a crime?"

Jesse Kanatawa stepped up to his side as Max waited in a ridiculously long line for snacks at the concession counter.

"Nope, not a crime."

Max heard the smirk in Jesse's voice and gritted his teeth. "You know you don't need to be here, right?"

"Uh-huh."

Max bit back another sigh as he reached the counter. "I guess this means you're seeing the movie, too. You want Milk Duds or M&Ms?"

"You know I don't eat that shit. Get me popcorn. So what torture am I being subjected to?"

Max ordered from the girl behind the counter who looked like she was being tortured with dull knives as she got their order.

"I have no idea what the movie is. Probably some chick flick."

Jesse grunted. "Great."

"You can leave."

Jesse lifted an eyebrow at him. "Uh-huh."

Max released his pent-up sigh as he paid for their snacks and shoved a soda and the bag of popcorn at Jesse then picked up his own soda and box of Junior Mints. "We've had no trouble."

"Which doesn't mean it isn't coming."

Max headed toward the theater where the movie he really didn't want to see was playing, Jesse right behind him. "I know that. I just..." He stopped just before entering the theater. "You're right. This is a mistake."

Jesse's hand in the middle of his back forced him to keep walking.

"Christ, you're easy." Jesse huffed. "It's been six months. Loosen the reins a little. You want to stalk the girl? Go for it. Just don't be a pussy about it."

Max curbed the urge to elbow Jesse in the stomach. He didn't want to draw any attention. As far as anyone here knew, they were two guys seeing a movie. Nothing out of the ordinary.

Luckily, this theater loaded from the back so Mary Alice Dubrosky wouldn't see him. Not that he expected her to care that he was here. Hell, the girl probably hadn't thought about him since she'd seen him weeks ago.

He, however, had become obsessed. And that was dangerous. Mainly for Mary Alice. But mostly to Max's sanity.

Cutting right into the half-empty theater's back row, they sat at the very end, backs to the wall.

The teenager in the center of the row, his arm around a girl, gave him a dirty look.

Sorry, buddy. Hate to cockblock you, but I've got a woman to stalk.

Max caught Jesse grinning at the guy, who quickly turned away.

"Don't scare the natives." Max settled into his chair, elbowing Jesse's arm off the armrest between the seats.

"Buzzkill."

"Fuck you."

Jesse laughed and Max saw the two women three rows in front of them glance over their shoulders. And linger long enough to smile at him and Jesse.

Max acknowledged them with a nod then looked away. He had no interest.

He and Jesse got a lot of double takes when they were together. Max knew he wasn't hard on the eyes but Jesse... Jesse looked like he belonged on a fucking billboard selling underwear.

Jesse had taken more than his share of shit from the other guys in their organization for his exotic looks, thanks to his Latino mother and half-Asian father, but now that he and Max had gone out on their own... Jesse didn't take shit anymore.

Max glanced at his best friend and realized Jesse hadn't even seen the women checking them out. Totally oblivious as he tossed popcorn in his mouth.

Out of the corner of his eye, he saw the women roll their

eyes at each other. Max figured he and Jesse had just been labeled gay.

Not true but they did have a closer relationship than most men ever would. Yes, they had sex together but always with a woman between them.

"So who's she with?" Jesse slumped into his seat, stretching his legs out in front of him. "And holy shit. When did they start making theaters with leg room and rocking chairs?"

"How the hell do I know who she's with? And I don't think I've been in a movie theater in more than a decade."

"Hmm. I think the last movie we saw was in high school so that's at least thirteen years. Want me to see if I can identify her?"

Max wanted to say no but he was an idiot so... "Yeah. Sure."

"I'm surprised you don't know already." Jesse tapped away on his phone. "How long have you been stalking her?"

Not rising to Jesse's bait took a concerted effort of will so Max popped Junior Mints in his mouth.

"Bethann Riedel," Jesse finally said. "BFF since first grade."

Max turned to Jesse with a grimace. "What the fuck is 'BFF'?"

"Best friend forever." Jesse grinned. "You know, like us."

Max gave Jesse the finger and turned back to the screen as the lights dimmed and the previews started but he breathed a silent sigh of relief.

Jesse seemed more like his old self every day. He'd been in a heightened state of awareness since he and Max had taken over parts of Mickey's former empire. Since they lived together, Max knew Jesse hadn't been sleeping more than a couple of hours a night.

Max tried not to make it obvious that he was worried about Jesse but...he was worried about Jesse.

And he knew Jesse was worried about him.

Especially because, yeah, he'd been stalking a certain redhead.

Christ, he really was an idiot. He shouldn't be here. He should be anywhere but here. But for the past six months, since the moment he'd met her, he'd been obsessed.

What the hell was it about her?

She wasn't conventionally beautiful. She was so sweetly adorable, she should come with a diabetes warning. He wasn't sure if it was the copper hair that fell to the middle of her back in loose waves or the pale green eyes or the button nose or the full pink lips that he wanted to crush under his.

Or watch as she used them to suck off Jesse while Max slid into her from behind.

Fuck.

He shifted in his chair, trying not to make it obvious he needed to relieve the pressure of his hard-on.

Of course Jesse noticed, his almost silent huff of laughter enough for Max to give him the finger. Again.

Now he heard Jesse's laughter above the ear-splitting volume for a preview for the next superhero blockbuster and then another for an action film starring Arnold Schwarzenegger. Hell, Jesse might actually like that one.

But he knew they'd never get to see it unless Mary Alice decided she was going and—

Fuck. This was such a bad fucking idea.

He didn't have time for a woman unless it was to relieve

stress for a night. Mary Alice wasn't that type of girl. Hell, he hadn't spent more than a few minutes at a time with her and he knew that for a fact.

Then why the hell had he followed her to a fucking movie theater just so he could sit twenty rows behind her? He didn't even remember making a conscious decision to follow her.

He'd been driving by Tristan and Adam's office with the intention of stopping to talk to Adam about something. Or had that just been an excuse? He didn't even know now.

Then he'd seen Mary Alice leave the building. He'd watched her walk into the nearest parking garage, watched her drive out a few minutes later.

The next thing he knew, he was following her. He hadn't thought about doing anything more than making sure she got home okay. And when she'd parked in the lot that was nowhere near her apartment, he couldn't help himself. He pulled in a few cars behind her.

Meanwhile, Jesse had used the GPS tracker on his phone to find Max.

And now, here they all were.

Which didn't mean a goddamn thing except they were in the same room.

So what the hell are you doing here?

Damn good question.

Shifting in his seat, he tried to ignore the obvious answer but Max hated lying to himself.

They were here because the last time he and Jesse had had a woman between them, Max's mind had been elsewhere. He'd gone through the motions and got off but the woman moaning in his arms wasn't the woman he wanted.

And Jesse had known. Which was why the woman that night had been a redhead. It just hadn't been the right redhead.

The theater went completely dark and Max tensed before he could stop.

God damn it to hell.

He'd been to enough therapy to know why he reacted the way he did. And he knew he might never get over it because childhood traumas were difficult to overcome, more therapy, blah, fucking blah...

In the next second, the screen erupted in brilliant color and sound as the film started and he began to breathe normally again.

He watched the first couple of minutes, long enough to figure out the movie was a sci-fi saga full of spaceships and aliens. Jesse would love it. Max would rather watch a political thriller than a film where things blew up every ten minutes.

So he returned to staring at the back of Mary Alice's head. He had the perfect view. Which was pretty fucking ridiculous.

He wanted her to be here between them, his arm around her shoulders, listening to her whisper in his ear about the film. Or the weather. Or anything at all.

He remembered the last time he'd seen her, last week at Adam and Tristan's office. He'd stopped to discuss a couple of issues with Adam and Tristan. After Adam's father and uncle had handed over the reins of part of their operation to Max and Jesse, Adam and Tris had become valued sounding boards. Adam, in particular, had a way of looking at things that Max sometimes didn't see.

And Tristan was a total boy scout who provided a completely different outlook. Which came in handy because Max and Jesse had worked for one of Philadelphia's biggest criminal enterprises before trying to go legit.

Max had a lot to deal with lately. He'd known he'd have to wade through a lot of shit to make this work, and he'd thought he was up to the challenge. Thought he'd understood that he'd have to give up a hell of a lot in order to make this work.

He hadn't expected to be blindsided by a tiny redhead who made his dick hard and stirred every protective instinct he had to protect her from the cold, hard world.

The world he lived in, which was no place for a woman like her.

God damn it.

What a fucking exercise in futility.

When the hell was this film going to be over so he could leave and get the hell as far away from her as he could?

Jesse was right. He put her in danger by being here. Hell, anyone in his immediate vicinity was potentially in danger if someone decided to try to take him out.

There were at least five people he could name off the top of his head who'd be happy to get rid of him. Even though he'd made it clear he wanted to go legit, he knew at least three men from the Philly underworld who'd take him out just because he might pose a threat down the road. And they wouldn't care if there was collateral damage.

Max would care. He might act like a stone-cold bastard most of the time but he wasn't. Not completely.

And he wasn't going back. He'd spent all of his life on the wrong side of the law. He was sick of looking over his shoulder, wondering when the ax was going to fall and whether it would be his neck on the block or Jesse's.

And if anything happened to Jesse—

Popcorn kernels hit him in the face and he turned to Jesse with a what-the-fuck look.

Jesse didn't even bother to return his gaze. "For chrissake, Max, shut your brain off for two fucking hours."

Then Jesse went back to shoveling popcorn into his mouth, gaze glued to the screen, looking totally relaxed.

Max took a deep breath and tried to unkink his muscles. But he couldn't completely relax. Neither of them could afford to let their guard down. Either one of them could be in danger at any time.

Probably don't want to think about that too much.

He glanced at Jesse, noting how intently he stared at the screen. Jesse had always loved movies. They'd taken him away from the reality of the drug-addicted mother who'd adored him but couldn't stay sober long enough to make sure he had food and a roof over his head. Or from the grandparents who held the fact of his existence against him and blamed him for his mom's addiction.

Max had retreated into books when his stepfather sank into a bottle and came out swinging on the other side. Or when his mother got in the way of those swings and ended up in the hospital. Or after Max ended up in the hospital when he didn't move fast enough to protect her.

Jesse had brought him books then, either taken from the library or stolen from the supermarket. Neither of them had had money to buy things like books or movie tickets back then. Hell, they hadn't had money for much of anything.

They'd learned what they'd needed to do to survive. To thrive.

They'd risen above. They'd continue to do it now. He'd take them legitimate or die trying.

Which wasn't just a saying.

So there was no way in hell he should be thinking about Mary Alice. He should be looking over his shoulder for an attack. Watching Jesse's back like Jesse watched his. No distractions. They'd only get him and Jesse hurt. Or dead.

So when did they get to enjoy legitimacy?

Fuck.

Silencing a sigh, he tried to take Jesse's advice and shut off his brain. He'd missed too much of the movie to pick up the plot so he went back to staring at the back of Mary Alice's head. In the bright glow from the screen, he saw her turn to her friend and whisper something in her ear that made the other girl nod and laugh.

He'd never heard Mary Alice laugh. Hell, she'd never smiled at him. Whenever he and Jesse showed up at Tristan and Adam's office, she scowled then wiped it away and pretended like she didn't care that he was standing in front of her desk.

If she found out he was here...

"Come on," Jesse muttered in his ear. "We better get out of here before she sees us."

Max flipped his attention back to the screen, where a man and woman kissed as a star burst into flame behind them. Could've been a planet or a spaceship or the freaking Death Star. Hell, he didn't have a clue.

"Don't you want to see the end?"

Jesse shrugged. "Already have. Watched the bootleg a week ago."

Figures.

Sliding out of their seats and out of the theater, they headed for the exit.

Since Max had parked his car in the same garage Mary Alice had used, they'd have to wait until she left before he and Jesse attempted their escape.

The August heat covered them like a blanket as they stepped out onto the sidewalk. They both wore slacks and long-sleeved shirts. Max had his rolled up to his elbows, exposing the stylized lily tattoo on his inner right forearm. Jesse wore an unstructured jacket. The better to conceal his shoulder holster.

Jesse never left the house without his gun. Someday, Max hoped, he wouldn't have to.

By unspoken agreement, they crossed the street to a coffee shop, where Jesse ordered the largest cup of the strongest brew they had. Max settled for a bottle of water. The coffee would negatively impact the effect of the alcohol he planned to have when he got back to the house they owned in Northern Liberties. They'd been rehabbing what had been two separate buildings into one for the past several year.

Max didn't think they'd ever be done.

A few minutes passed before Mary Alice and her friend left the theater. They must've stayed for the credits. Why the hell would anyone sit through a scrolling list of names?

He turned to ask Jesse but the words stuck in his throat when he realized the girls weren't heading for the parking garage.

No, they were headed in the opposite direction. Toward the clubs.

Shit.

Jesse sighed. "Let's go."

"You don't like her, do you?"

They got up to follow the girls, Max's hands shoved in his pockets, Jesse's hanging free at his sides. In case he needed to get to his weapon.

Jesse continued to stare straight ahead. "I never said that."

"No, you didn't. But you don't need to."

"So you're a mind reader now?"

"Yours? Yeah."

Huffing, Jesse shook his head. "You don't have a fucking clue."

The girls walked like they had a purpose, arms linked, laughing. Mary Alice's bright hair swung down her back. He wanted to wrap it around his hand and tug her head back until she stared into his eyes. He wanted her to see him coming when he kissed her. He wouldn't let her up for air until she was breathless.

Then he'd turn her so he could strip off that clingy blue top and skin-tight jeans while Jesse—

Fuck.

If Jesse didn't want her, there was no sense fantasizing. And he'd had some fucking awesome fantasies lately, all starring her and him...and Jesse.

"So enlighten me." Max slid Jesse a look but Jesse was doing his bodyguard thing. His gaze slid all the hell over the place, seeing everything.

Max had learned to be vigilant as a teenager, always

looking over his shoulder for the cops, but Jesse had been the one who had an early warning system hardwired to his brain. It'd saved their asses more times than Max could count.

"Enlighten you about what?"

"Don't play fucking word games. Do you have any interest in her?"

"Sonuvabitch." Jesse stopped, a smile curving his lips. "At least she has good taste in clubs."

Mary Alice and her BFF stood at the entrance to one of the clubs Max and Jesse owned. Well, hell. At least he'd be able to stalk her from the relative comfort and safety of his own property.

The girls had no trouble getting in. It was a slow night but these two wouldn't have had a problem getting in any night. And he'd make sure she never had a problem getting into any of his clubs. Then he'd make damn sure no one ever hassled her.

No one except you.

Shit.

As they made their way around the building to the back entrance, Max stepped in front of the door before Jesse could reach for the handle. Their eyes almost on the same level, Max made sure he could see Jesse's.

"You didn't answer my question."

Jesse sighed, shoving a hand through stick-straight, coal-black hair. He kept it long now because he could. A silent fuck-you to grandparents long gone.

"You want the truth?"

Max nodded, his gaze pinning Jesse in place. "That'd be nice."

Jesse shook his head but didn't drop Max's gaze. "She's exactly my type. Exactly *our* type. And we have *no* fucking right to involve her in our lives. Not now. Maybe not ever. We are in no way in the clear here. Mickey did as much as he could to make sure no one came after us but you know that's not a guarantee. You're still vulnerable."

Max's hands curled into fists against the need to rub at his chest, at the burn in the center. "And that might not ever change. But we're still here. And I'm sick of fucking waiting for what I want." He paused to breathe, trying to calm the runaway pounding of his heart. "I want her. I've wanted her since she stood in front of Tristan's office door and thought she could stop me from getting past her. But this isn't just about me."

Jesse straightened. "Maybe it should be. Or maybe you should stay the hell away from her. I know I should be very, very far away from her."

Max looked into his friend's eyes, searching for some kernel of truth in his words. And found none.

"Bullshit." He said that one word with enough force that Jesse couldn't mistake his meaning. "That's absolute fucking bullshit and you know it."

Jesse sighed again and shook his head, turning to stare back down the street as if he wanted to bolt. But Jesse would never run from Max's side. And Max would never leave Jesse to fend for himself.

After several seconds, Jesse finally turned back to him, dark eyes narrowed and his mouth a flat line. "You want to hear me say it. Fine. I want her. I want her naked and in bed with us. And I know how much you want the same thing and that makes me want it even more."

Jesse had moved closer until only inches separated them. Max knew he wouldn't come any closer.

"But this isn't just our lives, Max. You know that. What if something happens to her? Can you live with yourself?"

Can I?

Max shook his head. "There's never gonna be a good time. And I'm sick of waiting. At some point, we gotta take what we want. Or at least try to. And I want her. Do you trust me?"

Jesse sighed hard. "You know I do. Unconditionally. But this isn't about trust."

Max nodded. "Yeah, it kinda is."

2

"Are you sure you're okay with this?" Bethann grimaced at Mary Alice. "I honestly didn't know Danny was going to be here. He knows it's our night out and he promised he wouldn't intrude."

Mary Alice rolled her eyes at her best friend and laughed. "Seriously, Bethann. Just go dance with the guy. I know you haven't been able to see each other much because you're working opposite shifts. I'm a big girl. I'm completely capable of keeping myself amused."

"Well, at least come over and meet his friends. Who knows?" Bethann waggled her eyebrows. "You might find one you like."

Fat chance.

But because she didn't want her friend to worry, Mary Alice forced a grin then followed Bethann across the room to the booth where her fiancé waited with a smile and two other guys. Nice-looking guys who shook her hand and smiled at her, sizing her up like she was a Hooters waitress.

Though she kept smiling, she had to work hard to keep from grimacing because they were acting like dicks.

They were probably really nice guys…when they weren't drinking. Tonight, however, they'd obviously had a few too many. They shouted at each other over the music and crowded her on both sides of the booth, high-fiving about stupid shit and doing shots they really didn't need.

She wished she and Bethann had decided to go to a diner for a piece of pie or a chocolate milkshake but Bethann had wanted to unwind with a drink and dancing after the movie. And since Bethann was an emergency room nurse who'd just come off a four-day stint of twelve-hour shifts, Mary Alice had agreed.

Now she found herself wondering how she could get out of here without hurting her friend's feelings or getting an unwanted escort home.

When Bethann had suggested this club, Mary Alice had almost suggested another. But that would've meant admitting, if only to herself, that she had some objection to coming *here*.

She didn't. Of course she didn't.

The fact that Max Burdanov and Jesse Kanatawa owned this place meant nothing to her.

Yeah, right.

Then again, maybe she'd ask the bartender if the owners were here tonight. Then, if she had the nerve, she'd ask the bartender to tell Max and Jesse she wanted to see them.

Would they care? Or had she completely misread their interest?

And, oh my god, was she *crazy*? She had to be if she thought she should be anywhere near Max and Jesse.

Adam and Tristan had warned her to stay away from them. Actually, they'd told her flat out to "stay the fuck away from those two sons-of-bitches." Since she didn't think her bosses could read her mind, she had to wonder how the hell they'd known what she was thinking because she'd never said anything about Max and Jesse. Not one word about her ridiculous feelings about them.

About how, when she got near them, she got jumpy, twitchy. Hot. How she had fantasies she had no business having, fantasies she should never act on because she lived in her world and they lived in theirs.

Shit.

"So I told my boss there was no fucking way I was doing that."

She lived in the world where tools like these two on either side of her tried to show how big their dicks were without dropping their pants and proving themselves wrong.

She wanted to roll her eyes but controlled the impulse. Yes, she was twenty-two but she really didn't enjoy the club scene. Too many stupid people acting like idiots. Too much loud, stupid music that didn't have any real instruments. She'd rather be at her brother Tommy's bar in Kensington, shooting pool and talking to the regulars who'd known her since she was born.

All these fake people dressed to impress other fake people made her temples ache. She scowled then quickly covered it when Frat Boy Two offered to get her a drink.

Declining with the excuse she had to get up early tomorrow for work, she gave Frat Boy One a fake smile as he headed toward the bar.

"Was it something we said?"

Frat Boy Two leaned in a little too close for her comfort and she had to rein in her training so she didn't punch him.

Growing up with four older brothers, she'd learned to protect herself. They'd insisted she learn self-defense because they wouldn't always be there to protect her.

Her oldest brother hadn't been able to protect himself.

Shaking off that heartbreaking thought, she focused her attention on the remaining Frat Boy, willing him to back off. But he was either too drunk or too stupid because he shimmied even closer.

Damn, she really didn't want to make a scene. And she didn't want to have to break his fingers if he touched her. But she would if he tried.

She forced a smile and did nothing to hide the fact that it was fake. "Actually, I've had a really long day. I'm not going to be good company tonight."

The guy smiled from behind his perfectly trimmed beard. *Ugh.*

"You're doing just fine, sweetheart. Why don't you tell me what you do for a living?"

Did he actually think she was playing hard to get? Or that she was shy and needed to be coaxed? *Lord, save me from clueless assholes.*

"I really am tired. I think I'll just—"

"Here we go." Frat Boy Two returned from the bar, sliding one glass across the table to his buddy and another one in front of her.

"You can't leave now." Frat Boy One smirked. "Just have one drink. I'm sure your friend would want you to."

No, she really wouldn't. "I'm going to find my girlfriend right now and tell her I'm leaving. Have a good night."

She began to slide out of the booth but Frat Boy Two didn't move.

Damn it. This could get ugly.

She should've gone home after the movie, should've pleaded exhaustion to Bethann and taken her sorry ass back to her apartment.

"I'd appreciate if you'd move."

"Come on, ba—"

His sentence ended in an unmanly yelp as Frat Boy Two slid out of the booth. Quickly and not under his own power.

"I believe the lady would like to leave."

Jesse Kanatawa stood at the entrance to the booth, a large hand on Frat Boy Two's shoulder, fingers digging into the muscle hard enough that the guy looked to be in pain.

She couldn't honestly say that bothered her. He deserved whatever he got. She'd asked nicely and he'd been a dick.

What did bother her was her reaction to Jesse.

Breathe, damn it. Just breathe.

Without another word, she slid out of the booth and walked away, not looking back.

But she barely got ten feet before Jesse caught up to her.

"Are you okay?"

His voice was pitched low but she had no trouble hearing him because he'd leaned down to speak into her ear.

He had to lean down pretty far to do it. He towered over her but she'd never realized how much because he'd never gotten this close. She'd only ever seen him at the office where she worked for Tristan and Adam. And never without Max.

Together, they made her thighs quiver. Alone... Hell, alone he did the same.

She was afraid it wouldn't matter if she was alone with Max or Jesse. She'd have the same damn reaction.

"I'm fine. Thank you for making sure I didn't cause a scene by breaking the guy's nose. I'm going home now."

"Max would like to talk to you. If you have a few minutes."

No. No, no, no. That wasn't going to happen. "I'm sorry. I'm tired."

"Sounds to me like you're running scared because those assholes frightened you. And that means I'm going to have to crack some heads."

She stopped and looked up, seeing the absolute conviction in Jesse's dark eyes. "I'm not running."

Jesse's mouth twitched, as if he wanted to smile but wouldn't allow it. "Glad to hear it. Then you can spare Max a few minutes."

The challenge in his voice made her jaw set and her gaze narrow.

Damn him. "Fine. Just give me a second to tell my friend I'm leaving. And don't touch those boys. They're not worth the trouble."

He didn't acknowledge her last demand. "I'll wait for you by the bar."

Turning on her heel before she changed her mind, she headed for the dance floor, where Bethann and her fiancé Danny moved like a well-oiled machine. They'd been taking lessons together in anticipation of their wedding, but Bethann had always made everyone around her pale in comparison when she danced.

When Bethann saw Mary Alice moving toward her, she waved her hands in the air and started screaming. Not that Mary Alice could hear her. The music was too damn loud. Which also meant Bethann couldn't hear Mary Alice try to tell her she was leaving.

Or maybe Bethann just ignored her as she grabbed Mary Alice's hands and pulled her closer then coerced her into dancing.

Since it meant she avoided Jesse and Max for a few more minutes, she danced. Pushing everything out of her head for the length of the song, she let herself move to the music, a sexy Beyoncé remix that got her blood pumping. She let her body shimmy a little more, let her ass shake just a little more suggestively.

In her head, she was saying "fuck you" to the Frat Boys who'd thought they could intimidate her. And maybe, just maybe, it was the fact that Jesse was watching and Max probably could see her, too.

The song came to an end way too soon. Couldn't put off Jesse any longer.

Leaning in, she spoke directly into Bethann's ear. "Hey, I'm going to head out. It's getting late and I have to be in early. I'm sure Danny won't mind taking you home, considering you're going to the same place."

"Damn, I'm sorry." Bethann looked totally guilty. "I didn't mean to ditch you. Let me tell Danny we're going to skip out. We can get some coffee—"

"No, no. We're good, Bethy. Seriously. I really am tired and I know you need to blow off some steam."

"Are you sure?"

When Mary Alice nodded, Bethann gave her a tight hug. "I'll call you tomorrow. Not too early, of course."

"All right. Do you want Danny and me to walk you back to your car?"

"No, I've got an escort."

Bethann's eyebrows curved up. "Really?"

"Don't look so excited. It's a business associate."

Bethann's gaze now narrowed. "Do people really have business associates anymore? You sound like you're in a spy movie."

Mary Alice rolled her eyes. "He's just a guy who knows Adam and Tristan. I'll be fine."

"All right, but I want a text when you get home."

Mary Alice leaned in for a hug. "You got it. Love you. Have fun."

"I'd say the same to you but I know you too well. Talk to you tomorrow."

Mary Alice tried to shrug off Bethann's offhand comment about having fun, but it stuck with her as she made her way back to the bar where Jesse was holding up the end.

Watching her.

She knew how to have fun. She loved hanging with her friends, loved going to the movies and out to dinner and to bars where there were normal people. But she also loved her job. Loved managing the office for Adam and Tristan, loved the work they did, something different every day, and loved the fact that they helped people.

But lately, Jesse and Max had been creeping into her thoughts more than normal. And that was just stupid on her part. Because they were not just regular worker bees, droning along in some conglomerate.

No, they'd worked for one of the most profitable criminals in Philadelphia since they were teens and they'd just taken over part of the business.

Jesse watched her walk toward him, his expression perfectly blank, although she swore he was hiding a smile. And his eyes...those dark eyes glinted in the low light.

I am not attracted to him. I am not attracted to him. I am not—

Damn, who was she kidding? Certainly not her.

Stopping in front of Jesse, she expected him to turn and lead her away but he didn't. He just stood there, staring down at her.

Crossing her arms over her chest, she raised her eyebrows at him. "What?"

"Are you okay?"

She rolled her eyes. "It takes a lot more than two idiots pissing me off to make me not okay."

"You look tired."

Did she actually hear concern in his voice?

No, she must be delusional. She'd never seen anything in Jesse's actions toward her to indicate interest.

She sighed. "Maybe because I am. It's been a long day."

"Then why are you here?"

Now she rolled her eyes. "Because I had plans with my friend and I'm not eighty years old and I don't need to be in bed."

His gaze narrowed slightly as his gaze dropped to her mouth for several long seconds.

A blush heated her cheeks.

Oh my god, she must be more tired than she'd thought if

all it took for her to get flustered was for him to look at her lips.

No. No, no, no. No way in hell.

"You said Max wanted to talk to me." She made a brushing motion with her hand and his lips quirked. "Well, let's go. Since I look so tired, I should get home soon."

Now he smiled outright and her freaking thighs wanted to clench.

Jesus. She was crazy. Absolutely insane if she thought—

No, she wasn't even going to *think* those thoughts.

Jesse straightened away from the bar where he'd been leaning and waved her toward the door to the right.

Of course, he reached it before she did and held it open for her. The door wasn't all that wide and her shoulder brushed against his chest as she passed.

A shiver worked its way up her back but she refused to let it show. Instead, she tossed her hair over her shoulder and lifted her chin in the air.

She'd find out what Max wanted and she'd go home.

Alone.

Of course alone. Just like every other night.

Grr.

"Something wrong?"

Jesse walked at her side down a long hallway. They passed a couple of doors but Jesse didn't slow.

"Nothing's wrong."

"You seem a little tense."

"I'm fine."

He touched her shoulder, stopping her in her tracks. "Do I scare you?"

She looked up at him, shock evident on her face. "What?"

"You heard me." He stared down at her intently, which seemed to be his default setting.

Her face folded in a frown. "Why would you think that? Are you *trying* to scare me? Because if you are, you're failing miserably."

He didn't look convinced but he started walking again. "Glad to hear it."

Still shaking her head, she followed him another few feet before he stopped in front of the very last door at the end of the hall.

"Do you want me to wait out here?"

Why would he— "Oh, for… Just open the damn door, Mr. Kanatawa. You're starting to piss me off."

He didn't move. "You don't like me much, do you?"

If he only knew. "I don't know you well enough to dislike you."

Which was the truth. But not exactly the whole truth.

His lips curved into a smile now, and she had to make a conscious effort to control her breathing.

Because she *did* like his smile. Much more than she should.

"Fair enough, *carina.*"

Then he turned, knocked twice and opened the door, waving her through in front of him.

Already flustered, she realized this was a really bad idea. Because, hole-lee hell, these men made her mouth water.

Before she'd started working for Tristan and Adam, she'd been a typical teenage girl who thought guys only looked good in ass-hugging jeans and skintight t-shirts.

She'd realized her mistake after seeing the men parading

through the office and understood that a well-cut suit could be just as sexy. Even more so on some men.

Like these two. Of course, she'd never seen Max and Jesse in jeans so maybe she'd have to change her mind—

And no *way* was that going to happen. What the hell was she thinking?

Shoving those rogue thoughts out of her mind, she stopped several feet in front of the massive black desk Max sat behind.

Her heart beat faster than any death metal drummer and her throat dried to the consistency of the Sahara.

Max wanted to talk to her? Fine, he could talk. Didn't mean she had to respond.

Which made her want to roll her eyes at herself. She was being ridiculous. But she still didn't open her mouth.

He met her gaze and held her in place. "Mary Alice. How are you?"

"I'm fine, Mr. Burdanov. How are you?"

His smile made her swallow convulsively.

"I'm good. I understand you were being hassled in the club. We want you to know we don't condone that type of behavior and it'll be taken care of."

"Taken care of, how? There's nothing to take care of. I had it handled."

His gaze narrowed slightly. "I'm sure you did. That doesn't mean we should do nothing. If we don't do something, customers may think we condone men hassling women. And they couldn't be more wrong."

Criminals with standards. How HBO of them.

Not fair. So not fair.

"Fine. But as you can see, I'm in one piece and no harm done."

Max rose and rounded his desk, settling himself on the outer edge, much closer than he'd been before. She had to stick her feet to the floor so she didn't take an instinctive step away.

"I'm glad to hear it."

He exchanged a glance with Jesse, still behind her and out of her line of sight. They were communicating without words, and she had the feeling they were fighting though she had no idea why she thought that.

Their silent conversation only lasted a few seconds and then she had Max's full attention again. Her knees wanted to quake and she locked them tight as he continued to watch her.

"I'd like to take you to dinner tomorrow night. If you're free."

Her mouth dropped open for several seconds before she consciously shut it. But she still had nothing to say.

Completely taken off guard, she shook her head, wondering if she'd heard him correctly. "I'm sorry...did you just ask me out?"

He didn't look at all put off by her obvious confusion. "Yes, I did. I'll understand if it's short notice but then I'll just ask about the next night and the night after that."

She blinked. "Why?"

Max's expression didn't change. "Because I'd like to spend time with you and dinner is a safe option. You choose the restaurant. I can send a car for you if you don't want me to pick you up."

Her mouth opened but she had no idea what she should

say so she closed it again. Max continued to stare, waiting, like he had nothing better to do.

"You want to take me on a date?"

"Yes, I do. Has it been so long since you've had one that you don't remember what they are?"

"I—No! Of course not." Was he laughing at her? "I just don't understand what your angle is."

His head cocked to the side. "My angle?"

"What do you want with me?"

His lips curved up. "How about the pleasure of your company?"

She shook her head. "I'm sorry, I'm having a hard time believing you want to take me out. We don't really know each other."

There was that smile again. "I understand dates are good for that."

"But…"

She couldn't think of anything else to say. What she wanted to say was yes. She wanted to go out with him.

Okay, what she wanted a little more complicated than that but she'd settle for a date with Max. To start.

And that was where everything went off the rails because she shouldn't want to go out with Max. Shouldn't want—

What?

What she couldn't have.

"But what?" Max prompted.

He continued to watch her with those dark blue eyes that stood out against his pale skin, his Russian ancestry stamped so clearly on his face, he could never deny it. His auburn hair was at least five shades darker than her own copper curls and cut short on the sides with a little bit of length on the top. Suitable for business yet still a little rebellious. Or he just hadn't had the time to get it cut lately, what with trying to become a legitimate businessman after years of working for a Russian mob boss.

His eyes narrowed as if he'd read her mind and his mouth tightened. But his expression cleared in the next instant as if it'd never been there.

And since she wanted to believe she wasn't the type of person who held a man's past mistakes against him, she shook those thoughts out of her head.

"But nothing."

With a sigh, he stood and took the few steps to close the distance between them. She had to look pretty far up and she couldn't help a shiver of attraction.

Both Jesse and Max elicited the same response from her. They both made her breathless. That wasn't how normal relationships worked.

Except...her bosses were involved in a multiple-partner relationship and so were their lover's brother and his best friend. They were making it work.

Her parents would be horrified. Because wanting to have sex with two men, at the same time, was strange, right? Aberrant.

And not at all what Max was offering her. He'd asked her out and made no mention of Jesse. So all these fantasies running through her head meant nothing right now.

"I'm not sure that'd be a good idea."

He didn't look surprised by her answer. Which pissed her off.

"And why is that?"

Because you're not the only man I want to date and that scares me.

"Because I'm not sure I want to date anyone right now."

Lies, lies, and more lies.

One side of his mouth quirked, as if he knew exactly what she was thinking. Then he nodded and stood and she thought, for a brief second, that he might lean forward and kiss her.

Instead, he turned his back to her as he walked around his desk to sit in his chair before meeting her gaze again.

"I'm sorry to hear that."

So was she.

She nodded and blinked, shifting her gaze away from his way-too-perceptive one. "I really need to go. I have to be at work early tomorrow."

"Of course." Max's gaze flashed over her shoulder. "Jesse will walk you to your car. I have business I need to handle."

She nodded, mostly because she was afraid she'd make an idiot out of herself by stuttering if she opened her mouth. Then she turned to find Jesse by the door, his hand on the knob.

So anxious to get rid her.

She raised her eyebrows at him. "I *am* capable of walking myself to my car."

Jesse shrugged. "It's late. Humor us."

Us. Yes, she'd love to. God, she was so screwed up.

Shaking her head, she tilted her head back to look at him. "My brothers taught me how to take care of myself."

Jesse waved her ahead of him. "I'm sure they did. I'm still walking you to your car."

Because she hadn't really expected to win this battle, she nodded and headed toward the door.

"Mary Alice."

Max's voice stopped her in her tracks, and she drew in a quick breath before turning to look at him over her shoulder.

"Take care."

He sounded...so final.

And that made her want to tell him she'd made a mistake, that she really did want to go out with him.

She forced herself to walk through the door.

3

Jesse steered Mary Alice toward the service door at the end of the hallway so they wouldn't have to go out through the club.

They didn't speak as they walked out of the building and down the alley.

She barely came to his shoulder, and he had the almost overwhelming urge to put his arm around her and pull her against his side.

Or shove her up against the wall and kiss the hell out of her.

He hadn't been kidding when he'd told Max he didn't have a clue how he felt about this girl. When he thought about her, he had the urge to run the other way. And another, just-as-strong urge to put his mouth on hers.

But for the first time in his and Max's long relationship, they were out of sync.

Mary Alice was the reason. She could put a wedge between them they might never be able to fix.

As they walked in silence to the parking garage, she stared straight ahead. He tried to keep his attention focused on their surroundings. Never knew where the first strike might come from.

When she finally stopped at her car, she opened the door before turning back to him.

Blue eyes solemn, she stared up at him. "Thank you for walking with me but I think I can take it from here."

She didn't smile, but she didn't look scared. In fact—

No. No way did he see attraction in her eyes.

He nodded, watching her because he couldn't not. Because Max had him totally wrong.

"Good night, Mary Alice."

"Good night, Mr. Kanatawa."

Then she climbed into her red Jeep Wrangler. She looked tiny behind the wheel. Young. Defenseless.

Christ, he was a stupid, fucking idiot.

The Jeep started with a muted roar. Someone had obviously worked on that engine and put a little more power into it. Probably one of her brothers.

When she pulled out of the space, she glanced at him, raising an eyebrow as if to say, "See, no problem."

He stifled a smile.

The girl had a sharp tongue and a smart brain, and together they made his dick and every other part of him sit up and take notice.

How the fuck did Max not see that?

Maybe you just got good at hiding things.

The problem was, he and Max didn't hide things from each other. They never had.

They'd shared practically everything since Max had given Jesse half of his sandwich on Jesse's first day in fourth grade.

What Mary Alice didn't know was that he and she shared something, as well. Something darker and more painful and nothing she'd probably want to talk about with him.

When she finally drove out of sight, he headed back to the club. He entered through the front, nodding to the doorman, whose stiff back and sharp nod made him stifle a sigh.

Christ, he was tired of always having to be a hard ass.

Making his way across the floor, he nodded to a few other employees and ignored the women who smiled at him or blatantly rubbed against him as he passed by. He wasn't interested in any of them. Would never be interested in any of them.

Party girls held no appeal for him. The ones who got sloppy drunk and hung all over men and thought they were having a good time. Or the cold, cool ones who thought they were too good for everyone else and, if they stooped to your level for a little fun, well, you should be honored and fall at their feet.

Which meant he didn't meet a lot of women who appealed to him.

As soon as he walked through the door into the back rooms of the club, he breathed a sigh of relief. Stupid but true.

Who would've thought going legit would be so fucking terrifying?

Back at Max's office, Jesse stepped inside and Max looked up from the paperwork he'd been going through.

"Thank you."

Jesse knew why Max had said it but it pissed him off that Max thought he had to.

"What are those?"

Max sighed hard. "The previous owners kept double books. I'm trying to figure out if the club can sustain itself without the extra cash from the games and the girls and the drugs."

"And?"

"I think this one'll make it. We may have to unload one of the other two."

Which meant finding legitimate buyers for a property that was a well-known front for criminal activity because Max couldn't afford to sell that property to any other criminally oriented parties. Not if they wanted to get out of the life.

Jesse sank into his chair by the door. "How bad will that cut into finances?"

"Bad, at first. But after a few months, it should level out."

"And we can hold steady?"

Max sighed, pushing the files away from him as he leaned back in his chair. Closing his eyes, he rubbed them hard before opening them again.

Jesse's hands clenched on the chair arms. "You need some sleep or you're going to fuck something up. Let's go home."

Max shook his head. "I'm fine. And when the hell did you become my nursemaid?"

"See, you're getting cranky. You need some sleep."

"What I need is to get laid but that's not happening tonight."

No, it wasn't. Because the girl Max wanted had just left. And Jesse knew no one else would do now.

"Then I guess you should let me take you home so *I* can get some damn sleep."

Max cocked his head to the side, staring at him intently. "Jesse. What the fuck's going on with you? I feel like you've got this secret and I don't know what it is and it's driving me fucking crazy."

The problem was Jesse had secrets, one in particular he wasn't in the mood to share, but he'd give Max something because the guy was genuinely dumbfounded.

"I'm worried about you. About the long hours and the amount of alcohol you've been consuming and the stress you're putting on yourself. I'm worried about someone deciding you're vulnerable now that Mickey's gone and that I won't be able to protect you because we don't have the backup we had before. I'm worried that you won't let me hire additional guys for protection because you don't want to look like you're building a force.

"I'm worried about the Dominicans and the Mexicans and the Italians and the South Philly gangs who're starting to make a push north. I'm worried about the Baltimore Russians who gave Mickey a run for his money the last time they made a push into his territory. I'm worried that trying to go legit is going to get you killed, and you better fucking know that if they take you out, I'll be right behind you."

Jesse knew that was the one thing Max feared above all else. That Jesse would get hurt because someone came after Max. And that's probably exactly what would happen. Because Jesse's sole purpose was to keep Max safe. The problem was, that's what Max thought about Jesse.

After several seconds of staring at each other, Max finally drew in a deep breath. "Is this your way of telling me I shouldn't've asked her out?"

Was it? *Fuck.* Maybe a little. But more, it was everything that'd been building for the past few months since Mickey Oleksy and his brother had moved back to Moscow, given over most of their holdings to the Antonoff family, and left Max and Jesse with the rest, the businesses they were trying to take legitimate. That they could build into their future.

"No," Jesse said. "You're right about one thing. You still deserve to have a life. If that means we gotta be even more careful about shit, then I guess we do. So, you gonna ask her out again? She wanted to say yes. You know that, don't you?"

Max didn't answer right away, just continued to stare. Then he sighed. "She seemed pretty damn adamant to me."

"That's because you were too focused on what she was saying and not what she wasn't."

Max frowned. "And you're a mind reader now?"

Christ. Jesse didn't bother to hide his sigh. "I could see her expression, asshole. She likes you."

Shaking his head, Max gave him the finger. "Yeah, right. Which is why she turned me down." He thrust a hand through his hair. "Christ, you're right. It was a huge fucking mistake to ask her out."

"No, damn it. I'm being an idiot. Call her tomorrow and ask her out again."

"No. Adam will fucking break my head open if he finds out I've been stalking her."

Jesse shook his head. "When the fuck did you become such a pussy?"

"Fuck you, Jesse."

Silence fell for several seconds until Max shoved away from the desk. "You're right. I'm not gonna get anything else done tonight."

"Max—"

"No. Just...I don't want to talk about it anymore. Let's go."

Jesse watched Max head out the door before pushing to his feet to follow.

4

"Hey, Bethy. Is everything okay? What's going on? You sounded really upset on the phone."

As Mary Alice slipped into the chair opposite her best friend, she noticed Bethann's red-rimmed eyes and her pale complexion.

"No. Everything's really not okay. Oh, my god, Mally. It's bad."

Reaching across the table, Mary Alice took hold of Bethann's hand and squeezed. "What's going on?"

Bethann had called Mary Alice this morning and asked her to meet at their favorite coffee shop for lunch. Since Bethann's voice had trembled when she'd spoken, Mary Alice had agreed immediately, even though she'd woken with a headache, a result of tossing and turning most of the night.

After she'd nearly taken off Adam's head when he'd dared to ask her what was wrong, Adam and Tristan had practically tiptoed past her office and she'd figured it would do her good to get away from her desk for an hour or so.

Now, she wondered if she was going to be in a worse

mood when she left. Bethann didn't tend to be dramatic so something was definitely wrong.

"I don't even know where to start." Bethann shook her head, looking ready to cry again.

"Just spit it out, Bethy. Is someone hurt?"

"No, no. It's nothing like that. God, it's just…"

"What?"

"It's Danny."

"Did something happen to him? Come on, Bethy. I need a little more to work with."

Bethan's face crumbled. "He screwed up. Big time."

"How? Is he in jail?"

Bethann shook her head, tears at the corners of her eyes. "No, but he's in trouble. Bad trouble." She took a deep breath, as if she couldn't get enough air to say the words. "He wanted to make some extra money for the wedding, and a friend took him to a game. Only it wasn't just any game. It was some underground thing run by one of the city's crime families."

Mary Alice's lungs turned to stone for several seconds. "Who ran the game?"

"He said he's in debt to the Antonoffs. I've never heard of them but Danny's terrified. Some guys stopped us on our way to our car last night. I thought they were going to hurt us." The tears broke through and started to fall. "Danny wants to call off the wedding until he can pay them back. But…"

"But what?"

"It's a lot of money."

The pit in Mary Alice's stomach grew. "How much? I've got—"

"It won't be enough." Bethann kept shaking her head. "He owes them close to $50,000."

Oh shit.

Bethann picked up a napkin to wipe at her eyes. "I don't know how we're going to pay it. And if we don't... I don't know what they're going to do to him. I don't know what to do. Neither of our parents have that kind of money. No bank will give us a loan. I'm so scared."

Bethann drew in a shaky breath as Mary Alice's mind started to work through the problem. Which was why Bethann had come to her. She knew Mary Alice would be able to think of something. She always did.

Even if it was possibly the stupidest idea in the world.

And it really was.

Reaching across the table, Mary Alice took Bethann's hand. "All right, listen. I may know someone who might be able to help."

Bethann hitched in a breath. "What? Seriously? Oh my god, are you serious?"

"Yeah, I am." She was also crazy for thinking of going to him. Considering she'd just turned him down for a date last night.

Bethann shook her head, staring at Mary Alice like she'd just smacked her upside the head with a happy stick. "Who?"

"No one you know. And you can't tell anyone about this. You have to promise. Not even Danny. If I can fix this, no one can know I had any part in this."

As Bethann promised to keep her mouth shut on pain of death, Mary Alice was already trying to figure out how she was going to ask Max for the favor she needed.

She didn't have a clue.

When she and Bethann split after lunch, Bethann still teary eyed but at least not bawling, Mary Alice took the long way back to the office.

The heat and humidity closed around her and she was sweaty and overheated by the time she walked through the door. But she'd managed to work through the conversation she needed to have with a certain former Russian gang member.

Christ, was she serious about this? Did she really think asking Max—

"Hey, Earth to Mary Alice. You in there?"

Mary Alice's head popped up as Tristan rapped his knuckles on her door. Her fingers froze over her phone before she curled them into her palm and let her fist rest on her desk.

"I'm here. What do you need?"

"Adam and I have an appointment so we're leaving early, which means so can you." He paused and his eyes narrowed. "Hey, is something wrong?"

Hell, yes, there was something wrong. Her best friend's fiancé went and fucked up his life and now she was going to fix it. Hopefully.

"No, nothing's wrong. Why?"

"Because you've got that look on your face."

"What look?"

"Hey, did you— Fuck, what's wrong?"

Adam walked through the door and up to her desk, frowning, gaze narrowed to a squint.

Mary Alice rolled her eyes and pushed away from her desk. She wanted to bang her head against the desktop but knew that'd just freak out the guys even more.

She should've known they'd figure out she had something on her mind. She just hadn't realized how fast they'd be.

"I don't know." Tristan shot Adam a quick look before staring down at her again. "She won't talk."

Crossing her arms over her chest, she glared back at them. "Because there's nothing to say. Nothing's wrong."

Adam and Tristan exchanged a glance.

"You were out last night, weren't you?" Tristan's head cocked to the side. "Did something happen?"

"No, nothing happened. Why do you think something's wrong? I'm sitting here working. How does that equate to something being wrong?"

"Don't ever play poker for high stakes." Adam dropped into the chair opposite her desk, watching her like a hawk watched a mouse in the field. "No poker face at all."

She loved her bosses. She really did. But she was going to strangle them one day. And they'd never see her coming.

Right now, though, she *did* have something to hide and it pissed her off that they'd been able to read her so easily. So it was their own fault she was about to torture them. Even if she was going to lie to them. Just a little.

"Fine. You really want to know? I'll tell you. My best friend is freaking out about her wedding and wants me to wear a bridesmaid's dress that makes me look like a hooker in an eighties prom dress. My mom keeps wanting to set me up with some nice guy from church who looks like my Uncle Jim, bald head and all. I'm PMSing and jonesing for chocolate, which I don't keep in the office because I will eat it if it's here. And my bosses want to interrogate me. Where would you like to start?"

She waited for them to run for the door. They were guys, after all. Usually if she mentioned PMS and weddings in the same conversation with any of her macho brothers, they left so fast, they left marks on the floor.

Tristan and Adam exchanged a look, communicating without words. She'd seen Max and Jesse exchange that same look.

Damn them. They didn't leave, just continued to stare at her. But she refused to let them win this one.

She lifted her eyebrows at them, determined not to crack.

Finally, Tristan shook his head and sighed. "You're not in trouble, are you? Not hurt?"

And then they did this and she wanted to hug them.

"No. No trouble. Not hurt. It's not me, okay? I swear."

"And you'd tell us? If you needed anything?"

"Yeah. I would."

Except she couldn't tell them about this. And they couldn't help her.

Adam shook his head and gave Tristan a disgusted look but he finally turned toward the door, Tristan on his heels.

Before they left, Tristan turned one more time. "Mally, you know, whatever you need, you just have to ask."

Except when she knew they couldn't help her and would be furious if they knew who she was going to ask for help.

She nodded, biting her lower lip to fight back tears.

When they finally left her office, she sighed in relief.

But that hadn't been the hardest part. She still needed to make a phone call.

Which would have to wait until she got home.

Giving her more time to stress.

Goodie.

Max had almost managed to put Mary Alice out of his head by lunch the next day.

Having an emergency at one of the businesses helped. Pipes had burst in one of the buildings he and Jesse now owned. The travel agency occupying the first floor had had some damage, but Jesse knew to tell the owner they'd be sure to cover all expenses.

Jesse had gone over to handle cleanup while Max handled the other emergency that'd come up after Jesse had left. They'd had trouble at one of the other clubs they owned last night. A fight, nothing major, but the cops had been called so he'd have to talk to the lawyers and make sure there'd be no legal problems.

They'd been so damn careful these past few months. They'd made sure every building was up to code, made sure every license was paid, every T crossed and I dotted on every contract and legal document they signed.

They'd paid off as many outstanding debts as they could without leaving themselves in a financial hole. Which shouldn't be a problem because David had made sure they'd had enough capital to hold on to what they'd taken for at least two years. After that, the businesses they now owned should be making them enough money to keep them afloat.

Hell, they should do more than keep them afloat. Max intended for them to make him and Jesse rich. They'd never have to serve another master again, not even one who'd been as good to them as David.

And they'd do it legitimately. At least, as much as they could. Yeah, there might be a few things they'd have to skim a few corners on, but damn it, he didn't want Jesse to have to watch their backs constantly.

Two years, Max had estimated. Two years to put all the illegal shit behind them and give them the chance to make it without relying on muscle or weapons or drugs or games or sex.

Maybe in two years, she'd—

Max shook his head. Fuck that. He wasn't going there.

The phone rang and he didn't bother to check the number because he knew the ringtone.

"What's up?"

"I don't think it was anything more than an accident," Jesse said. "But we should probably take a look at the other buildings to make sure nothing's been tampered with."

They owned five commercial properties in the city, a mix of businesses and apartments, in addition to the three clubs, two restaurants, and the small craft brewery the Oleksy brothers had gotten as the result of a gambling debt. The owner was a genius with hops. Not so great at cards. David Oleksy had kept the guy around because he made damn fine beer, and Max had gone a step farther and given the guy a share in the ownership.

Not only would it keep the guy from going off on his own but it'd engender some goodwill.

"Check with Reece at the brewery first. He said something to me last week about some mechanical problems. Could be nothing."

"Or it could be somebody fucking around with us."

Yeah. Or it could be that.

"Let me know what you find out."

Jesse paused. "Everything else okay?"

Max bit back a sarcastic comment that only would've made Jesse more concerned. "Yeah. I've just been buried in numbers all morning and you know how much I love that."

Another pause. "You wanna go out tonight?"

If out meant pick up a woman and get laid, no, he really didn't. "Probably not. I want to work on that downstairs bathroom tonight."

They'd finally finished the two bathrooms on the second floor of their house, and Max had discovered that ripping out tile was a really good way to work out his frustrations.

Of course, Jesse knew that. "All right, I guess we can order in some pizza and tackle that."

"No. Go out. I don't need a damn babysitter. I need a few hours of solitude."

Max wanted to cut his fucking tongue out. God damn it. Why the hell couldn't he keep his goddamn mouth shut?

"Jesse—"

"Nah, you're right. I get it. As long as— Never mind. I'll go out."

Fuck. "Good." *Fuck.* "That's good. Just...I'll see you at home."

"Yeah."

Jesse hung up.

And Max was left to wonder how the fuck he was going to fix what was wrong between him and his best friend.

Jesse hung up and had to curb the urge to throw his phone across the room.

"Everything okay?"

Shit, he was scaring the natives.

He pulled out a smile for the building manager, a thirty-year-old divorced blonde who'd made it pretty damn clear that if Jesse ever wanted to mess up her sheets, she'd be more than happy to oblige.

"Yeah, everything's fine." Which was bullshit. "I'll get a crew in to fix the damage, hopefully by the end of the week."

"Will you be overseeing the work yourself?"

Couldn't mistake that blatant invitation…only it made him want to cringe.

Jesus, he was fucked in the head.

"Unfortunately, I've got a lot on my plate the next few weeks." He smiled. "It was nice to see you again, Vickie. Maybe we can get a drink another time."

"Sure." Her smile widened. "I'd like that."

Christ, you're such a fucking liar.

They'd never get that drink. He had absolutely no desire to see Vickie in any way other than business. He only had one woman on the brain and that wasn't going to happen so…

Jesse left so fast, he probably left skid marks.

He had a million other things on his to-do list today. When they'd taken over some of David's assets, he and Max had divided the work the way they divided everything—Max handled the mental stuff and Jesse handled the physical.

It worked for them, played to their strengths. It's why they made a great team.

Usually. The last week or so…

Fuck.

Since he did have places he needed to go and things he needed to do, Jesse forced himself to shove all the shit relating to Max into the back of his brain so he could concentrate. He'd learned at an early age that if he didn't compart-mentalize shit, he'd spend most of his days staring at a wall.

Seven hours later, Jesse pulled his truck into the garage attached to their building, noting the empty space next to his.

Either Max was still at work or... He'd gone out without telling Jesse.

He tried not to be pissed off about that. More than likely, Max was still at the office. It wasn't unusual for him to eat dinner at his desk and not leave until seven or eight at night.

But Jesse had the feeling Max was avoiding him. And that made Jesse's chest ache like he'd taken a punch.

He reached up to rub it away then shook his head and shoved out of the car. He'd told Max he was going out so, god damn it, he was going out.

Even if that was the last thing in the world he wanted to do tonight.

Fuck.

Getting out of the car, he headed for the door leading into their home.

Technically, Max owned the building. The world they lived in, men didn't share a house. Jesse owned a condo a few blocks away. He never stayed there now but if anyone asked, that's where he could be found.

In truth, they each had their own rooms in this building, a three-story former industrial building. They'd been rehab-bing it for the past two years. Making it into the home they'd always wanted, figuring by the time they had it finished, he and Max would've gotten out.

Well, they'd gotten out but Jesse wasn't sure their lives would ever be safe.

At least, not safe enough.

Excuses, excuses.

Maybe. Then again, who really knew?

A decade ago, their lives had been in danger every time they stepped outside. Mickey had been in jail and David's organization had been under attack. Hell, Jesse didn't remember who'd been after them that time. He only knew, for midlevel members like Max, it'd been dangerous to go anywhere without someone to protect his back.

That'd been Jesse's job for as long as they'd known each other. Not that Max couldn't take care of himself but, in their world, appearances were everything. Jesse made Max appear untouchable.

Together, they had each other's back. Life was still dangerous, and just because they were trying to go legitimate didn't mean people weren't still out to kill them. The threat may have lessened but it hadn't gone away.

When Max wasn't where Jesse could cover his back, Jesse got twitchy.

And pissed off.

So when the doorbell rang, he reached for the gun holstered at his back.

After checking the peephole, he released the gun as if it'd shocked him.

Well, shit. Maybe he wouldn't be going out tonight after all.

5

ucking pussy. Just leave already.

Max shoved away from his desk with a grunt, checking the clock.

He was hungry and he had a headache and he needed to go the fuck home and take a shower. And he needed to apologize to Jesse.

He'd taken out his frustration on the one person he shouldn't have and he had to make that right. But Jesse having a night out alone wasn't a bad thing. And since Max had fucked up with Mary Alice...

Yeah. Maybe he'd take a sledgehammer to a few tile walls before that shower. Work out some of this aggression.

And try not to wonder where the fuck Jesse was. Or think about Mary Alice.

Man, he'd fucked that up completely.

All the way home, he thought about how he could fix it, what he could do differently. He was good at handling people. Usually. Of course, most of those people wanted something from him and he knew how to play that to his advantage.

Mary Alice didn't want anything from him. And apparently, she wanted nothing to do with him. He needed to come to terms with that.

By the time he got home and parked his car in the garage, he sighed in relief when he saw Jesse's car parked there already.

Yeah, it meant Jesse hadn't gone out. But it also meant Max wouldn't be alone tonight.

Christ, they really did need to spend less time together. Otherwise…

Otherwise, what?

They'd die alone in their renovated building with a hundred cats, with their hands around each other's necks, strangling each other.

Idiot.

Absofuckinglutely.

Pushing through the door into the main building, he barely noticed the unfinished mudroom as he headed for the oversized kitchen neither of them had the time to use except to make coffee in the morning and throw a pizza in the oven at night.

Come to think of it, tonight was the first night in at least a week he'd been home before ten. If they weren't at the office, they were at one of the clubs or restaurants, checking books, talking to staff, familiarizing themselves with the operations.

Through the kitchen, he walked through the unfinished room they planned to make into a dining room and into the room he'd chosen for his office. The bare walls only needed a couple coats of paint to be finished, but he hadn't had time to even think about what color he should paint them.

And, honestly, he couldn't have cared less. Jesse had jokingly suggested they get a decorator to finish the place when they were done with the renovations, but Max knew it'd never happen. Neither of them wanted anyone in their space, fucking around with their things.

Hell, they'd never actually had anyone in the house, other than a building inspector and a few men they trusted unconditionally. Max could count those on one hand.

So when he heard a female voice coming from the front of the building, he figured it was the TV. Until he realized he recognized the voice.

His heart skipped a beat, which just pissed him off.

What the fuck was she doing here?

He took several steps toward the voices before he stopped, took a breath. His brain stuttered and he sucked in another breath.

Had she changed her mind? How the hell had she found them? It wasn't like she could look them up in the phone book or online. Had she asked Tristan or Adam?

No. He couldn't believe she'd do that. If she had, either of those men would've been in his face, wanting to know why she'd been asking about them. So she'd had to put some effort into finding them.

As silently as he could, he approached the living room, stopping just outside.

"Are you sure I can't get you something to drink? I texted Max, but he's a boy scout when it comes to using his phone when he drives."

"No, thank you. I'll just wait until Max gets here."

"And you're sure you don't want to tell me what's going on?"

"I'd rather talk to both of you at the same time."

She needed something. Of course. Why else would she be here?

And that was their opening.

Are you really going to leverage her need against her?

If it meant he could have her... Yeah, he was.

The thought left a bitter taste in his mouth but he quickly swallowed it. She knew who he was, what he was.

He stepped into the doorway.

Max knew Jesse had realized he was there before he showed himself. The security system sent alerts to their phones if the doors or windows in the building opened. But Jesse deliberately shifted his gaze so Mary Alice knew he'd arrived.

She sat alone on the couch, her back stiff. Jesse sat across from her on one of the two huge recliners.

Her head turned and she bounced off the couch to her feet. Dressed in a long patterned skirt and a tight purple t-shirt, she looked young. Really fucking young. And completely out of place in their man cave, with the TV that took up most of a wall, the electronics and the Xbox and the pool table behind the couch, where he and Jesse spent a hell of a lot of their down time.

Lately, they'd barely had time to sleep much less play games. But now he couldn't help but think about what games they could play with Mary Alice on that couch.

He made sure nothing of his thoughts showed. He didn't want to scare her off. Not now when he had her exactly where he'd wanted her since the moment he'd met her.

"Hello, Mary Alice."

She swallowed hard. "Hello, Max."

"Is everything okay?"

She blinked. "I'm fine, thank you."

"That's not what I asked."

Her eyes narrowed, as if she wanted to get angry but didn't want to piss him off.

Fuck that. He hated thinking she might be afraid of them.

"I'm not here for me."

That made sense. "So why are you here?"

She didn't answer right away. Instead, she seemed to be figuring out what to say. He had a hard time believing she hadn't memorized her speech. Mary Alice didn't seem like a woman who'd leave anything to chance. They had that in common. Or so he'd thought.

She faltered now. Which fascinated him. What could she possibly want that would make her this uncomfortable?

Her gaze skittered back and forth between him and Jesse before she took a deep breath.

"I need a favor."

So he was right. Which both pissed him off and made his brain begin to churn. He waited for her to continue, but she took another deep breath and looked away.

"Mary Alice, just—"

"My friend's in trouble and I need your help."

He flashed a glance at Jesse, but he had his gaze pinned on Mary Alice.

"What kind of trouble?"

Her chin lifted. "The kind that comes from owing too much money to the wrong people."

Ah. "And those wrong people are..."

She swallowed hard and flashed a glance at Jesse before looking back at Max. "The Antonoffs."

Of course.

He swallowed back a grimace. "And what makes you think I have any sway with the Antonoffs?"

Her chin lifted. "Because I know they took over the illegal parts of the Oleksy organization."

That wasn't common knowledge though he wasn't surprised she knew. She worked for Mickey's nephew, after all.

"That doesn't explain why you think I can help you with this problem."

"Because I don't know anyone else who might be able to. Except you."

The hope in her eyes made him want to be her damn hero. But he saw an opening and, even though he knew that made him a Class A prick, he wasn't going to pass up the opportunity she'd handed him.

He caught Jesse's gaze for a few brief seconds over her shoulder. His best friend knew him well, knew exactly what he was going to do.

Jesse didn't like it. But he didn't tell him not to.

"Tell me everything and I'll tell you what I can do."

Taking a deep breath, she laid it all out. Names, dates, amounts. What she didn't give him was why. As if she could keep this a strictly business transaction.

Not gonna happen, sweetheart.

But he'd let her keep her illusions for a few more minutes. She needed something only he could give her. And he wanted her so he'd take her any way he could get her. He'd worry about more later.

"Is there a reason he was gambling or is he an addict?"

Her head cocked to the side, all that pretty copper hair falling over one shoulder. He wanted to see it spread out on his bed, wrapped around his hand, trailing over his chest. His cock twitched but he throttled back his response.

This will work. Just don't get ahead of yourself.

"He's getting married in a few weeks to my best friend. He was hoping to win the money to take her on a honeymoon."

Her movie companion from the other night. He recalled her face but couldn't remember her name.

"And she asked you to get involved?"

She shook her head. "She came to me to vent and I told her I may be able to help but I didn't tell her who I was asking for help. I didn't want to get her hopes up because I wasn't sure you'd want to help, much less be able to do anything."

Now, that was a challenge if he'd ever heard one.

His lips twitched, wanted to curve in a smile, but he kept his expression neutral. "And what is it you think I can do?"

Her nerves showed as she brushed her hair over shoulders, straightening her back. He watched her every move. Couldn't help himself.

"Ask the Antonoffs to back off and give Danny time to pay them. It won't be much at first but they'll get their money. I give you my word."

"You're willing to put yourself on the line for your friends?"

She blinked. Something about that question made her nervous. Not that he blamed her. The Antonoffs had a reputation for ruthlessness, and he and Jesse knew it wasn't just a reputation. They backed up their threats with action. And while they weren't known for deadly solutions to money problems, they were known for creative methods of getting blood from stones.

"Yes, I'm willing to help, in any way they need."

Which was a problem, because he wasn't willing to let her become a tool for the Antonoffs.

Shit.

Behind her, he saw Jesse close his eyes for a brief second and shake his head, frustration in the tight lines of his mouth.

Max knew if he thought about the situation a little more, he could come up with a solution other than the one he had in mind. One that didn't require her to give in to his demands.

But he wanted *her*. And this was how he'd get what he wanted.

He sat on the chair across from the couch, projecting a calm he didn't quite feel. "How far are you actually willing to go? I might have a solution to your friend's problem, but it'll require a sacrifice from you."

She held his gaze and he found himself locked onto her eyes. He had the all-consuming urge to grab her and lay her out on the couch. Shove up that slim skirt and put his hands on her skin. He'd stroke his fingers along the outside of her thighs until he reached her hips. Then he'd flatten his hands and move them to the inside of her thighs, where he'd push them open—

"I guess it depends on how much you ask from me."

She held his gaze, her chin tilted up at a slight angle that made him want to smile. He didn't. Didn't want to give her the wrong impression.

Now he looked at Jesse, who held his gaze steady, no opposition visible in his expression.

When he looked back at Mary Alice, her cheeks were flushed. He wondered if they'd be that same color when he finally got her spread out between him and Jesse.

As if she'd read his mind, that flush deepened. But she didn't drop his gaze.

Mary Alice had come here tonight knowing the answer to the question Max hadn't asked yet.

All afternoon, she'd wavered back and forth, going over the pros and cons, all while knowing exactly what she was going to do if Max offered her a solution for her friends.

She had a few stipulations of her own, but if this played out like she thought it would, she already knew her answer to his proposition.

Now she waited for him to say it, holding her breath while trying not to show how worried she was.

What if he doesn't take the bait? What are you going to do if he tells you he can't help?

Then she'd have to find another way. Like offer herself on a platter.

Are you crazy?

Maybe a little.

Because she'd regretted turning him down since the moment the words had left her lips.

She'd cursed herself for being scared, for being unwilling to take what she wanted for herself.

But now she had an excuse. And she was taking it.

If she'd read Max right.

Finally, he took a deep breath and leaned back in his chair.

"I need a companion for certain events, dinners, and cocktail parties. Someone with an unimpeachable reputation."

That...wasn't what she'd been expecting. She faltered, her lips parting as her brain spun. She'd thought he'd demand a date. She'd wanted him to demand she go out with him. She'd planned to add her own caveat.

Now what?

Her gaze narrowed. "You want to be seen with me because I'm not associated with your..." *criminal* "...former life."

The corners of his mouth quirked into a faint smirk. "Are you so sure it's former?"

No, she wasn't. And even though she knew she should have nothing to do with either of them, here she was.

Because whenever she thought about Max and Jesse, heat swept through her like a flash fire. Like it was now.

Her body must've betrayed her because the look in his eyes built into an inferno. Her stomach clenched and her lungs stuttered. She literally ached with desire. She had to stop herself from clenching her thighs together. Never in her life had she been so turned on.

Dangerous territory.

She continued to hold Max's gaze, determined not to falter. "No, I'm not sure."

"Max."

Jesse's rough voice stoked the raging heat and she looked

over her shoulder at him. His expression held a warning. But not for her. Jesse stared at Max.

Max's attention stayed on her. "Then why are you here?"

"Because I need you to help my friends."

Liar. He sees right through you.

"And you're willing to do anything for them."

Was he waiting for her to back down? "Yes."

He held her gaze for several long seconds before he deliberately looked at Jesse and held his gaze for several long seconds before he focused back on her.

"I may be able to help."

She tried not to cry in relief. "And your terms?"

Max's lips curved in a hard smile and her heart pounded against her ribs.

Jesus, I sincerely hope you haven't screwed yourself six ways to Sunday.

"We have several upcoming events where we'll need a companion. Some are private. Some are public. There could be press. There'll probably be gossip. Adam and Tristan will find out. Your family, your friends. They're going to tell you you're making a mistake. They're going to tell you you're ruining your life. That you're putting yourself in danger. But if you agree to the deal, there's no backing out. You'll have to see it through for six months."

The flat demand in his voice made the hackles on her neck stand up. He didn't scare her... At least, that's what she told herself.

And if she was lying... Well, maybe she kind of liked it.

She also liked the fact that he'd used "we."

"We have..." "We need..."

Not "I."

Am I really going to go through with this?

She took a quick breath. "Are you saying I'd be dating both of you?"

If she'd surprised him, he didn't show it.

Behind her, she heard Jesse shift, felt the air move around her, and knew he'd stood. She could feel him at her back, not close enough to touch but close enough for her body to crave his touch.

"Max." Jesse's voice, hard and clipped. "We need to talk. Now."

Max didn't release her gaze. "That's exactly what I'm saying."

"Max." Jesse didn't raise his voice but she heard the command in it.

Max ignored him. "How much do you want to help your friends, Mary Alice?"

"God damn it, Max." Jesse's voice sounded strangled. "Stop—"

"My answer is yes."

6

Jesse's hands curled into fists, ready to take a swing at Max.

But the bastard kept pushing Mary Alice. He knew how much Max wanted her but this wasn't the way. Not under pressure. Not afraid for her friends and willing to do anything to help them. The girl was too damn soft-hearted and Max would exploit that weakness to get what he wanted.

And that didn't sit well with Jesse. Especially since Max insisted on dragging him into it. No way did he want to be responsible for causing her any more distress. Forcing himself to loosen his fists, he gave Mary Alice a wide berth as he stalked toward Max, stopping in front of him and forcing him to look at him.

Jesse saw fierce triumph in Max's eyes and Jesse's jaw tightened so much, he could barely get the words out.

"In the other room. Now."

"Jesse."

He ignored her, didn't want to see the fear on her face. That'd just make him want to punch Max harder.

"God damn it, Max. Move."

Max held his gaze. "I believe she wants to talk to you."

"You're being a prick."

Max's eyebrows rose. "I believe I'm helping her with a problem. How is that being a prick?"

From behind, he heard her huff out a sigh. "Jesse, if you want out of this arrangement, that's fine. Just don't presume to understand what I want without talking to me."

Something in her tone made him turn.

Her expression held no fear, pretty green eyes steady as they held his. But Jesse read body language like a goddamn professional profiler and he knew she wasn't as okay with this as she was trying to front.

"Fine. You want me to talk to you? Then answer my question. Do you honestly understand what he's asking for? What he wants?"

Her gaze never wavered. "Yes."

"And you're willing to be seen in public with the two of us, knowing everyone—your friends, your family, everyone —will think you're sleeping with both of us?"

"I don't believe that was part of the deal."

He took a step closer, noting that she didn't move an inch. If she was scared, she hid it well.

"It doesn't matter if it's part of the deal. People will talk. They'll gossip. They'll tell other people. Are you really willing to play the whore for friends?"

He heard Max's muttered, "Fuck," but he only had eyes for her.

And in her gaze, he finally saw something that wasn't fake or studied.

She was pissed.

Good. Because he wasn't willing to sacrifice her to Max's goddamn lust. Or his own.

But he realized being angry just made her even sexier.

Hands on her hips, she glared at him. "I'm not willing to play the whore for anyone and if you think that's what's going on here, you're going to be disappointed. I'm willing to provide you and Max with an escort, which is all he asked. I'm willing to do that for my friends because I love them. Nothing Max said indicated that I would be required to fall into bed with either or both of you. Am I wrong, Max?" Her gaze flicked over Jesse's shoulder. "Did I misunderstand you?"

"No." Max's voice held a hint of amusement. "You didn't misunderstand me. I don't require you to have sex with us to complete this deal."

God damn you, Max.

Her gaze pinned him again. "Then I guess you have a decision to make, Mr. Kanatawa. I'm willing to agree to Max's terms. If you're not, then you can take yourself out of the equation. But," she took a step forward, still not close enough to touch but close enough for him to want her to, "I know that where Max goes, you go. If you decide you don't want to be part of this arrangement, that's your choice. But don't think you're doing me any favors."

Turning, she grabbed her purse off the couch and took out her keys before heading toward the front door.

He and Max watched her go, neither of them following her.

Before she disappeared, she looked over her shoulder at them. "I expect you to contact me as soon as you have any details, Max."

"There's one more thing."

Jesse watched Max walk toward her, watched him put his hands on her face. Then he leaned down and kissed her.

From where he stood, Jesse couldn't see her reaction, couldn't see the actual kiss.

And he wanted to see.

But it was over in two seconds and Max stepped away.

Jesse saw Mary Alice's wide eyes, her parted lips, and the flush on her cheeks. Then she turned and headed out without another word.

Max followed her to the door, standing in the entrance until Jesse heard a car start and drive away.

Then Max turned on him and Jesse braced for a fight.

***

Holy hell.

Mary Alice had let him kiss her.

She hadn't backed away when she's seen him coming, hadn't pushed him away when he'd cupped her face in his hands.

She hadn't responded either but he had time. Hell, she'd offered herself up on a platter with this arrangement to save her friends, given him the opening he needed.

And Jesse had nearly fucked it up.

His gut rolled with anger. The best thing he could do now would be to go upstairs to his suite. He had a TV in his bedroom and a complete office in the adjoining room. He should go upstairs and shut himself in because if he had to talk to Jesse now, he'd say something neither of wanted to hear.

Or he'd hit him. And that wouldn't be good for either of them.

"Max."

He could practically hear Jesse grinding his teeth, trying not to let anything else escape.

Max did the same. And bit his tongue for good measure.

Turning, Max headed away from the living room where Jesse stood and headed for the kitchen. They were still working on this room. They couldn't agree on anything. Not the cabinets or the floor or even the wall color. Max wanted light, Jesse wanted dark. Max modern, Jesse rustic.

So the walls were unpainted drywall and the cabinets had no doors. At least they had appliances because they'd both agreed on stainless.

Max grabbed a beer from the massive fridge and headed for the stairs at the back of the house.

"God damn it, Max. We've gotta talk about this."

"Nothing to talk about now." He took the stairs two at a time. "You can give her your decision tomorrow."

"You practically fucking twisted her goddamn arm to get what you wanted. How the fuck—"

"Fuck you, Jesse." Max turned on Jesse, the enclosed staircase not the ideal situation for this conversation. Neither of them liked confined spaces but they'd needed a second stairwell in the building, another escape route. "Is that what you really think of me? That I took advantage of her?"

"Didn't you?"

"Christ, Jesse. I gave her a way to take the offer and not feel bad about going out with us."

"So you used her fear against her?"

"She's not afraid of us." Max shook his head sharply. "You didn't see her face—"

"No, I didn't. But you can't tell me you didn't see how she shook. She's frightened, Max. Whether she's frightened of us or just of what people will think when they see her with us. She's not a toy or a chess piece. And you're fucking with her life."

"She's an adult, able to make her own damn decisions. She knows what she's doing. And did you stop to think for one minute that maybe we're exactly what she wants?"

Jesse sneered. "No. No fucking way. Now who's being delusional?"

Max's right hand curled into a fist and he had to make a conscious effort to loosen it.

"Think what you want. I need to do some work."

He was almost at the top of the stairs when Jesse called to him from below. He hadn't followed any farther.

"She's not going to be what you want, Max. She can't. She's just not that kind of girl. She has no idea who we are or what we're like and she won't be able to handle us. It's a fucking disaster in the making."

Even though Max knew where Jesse's fear came from, it didn't make him any less pissed off at his best friend. "Neither of us know what kind of girl she is. But I intend to find out."

Retreating to his office, Max figured he'd use this pent-up energy for a purpose.

He never had enough time to do everything that needed

to be done. He usually spent his time at their official office in Center City dealing with anything related to their legitimate business dealings. They hadn't hired an accountant yet because Max wasn't sure the books were clean enough to pass a third party without raising flags. So for the time being, he handled everything. Damn good thing he had a master's in business management from the Wharton School of the University of Pennsylvania and had aced all of his accounting classes.

Didn't mean he enjoyed it, just that he could do it on his own.

But after an hour staring at spreadsheets, he shoved away from the desk, more frustrated than he'd been when he started.

The books for one of the clubs they'd taken were so fucked up, Max was almost convinced there had to be a third set of books. Or maybe the previous manager really had been that incompetent.

Or maybe this shit with Jesse and Mary Alice messed with his brain more than he'd thought.

He'd been waiting to make a phone call to Larisa Antonoff. As the daughter of Arkady Antonoff, head of the family, she'd be able to help Max broker some kind of deal for Mary Alice's friends.

Glancing at the clock, he figured it was late enough to call.

He and Larisa had a friendship dating back more than a decade. He'd been David's heir apparent and she was Arkady's beloved only daughter. Arkady was never going to be happy with any man Risa brought home, but he'd seen the appeal of having ties to the Oleksy family so he'd allowed Max to be friends with her.

There'd never been anything romantic between them. Not that Max hadn't considered it. Risa's cool Russian beauty attracted men like bears to honey. But those men who tried to get close discovered Risa's claws fairly quickly.

Risa didn't trust many men and with good reason. But they'd shared a bond of experience.

He knew he could count on her help with this and still manage to keep him from being pulled back into the life he was trying to leave behind.

Jesse...

What the fuck was he going to do about Jesse?

Jesse hadn't seen the look in Mary Alice's eyes when he'd told her he could help. He hadn't seen the flash of disappointment when Jesse had tried to make Max stop.

Max wasn't wrong about her. She'd just needed an excuse to be seen with them. And he was going to capitalize on it as much as he could.

And so would Jesse. Jesse had to come around. Max couldn't believe he wouldn't.

Opening his desk drawer, he retrieved the burner phone and texted Risa then set it on his desk, not expecting to hear from her until morning. He checked the phone twice a day, morning and night, just to be sure he didn't miss any messages. He had no idea if she did the same or if she only checked once a day.

But he knew she'd get back to him. She always did.

When the phone vibrated five minutes later, he had to admit he was surprised.

· · ·

Can't sleep? Or is something wrong?

And that was Risa in a nutshell. Straight to the point, no bullshit.

Nothing's wrong. Need a favor. Can you talk?

Several seconds passed. Then a minute.

Finally the phone rang.

"Wow. Three words I never thought I'd hear from you. What's wrong?"

Max smiled. "Nice to talk to you too, Risa."

"Yes, yes. I know it's been a while. What's wrong, Max? Did something happen? What do you need?"

"I need a favor for a friend. You're not going to like it, though. It involves a debt to your family."

"How much? What for? And why?"

Max's grin widened. "I have this mental image of you with a little black notebook and a pencil, writing this all down."

Which was ludicrous because Risa barely picked up a pen unless it was to sign a receipt and that barely ever happened because the stores she shopped in all knew her by name and automatically sent the bill to a tab.

"And I have an image of you in your underwear kicked back on the couch watching some sports show with a beer in your hand. We both know how foolish that is because you're probably sitting at one of your many desks working on spreadsheets."

He winced. "Guess we know each other pretty well."

"Which is why I'm trying not to freak out about you needing a favor."

"Would you freak out a little less if I told you it's for a woman?"

She paused but he swore he heard her suck in a startled breath. "Well, now I am interested. Tell me more."

"Nothing to tell yet. She asked for a favor because she knew I might be able to help. I offered because I want her."

Risa would understand that, Max wanting something in return for granting a favor. That's how her world worked. Hell, that's how his world had always worked.

Something else he was trying to change.

"What? You can't just finesse her into bed? I think I need to meet this woman who makes mighty Max grovel."

"I'm not groveling." He'd never grovel. Nothing and no one was worth debasing yourself. "I'm trading favors."

Risa sighed. "Sorry world we live in, isn't it?"

Max paused, hearing genuine sadness in her voice. "Something you want to talk about?"

"No. Now, what do you need?"

He thought about pushing her but knew if the shoe was on the other foot, she'd let him slide.

"I need to pay off a debt but I don't want the debtors to know the debt's been covered. And I need you to make sure no one knows where the money came from."

"You sound so business-ey, Max. Makes my heart quiver."

He snorted out a laugh, shaking his head. "Only you would be turned on by that."

"You'd be surprised by the amount of women who'd be turned on by a man talking business."

"Yeah, well, I haven't met any."

"Then you're not looking in the right places. But never mind that now. Give me the specifics and I'll fix this for the woman you want to get into bed."

7

ary Alice opened the door to the second-floor Bella Vista apartment she shared with two roommates.

She really didn't want to talk to anyone so she tried not to make any noise. She loved Isabella and Damaris like sisters but, like sisters, they'd take one look at her and realize something had happened.

Something huge.

Practically holding her breath, she closed the door behind her and listened.

No TV, no talking. Silent.

Thank God.

Sucking in a deep breath, she practically ran for her tiny bedroom, shedding clothing as she made her way through the small living room. Tonight, she barely noticed the bright colors of the hand-me-down furniture and the framed posters covering most of the institutional-beige walls.

Since she'd been the last to sign the lease, she'd gotten the much smaller room that was no bigger than a walk-in closet, but she didn't mind. She loved living on her own, paying her own way and being an adult.

And she definitely loved that she didn't have to face the firing squad of her mom, dad, and older brothers, which she would if she still lived at home in Kensington.

With the door to her room shut behind her, she fell flat on her back on the bed and stared at the paint peeling from the ceiling.

He'd agreed. She still couldn't quite believe it. Danny would be in one piece for the wedding and Bethann would be able to stop worrying.

Yeah, but have you sold your soul to the devil for them?

Max wasn't the devil. He just wasn't a man anyone in her family or her friends would want her to date. And she wanted to do so much more than date him. Not even that kiss had been enough. And it had been one hell of a kiss.

Add Jesse into the equation and she could barely breathe just thinking about the possibilities.

Which would be great except Max wanted her as a business asset and Jesse didn't seem to want anything at all to do with her.

So where did that leave her?

Lying on her bed alone, wondering what the hell she was going to tell her mom when anyone found out she'd accompanied Max and Jesse to some dinner or function.

With a groan, she pushed up onto her elbows and stared at herself in the mirror on the back of the door.

What did Max see when he looked at her? A woman he wanted or a tool he could use? And did Jesse even see the woman or only the pain-in-the-ass broad who'd barged into their lives and traded her reputation for their help?

Jesus, what the hell was she going to tell Adam and Tristan? She couldn't even think about telling her brothers. They'd freak.

With a sigh, she stripped off the rest of her clothes and headed for the shower across the hall.

But the more she thought about the situation, the more she realized she was going to need someone on her side. Someone who had shared experience.

Half an hour later, dressed in comfy cotton shorts and a stretched-out old Flyers t-shirt, she picked up her phone. Then put it down with a sigh. Then picked it up again with a huff.

Just do it.

Scrolling through her favorites, she pulled up Kat's number and, before she could chicken out again, she pressed the number.

It was only nine at night but it took five rings for Kat to answer. She'd almost given up when the call connected.

"Hello, Mally. Is everything okay?"

"Hey, Kat. I'm sorry to call so late but—"

Kat's laughter cut her off. "It's nine o'clock and I'm about five years older than you. I'm not quite ready to retire for the night with my hot pad and Geritol. What's up?"

"Are the guys there?"

"No. Do you need them? I can—"

"No. No, that's not— I don't need Adam or Tris. I need to talk to you."

"Sure. What's up?"

Now that she had Kat on the line, she wasn't quite sure how to ask what she needed to know. But she needed something from Kat before she started.

"I know this is asking a lot but I need you to promise me you won't tell the guys that we talked."

Kat paused. "Are you in trouble?"

"No, it's nothing like that."

"Okay." Kat dragged the word out to at least four syllables. "You've got my attention. What do you need?"

"Some advice."

Another pause. "Legal advice?"

"No."

Kat laughed. "I'm going to need a little more to go on if you want my help."

"It's about your relationship."

Silence again. "Mally, just spit it out. What do you want to ask me?"

"I guess...I want to know how it works. How you handle two men. At the same time."

"Are you saying you're considering dating two men?"

She sucked in a breath and admitted aloud what she'd only been saying to herself. "Yes."

"Are you going to tell me who?"

"Yes, but you have to promise not to—"

"I won't repeat a word you say. I promise. But now you have to tell me what's going on."

Another deep breath. "Max Burdanov and Jesse Kanatawa asked me out."

Okay, not exactly the truth but not completely wrong either.

"Hmm. I can see why you don't want Tris and Adam to know." Kat's dry tone made Mary Alice want to cringe. "Are you sure you know what you're getting yourself into?"

"No. If I did, I wouldn't need advice, now, would I?"

"True. But, Mally, are you really sure this is what you want? A relationship between three people is a hell of a lot more work than a relationship between two people. Tris and Adam have known each other for years so they already had the base relationship in place. It was strong enough to withstand the mess I made with them at first. How much do you know about these men?"

"I know they've been friends since they were kids. I know they're practically inseparable now."

"And I know they worked for David Oleksy."

Mary Alice heard no condemnation in Kat's voice and breathed a sigh of relief. She'd been worried Kat would immediately condemn them both. "Yeah, they did. But when David left, they got out. They're legitimate businessmen."

"And do you trust them?"

"Yes. I have to or I wouldn't even consider this."

"All right. So...lunch Monday? This is a conversation we really should have in person. I've got court tomorrow and the guys and I are going to Boston to visit Tristan's parents Saturday and Sunday."

Mary Alice breathed a sigh of relief. "Yes. That would be great, Kat. Thank you."

"Well, don't thank me yet. We haven't talked."

"I know but... I really need someone to discuss this with, and I appreciate that you're willing."

"Well, it's kind of a small club. They don't really have support groups for women in multiple-partner relationships. At least none that I've ever encountered. The only other woman I know is my brother's partner. I like Jules but it's a little awkward sometimes talking to the woman who's sleeping with your brother and your ex-fiance. And it'll be nice to talk to someone who doesn't look at me like I have three heads when I talk about my two lovers."

Jesse had the coffee going and sat at the breakfast bar when Max entered the kitchen the next morning.

Like an old married couple, they had a routine. Jesse usually woke first so he started the coffee then went out for a run or joined Max in the basement gym. Max hated to run so they had a rowing machine and a stationary bike in addition to the weights.

After they worked out, they'd go over their schedule for the day while they ate and discuss anything that'd come up overnight. Something almost always did.

"Shivers had a small kitchen fire last night. No one hurt. The staff had it under control in a few minutes but I figured you'd want to know."

Jesse watched Max as he got a bowl and filled it with Froot Loops. How the hell Max didn't weigh five hundred pounds was beyond Jesse.

Max met his gaze head on as he sat across from him, his voice distant. "Are we going to need someone for repairs?"

Jesse stifled a sigh and bit his tongue so he wouldn't say something to make the situation worse. "Don't know yet. I'm heading over there this morning to check it out."

"Fine. Let me know."

Max let his gaze fall to his bowl and Jesse had had enough.

"God damn it, Max. Are we going to talk about last night?"

Max's gaze snapped back to his, his expression hard. "Have you changed your mind?"

Jesse's jaw locked. "This is a bad idea."

Max's expression didn't change at all but Jesse saw anger flare in Max's eyes. "No. It's not."

Jesse had to loosen his jaw before it cracked. "I assume you already contacted Larisa."

"Last night. She'll get back to me with details."

"And you're going to call Mary Alice and tell her you want her to go with you Monday night, aren't you?"

Max nodded. "You know I am. And you know what I want. The question is, are you going to get off your ass and get on board?"

Jesse's jaw tightened again. Max had been invited to a mixer for local business owners, an event designed for networking. Max had to go, had to show the community he was serious about his transition to business owner.

He had to charm them but mostly he had to convince them. They had to believe him, had to accept him if Max and Jesse were going to make this bid for legitimacy work.

"Fuck."

Max's muttered curse snapped Jesse out of his thoughts. "What?"

Max shook his head, his expression showing an emotion Jesse hadn't seen in a long time.

Defeat.

"Max—"

"No." Max slashed a hand between them. "No more bull-shit. Yes or no."

Jesse looked Max straight in the eyes. And lied. "No."

And then it got worse.

Max's lips pursed until his lips practically disappeared. "Fine. But I'm not giving her up. Not now."

Jesse knew that. Which is why he was lying through his teeth.

"I didn't expect you to."

He had his reasons for lying. Damn good reasons. None of which had to do with the woman.

Jesse had to make sure this rash of breakdowns and accidents really were simple coincidence and not a coordinated strike. If his instincts were right, they were about to have bigger problems.

But, god damn it, this was going to suck.

For a minute, Jesse wasn't sure Max was going to let it go. Jesse almost wished he wouldn't. But he'd made his decision and he wasn't going back on it now.

After another few seconds of tense silence, Max picked up his spoon and opened the paper. They finished breakfast in silence.

Max heard from Larisa around ten that morning and he wasted no time calling up Mary Alice's number.

Now that he'd made up his mind about her, he was sick of waiting to take the next step forward. If only Jesse—

His hands clenched into fists and his phone gave an ominous creak.

Damn it. He'd sworn he wasn't going to obsess over this. Jesse had made up his mind and Max knew he wouldn't be able to change it.

They'd both have to live with their decisions. For now, at least.

Fuck.

Punching in her contact number, he leaned back in his desk chair in his office above Fives Restaurant in Old City.

Max loved this section of the city. Loved the history, loved the sense of excitement. There was always something to do. Maybe it was the fact that he'd never had the time for a night off to spend in the art galleries or the clubs.

He'd always been working.

As her phone began to ring, he took a breath, trying to throw off this pissed-off attitude and be charming.

Charming wasn't something he considered one of his strengths. Jesse disagreed. Max had no clue why except that he had to be. It was part of the job description now. Jesse had taken on the role of enforcer, leaving Max to be the public face of their venture.

Which wasn't how he'd imagined this going. He'd wanted a partnership. Jesse wasn't—

"Hello?"

"Mary Alice. It's Max."

Silence for a very long second. "Hi."

Did she actually sound slightly happy to hear from him?

Yeah, you're about to fix her friend's problem. Why wouldn't she?

"Hello. How are you?"

"I'm good." Pause. "And how are you?"

Obviously small talk wasn't his deal. "I'm fine. I spoke to my contact and I've worked out a deal for your friend."

Through the line, he heard her sigh and the relief in her tone made him feel like a conquering hero.

Idiot.

"Thank you, Max. I don't... I'm grateful. I...What should I tell my friends?"

"I'll send an email detailing their end of the bargain."

"Great. Thank you." Another pause. "So...our arrangement. When do we begin?"

She sounded less enthusiastic now, which made a small pick start chiseling at his left temple. But he wasn't going to back down. He'd fulfilled his part of the bargain. Now it was her turn.

"Monday night, I have a Chamber of Commerce mixer I have to attend." He'd almost added "I'd like you to attend." But that wasn't how this was going to work. "I'll pick you up at seven...unless you need longer to get ready after work?"

"No. Seven is fine. How long is the event?"

"Until ten."

"Okay. That's fine."

How civilized. Max could almost pretend this was a real date. That he'd called her and asked her to accompany him without the deal they'd made hanging over their heads.

Except that it'd be a lie.

"Will Jesse be with us?"

Her question made him pause. He heard something in her voice he couldn't identify. Something that made him think—

No. No way. Wishful thinking on his part.

"Only as our driver."

"Oh. Okay. I— Okay, that's fine. I just thought— So. Monday at seven. I'll be ready. Is this business or fancy?"

His brain still on the fact that she seemed upset that Jesse wouldn't joining them, he wasn't quite sure what she was asking. "This is strictly business for me. These aren't people I'd choose to spend a free night with—"

Her quiet laughter stopped him cold. What the hell had he said?

"I'm sorry. Did I say something amusing? Maybe you can let me in on the joke."

She went quiet with a little indrawn breath. Like he'd frightened her.

Jesus. What the fuck is wrong with you? Great way to get her to relax and trust you, asshole.

"I'm sorry, I didn't mean—"

"No, Mary Alice. I'm sorry. I shouldn't have spoken—"

"—to laugh. I really wasn't laughing at you. What I wanted to know was, what should I wear?"

He shut up immediately. Christ. He really was an asshole. And he had no idea how to answer her.

"I believe other women wore dresses the last time."

"Were they sparkly or just black?"

Was that a trick question? Then he gave some thought to her question and realized what she was asking. "I don't believe I saw sequins or rhinestones."

"Then I think I know the dress code."

Did she actually sound interested in going with him? Or was he reading something into her tone that wasn't there?

And what did it matter? She'd be going with him.

He found himself not wanting to hang up, but he had businesses to run. And no more small talk.

Finally, he forced the words out of his mouth. "Then I'll see you Monday night. Have a good weekend."

"I... Sure, okay. I'll see you Monday."

He hung up before he could say something else awkwardly off-putting.

8

Sitting at her desk Monday afternoon after her lunch with Kat, Mary Alice couldn't get Kat's question out of her head.

"I talked to Max Friday morning. Our conversation was...not really a conversation. It was more like he was doing a business transaction."

"And isn't that what you have? A business arrangement?"

She and Kat had been able to slip out to lunch without any interference from Tristan and Adam, who'd been out of the office.

But Mary Alice might possibly be more confused now than before.

Kat had tried to explain the dynamic of her relationship with Adam and Tristan, but Mary Alice felt like she hadn't known the right questions to ask for what she needed to know. And now frustration ate at her so badly she couldn't concentrate. Having all weekend to stew about her situation hadn't helped.

"Hey, Mally." Tristan appeared in her office door, making

her head pop up from behind her monitor. "I overheard you say you have plans tonight. And," he held up one hand to stop her immediate response, "before you go off on me, you had your door open and you weren't exactly trying to be quiet."

True. She'd been talking to her brother, so she hadn't been divulging state secrets. God, when her brothers found out she was dating Max...

She shrugged off a shudder and fought the urge to stick her tongue out at Tristan, because sometimes he and Adam were just as bad as her own brothers. "Just dinner with a friend."

Which is such a lie. It isn't just dinner and it isn't with a friend.

"Oh yeah? Anyone we know?"

Loaded question. And she had absolutely no intention of telling Tris who she was going out with. "No, just friends. What's with the third degree?"

Tris had the good sense to look a little embarrassed, his smile rueful. "Yeah, sorry about that. Hazard of the job, you know that. Anyway, we're heading out now so lock up when you leave. And have a good time."

She gave him a noncommittal smile. "Sure. You, too."

Adam's blond head suddenly appeared beside Tristan's. "Hey, you going out tonight? Be careful. And if you need someone, don't be afraid to call."

Letting herself sigh, she shook her head. "What's with you two? I'm going out to dinner. It's not quite the dangerous situation."

Adam's eyes narrowed. "Don't you watch the news? There've been several robberies in your neighborhood."

She didn't have to watch the news. She had brothers. Her second oldest brother, the cop, had called two days ago. "You'll be happy to know you're too late with the warning. Mike already called."

Adam shrugged. "Never hurts to have backup, hon."

Tristan's lips twisted in a wry smile. "And now we better leave before she starts throwing things at us. Have a good night. See you tomorrow."

Shaking her head, a smile flirting around the edges of her own lips, Mary Alice waved her bosses out of her office and watched as they left through the front door, discussing something as they went.

Both of them looked happier than she'd ever seen them, and a large part of that had to do with calm, cool Kat Riley. Who had the ability to handle two men.

Sure, Mary Alice knew their relationship hadn't been all hearts and flowers from the beginning. But now they'd settled into happy-ever-after land.

Which made her think maybe, just maybe, she could have the same.

The question was, did she want it?

And aren't you getting a little ahead of yourself?

Only Max had asked her out. Not Max *and* Jesse. They probably had no idea she even thought about dating them both. Okay, not only dating.

Hell, they'd probably be skeeved out if they knew what she wanted. It's just that... Well, she couldn't stop thinking about it now.

She'd thought about it all weekend. Had considered trying to talk to Bethann when her friend had called her, sobbing, to say thank you for whatever she'd done to get the Antonoffs to back off her fiance's debt.

Mary Alice hadn't believed Max would be able to work so fast. Obviously, she'd underestimated him because someone had called Danny to tell him about a new, totally doable payment schedule without one threat of violence.

But she hadn't been sure Bethan would understand or even hear her through her tears.

Oh hell. Who was she kidding? She barely understood herself. She hadn't even known what to ask Kat to clear her own confusion.

With a sigh, she cleaned up her last few pieces of work then headed back to her apartment.

She hadn't decided what to wear, and neither of her roommates would be home. They both worked odd hours and they'd left a note on the fridge for her not to expect them until around eight tonight. And she'd leave them a note telling them not to expect her until ten. Maybe they'd catch up tomorrow morning for breakfast.

Or maybe you won't be here for breakfast.

The thought made her breath hitch in her chest because, well... Sex. With Max.

Okay, if not sex, at least maybe a little heavy petting. Or a lot of heavy petting. That kiss last week had made her toes curl, for chrissake. She wanted more. Hell, she wanted a lot more.

She just wasn't sure she'd get more. At least not tonight.

"Okay, time to get serious."

She needed a dress for a cocktail party that wouldn't make her stand out but also wouldn't make her feel like a frump.

Opening her closet door, she braced her hands on either side of the opening and took a deep breath.

She had no trouble admitting to being a girly girl. She liked clothes, especially dresses that made her look like a woman.

"Let's see...something not too revealing," which wasn't difficult because she didn't own many things that fit in the hooker chic category, "and not black."

At least, not all black. But nothing with too much color either.

She groaned. "Damn it, picking clothes shouldn't be this hard."

And it wouldn't be if it'd be any man other than Max or Jesse.

After pawing through her clothes twice, she sighed and reached for the dark green wrap dress with the vee neckline that showed off just enough breast and the skirt that made her legs look a mile long.

"Hell, might as well flaunt it while I've got it."

An hour later, she began the countdown to Max's arrival. She had no doubt he'd be on time so she wasn't surprised when he knocked on her door at precisely seven.

Taking a deep breath, trying to calm her racing pulse, she opened the door.

"Oh." She blinked, taken off guard. "Hi."

Jesse stood in the hall outside her apartment, staring at her with those dark eyes and a poker face.

She realized she'd never seen him smile or heard him laugh. And she really wanted to. Which was stupid because he didn't want her.

"Hi." His deep voice made her heart pound and that

pissed her off. Damn him. "Max got tied up in a meeting. He'll meet you at the hotel."

Did he sound unhappy that he'd been sent to fill in for Max? Or maybe it was the fact that she was glaring at him?

She was too nervous and excited to temper her response right now. Blame the red hair. It was an easy excuse.

"Does this happen a lot? You getting sent to pick up Max's dates?"

"No." His jaw tightened. "Are you ready? We should leave. Traffic's getting bad."

Could he make it any clearer that he didn't want to be here, talking to her? Only if he came out and said the words.

That'll teach you to be careful what you wish for, won't it?

Turning away before he saw her grimace, she reached for her pashmina and draped it over her arm. When she turned back, she thought she might've caught Jesse checking out her ass but couldn't be sure.

She'd bet her life savings he cleaned up at the card table.

"All set." She smiled at him, just to see what he'd do.

No reaction except to wave her toward the front door.

Well, if that didn't tell her he wasn't interested, nothing would, right?

With a sigh, she dropped the smile and walked through the door. She waited for him to follow then locked the door and followed him down the hall to the stairs.

Silence descended, oppressive and slightly uncomfortable. What should she say? Hell, maybe he didn't want to talk to her.

Maybe he just doesn't like you?

What had she ever done to him?

It was on the tip of her tongue to ask when he reached the door to the street and pulled it open for her.

She had no trouble picking out his car. Had to be the black SUV with the tinted windows. Probably had bullet-proof glass and armor plating.

Are you really sure you want to do this?

Yeah, she really was.

When he clicked the remote and opened the back passenger side door for her to get in, she stopped on the curb and gave him a look. Tristan, Adam, or any of her brothers would have known that look.

Jesse's gaze narrowed.

One hand went to her cocked hip. "Seriously? You want me to sit in the back?"

Had he almost smiled? Or was she seeing things?

"I figured you'd be more comfortable."

"You figured wrong. I am not sitting in the backseat by myself. Unless you don't want me in the front."

His expression never changed. "Of course you're welcome to sit in the front."

Then he closed the back door and opened the front.

The SUV was too high for her to get into without using the step, and Jesse stuck his hand out to help her in.

She took it, trying to ignore the shiver that ran through her entire body at the touch of his skin against hers. Damn, the guy had big hands. Not Hulk-sized or anything, but big enough to make hers feel tiny.

She wondered what they'd feel like on her—

Nope. Not gonna happen. Don't even go there.

She released him as soon as she could without making it

seem like she was afraid of him. She wasn't. But, oh man, she couldn't stop her imagination from roaming.

Maybe she should've sat in the back.

Because when he climbed into the driver's seat, without needing a step, she couldn't stop herself from watching him. One of those big hands wrapped around the steering wheel, making her breath catch in her throat. The other punched the start button before reaching for the gear shift. No automatic transmission for this guy. He wanted total control.

Okay, enough of that.

Tearing her gaze away, she stared out the front window, although she didn't see much of anything.

Instead, she tried to regulate her breathing because she seemed to be on the verge of hyperventilating. Which was so stupid.

She'd been on dates before. Hell, she'd been on a lot of dates. She'd been dating since she turned sixteen and her dad finally agreed to let her go out with Chris Edmond, who tried to get to third base at Annie Lenkowicz's birthday party.

Luckily for Chris, she hadn't had enough strength to break his fingers but her brothers had made sure she knew how to defend herself. Chris had needed help leaving that night.

"Is everything okay?"

Jesse's quiet voice drew her out of those memories and she took a breath before answering. "Of course. So where exactly is this reception?"

"At Haven."

Impressive. "I've heard the food is great. I've never been there."

"It is."

"You've eaten there?"

"We know the owners."

"Are they friends?"

"Acquaintances."

Interesting. The Golden Brothers were Philadelphia blue-bloods. How would they know Max and Jesse? "So what are you going to do while Max and I are at this reception? Hang out on the street smoking and gossiping with the other drivers?"

His hands clenched around the steering wheel. And she scored one for herself.

"No."

Damn him. "So what are you going to do? Sit around and wait for us to be finished?"

"I have a few things to check on."

"Oh, like what?"

"We have a restaurant down the street."

"You mean you and Max own it?"

"Yes."

"Do you own other restaurants?"

"Yes.

Okay, he wanted to play this game? She had four older brothers. She knew how to play the question game. "How many?"

"Three."

"Do you own any other businesses?"

"Yes."

"What are they?"

She heard him sigh. "Why don't you ask Max these questions?"

"Because I'm asking you."

"I'm not the one you're dating."

As a conversation killer, it worked like a charm. Silence fell, which probably suited him just fine.

But her...not so much.

"Are you dating anyone?"

And there went his hands again, tightening on the steering wheel hard enough that she swore she heard it creak.

"No."

"Aren't you interested in dating?"

"If I say no, will you drop the third degree?"

Now she had him on the ropes. "I'm just making conversation."

"Uh-huh."

"What? I can't be curious? I've never dated anyone with a past quite like yours and Max's before. I'm intrigued."

"You should be running in the other direction."

Interesting. "Why?"

Jesse's jaw looked like it was about to crack. Her brothers would never know how well they'd trained her.

"Because you're not—"

His abrupt silence made her gaze narrow. "I'm not what?"

Another sigh. "Forget it."

"Oh no. I'm fascinated." And starting to get a little angry. Obviously he had some preconceived ideas about her. She wanted to know what. "Please continue."

His mouth flattened. "Do you have no self-preservation at all?"

"Of course I do. I just don't perceive you as a threat."

Did he actually look offended by that? Good.

Shaking his head, he took the corner a little sharply into the underground parking garage at the hotel, which she hadn't realized they'd already reached.

She didn't bother him while he parked, and if she couldn't help but smile when he jumped out of the car without another word, well, he couldn't see her.

Her door opened in the next few seconds and she turned to slide out. But before she knew what he intended, he reached in, put his hands around her waist, and lifted her out of the car.

When she landed on her feet, trapped between him and the car, she realized not only was she not afraid of him, she was really, really turned on by him.

Her nipples peaked and her thighs clenched and, oh my god, she actually went wet. She couldn't stop staring up into his eyes, so dark and so intently focused on her.

When he bent closer until she almost couldn't see him clearly, she swallowed hard. But only because she wanted to lean closer and lick him. Yes, she absolutely wanted to taste him.

"You never have to be worried about me hurting you." Now she watched his lips move. "But you damn well should be frightened of me because I am *not* the kind of man you need in your life."

If he thought she'd quiver and cower and meekly agree, he had no idea who he was dealing with. "And what kind of man is that, Jesse? Hmm? Please, enlighten me because I am dying to know."

Now those eyes narrowed and she swore she felt the heat

coming off his body. "One who'd want a hell of a lot more than you're willing to give."

He took a step back but she followed, needing him to see that he wasn't frightening her at all.

"And you have no idea what I'd be willing to give, Jesse. Too bad you're too much of a coward to find out."

With a sharp smile, she sidestepped him and headed for the elevator to the lobby. She didn't wait for him as she pushed the button and stepped inside when the doors opened. She wasn't surprised to find him right behind her, his jaw clenched. He refused to look at her as he pressed the button and stood with his back to her.

She kept her smile until the elevator doors opened and Jesse stepped out. Then she let her smile fade and took a deep breath.

You can do this.

Damn right she could.

Smile back on and fortified, she stepped out into the lobby.

And nearly lost it when she saw Jesse standing next to Max.

Oh my god.

Did they have any idea that the other women in the lobby were devouring them with their eyes? That those women would love to insinuate themselves between their bodies? Preferably naked.

Max's gaze caught hers as she was thinking she might have to warn a few of the other women away.

But they're not yours. This isn't a date. This is an arrangement.

Max needed a date. Not a girlfriend.

She needed to keep her expectations for tonight in check.

Then again the way Max looked at her...

Maybe she'd get more than she'd expected.

She could only hope.

What was she thinking?

Max hadn't wanted to immediately attach Mary Alice to his side, but the way she was looking at him made him think maybe his night wouldn't end in frustration.

"You're not gonna listen to reason, are you?"

The disgust in Jesse's voice didn't bother Max. What bothered Max was the fact that Jesse wouldn't budge on his decision.

"You're not being reasonable."

He stepped away from Jesse, reaching for Mary Alice's hand.

"Hello, Mary Alice."

Damn, her smile made his body respond as if she'd put her hands down his pants. Thank god she couldn't read his mind. And he wished like hell her smile wasn't just for show. And he had no doubt that's exactly why she was smiling.

"Hello, Max. How are you?"

He wondered how she'd respond if he told her exactly how he felt. And what he wanted.

Leaning down, he brushed a kiss against her cheek, deliberately getting close, into her space. He expected her to pull away.

She didn't.

Holy shit.

When he stepped back, he found her watching him, her eyes wide. But he saw no fear.

He wondered what she saw in his eyes. Hopefully nothing he didn't want her to see.

"The reception's in the atrium. We should probably go."

Deliberately avoiding Jesse's gaze, he took Mary Alice's elbow and steered her toward the atrium in the middle of the hotel.

He had no idea what Jesse was going to do. He didn't want to care or think about it all night so he focused on the feel of her skin beneath his fingers and the fascinating shades of her copper-colored hair.

"You look beautiful tonight."

She turned to look up at him but this time her lips curved in a sweet smile. "Thank you. I'd say the same but you always look put together. I don't think I've ever seen you in jeans."

Was that a dig? "I do wear them."

Her smile widened. "I think I'd have to see that to believe it."

They reached the atrium before he could respond and he drew in a breath before opening the door for her.

He'd never admit it but he hated these damn things. He had no trouble making small talk and ignoring those who talked about him behind his back. Most of these people didn't know the first thing about him except what they'd heard from someone else about the rumors of his criminal past.

No one here would have the balls to ask him about it. If they did, he might actually tell them the truth. And they wouldn't give a shit if he told them.

Just like he wouldn't give a shit about these trust-fund babies, except for what they could do to further his business goals.

Stopping just inside the door, he looked over the crowd, trying to determine whom he should talk to. He recognized a few faces and picked a few targets.

"I didn't realize there'd be so many people."

He shot a look at Mary Alice but couldn't tell what she was thinking. "Regretting our arrangement already?"

Her haughty look made his lips quirk into a smile. "You don't know me very well so I'll let that one slide."

"You're right. I don't. What would you like to drink?"

"Is this your way of getting to know me?"

"This is my way of asking if you'd like a drink." He had a feeling he was going to need one, even though he'd only allow himself to have one. He couldn't afford to even give the appearance of impairment.

"Not much on small talk, are you?"

He couldn't tell if her dry tone meant that was a dig. "No."

The look she gave him was pure exasperation. "Do you and Jesse make a pact to speak in as few words as possible?"

So Jesse hadn't been very talkative either. Christ, why the hell was this so damn hard with her? He didn't usually have trouble talking to women. Then again, he didn't have to talk to them. Jesse carried most of the heavy lifting there.

Fuck.

"No."

Goddammit.

"Okay. Sure, I'll have a drink. White wine. Whatever they have. I'm not picky."

Not picky. Just picky enough not to want to go out with him.

As they walked through the crowd to the bar, he nodded to a few people he'd met at the one previous mixer he'd attended and ignored the stares from strangers, several of whom actually narrowed their eyes and watched him the entire way, as if he might break out an AK-47 and start mowing them down.

Yeah, he might be reading too much into other people's reactions. Then again, probably not.

He didn't need these people to like him. He just needed them to know he wasn't the bogeyman. Which was why he had Mary Alice by his side.

So yeah, he was using her. And he refused to feel like a prick about that.

He couldn't afford to.

Mary Alice realized about five minutes into the mixer why Max needed her by his side at this shindig.

These people were sharks, with their shiny white smiles and flat, dead eyes. They sized you up as either chum or another predator in seconds then held out their hands like they were doing you a favor by allowing you to shake it.

Yes, she was exaggerating a little. She knew a few people here tonight, mainly through her work with Tristan and Adam. Those she gave big smiles and hugs and let her guard down for a few seconds. The others... Some gave her the actual creeps. The rest just pissed her off.

That last bunch looked at Max like he was the devil and she was either a fool or a whore for standing by his side.

Of course, some of the women gave her jealous little smiles and that was okay, too. At least those were understandable, considering Max was one of the most handsome men in the room.

He had that whole cool-Russian thing going for him. The piercing blue eyes and the strong jaw and those cheekbones. She wanted to kiss her way across those cheekbones then work her way back down to his mouth—

Yeah, probably best not to think about that too much. She had no idea if tonight would include any intimate contact and she didn't want to get her hopes up.

So for two hours, they mingled. Well, Max kind of mingled. Mostly, he targeted specific people and spoke to them. She had no idea how he chose his targets but she knew he must've had a specific goal with each one.

Fascinated, she stuck close to his side as he worked the room. Occasionally, he'd deliberately draw her into the conversation, but mostly he let her join in as she wanted.

Which gave her a lot of time to watch him work.

"I hope you weren't too bored."

As they headed for the elevator, among the first to leave the event, his question surprised her into taking a hard look at him.

"No, not at all. Did you think I was bored?"

"No. And I have no clue why you weren't."

She laughed at the genuine bemusement in his voice. "I like to watch people. They can be amusing."

"Or completely and relentlessly boring."

His dry tone didn't fool her. He was amused too. Just in a different way. More like a lion playing with a mouse. "You don't fool me. You had fun playing the part."

His eyebrows rose as they entered the elevator and he punched the button for the parking garage. She hadn't seen Jesse waiting for them in the hotel lobby so he must have left. Maybe he and Max weren't as attached at the hip as she'd thought.

"What part?"

"The part where you're just an average guy trying to get along in the world."

She caught him staring at her in the mirrored walls of the elevator and swallowed hard at the heat blazing there. All night he'd been so coolly polite, not just to everyone else but to her as well.

She'd almost convinced herself he didn't want her. That she'd been completely wrong to think she'd seen something in his eyes that made her think he wanted her.

Because right now... She could barely breathe.

"I am an average guy."

"No, you're definitely not. And you know it."

The doors opened and he stepped forward, his gaze checking out the garage before he waved her ahead of him. It took less than two seconds for him to do it, but it reminded her of who he was and why she shouldn't be thinking about how much she wanted to him to kiss her again. But this time, she wanted to kiss him back. Wanted to wrap her arms around his shoulders and press herself against him. Let him know she wanted him.

But it looked like she might actually have to make the first move herself because he wasn't making any moves at all.

And how awful would it be if he didn't respond?

The guy was throwing off some seriously confusing vibes.

Luckily for him, she knew what she wanted.

There was no one else around as he walked her to his car, a black Mercedes that screamed "Look at me" while trying hard not to appear too impressive.

Opening the door, he waited with one hand on the window as she stepped up to the car...but didn't get in.

Instead, she looked up at him and laid her hand over his on the top of the door frame.

"I'm not ready to go home yet."

If he was surprised by her statement, he didn't show it. Then again, she hadn't exactly been acting like someone who'd been coerced into this date.

Which should've totally messed with his head.

"Where would you like to go?"

He hadn't offered an option, probably because he wanted to see what she'd say. She couldn't ask him back to her apartment because her roommates were probably there.

But she wasn't sure she had enough nerve to ask herself back to his place. So maybe—

"We'll go to the club. We can have—"

"I'd rather go somewhere quiet."

His gaze narrowed and she knew he was trying to figure out what angle she was working. She started to wonder if maybe she should just come out and tell him she wanted to go to his place when he asked, "Would you like to come to my home for a drink?"

She tried not to smile too brightly. "Yes, I would."

Nodding, he waited for her to slide into the passenger seat

then closed the door when he was sure she had her legs inside. She had a few seconds to take a deep breath and congratulate herself on getting what she wanted before he slid into the driver's seat and started the engine. She swore she could hear her heart pounding as he turned the key. Something made a discreet chime and then...the nearly silent hum of the engine.

He didn't speak as he got them out of the garage and out onto the street. She let him have his silence, for now. She'd use this time to make a plan of attack. She wanted him to kiss her again. If she were honest, she wanted more than a kiss. Just how much more...

"Are you rethinking your decision?"

His voice pulled her out of her thoughts. "No. Why would you think that?"

"You've gone quiet."

"You're not exactly a fount of conversation yourself."

His eyebrows rose slightly, acknowledging her point. "So what would you like to talk about? Ask me anything."

Seriously? Her brain went blank.

He huffed out a quiet laugh. "Damn. I can't believe it. I shocked you."

She bit back a smile at the amusement in his tone. "I'm not shocked. Just thinking. I need to be sure I ask the right questions. You're giving me the keys to the kingdom."

"Are you that curious?"

Did he really have no idea how fascinated she was with him and Jesse? He couldn't be that dense. Then again, he was a man.

"Will you tell me how you got involved with David Oleksy?"

His hands tightened on the steering wheel but he didn't'

ignore her. "There's not much mystery. My family was poor and we lived in a miserable section of town. Working for David meant protection and money. I was good. I got better. David noticed."

"And Jesse?"

"He's my best friend."

Simply spoken, but he revealed so much.

"And do you do everything together?"

His jaw shifted. "Usually, yes."

She drew in a short breath. "Women?"

He drove quietly for several seconds and she realized they weren't far from his home. "Sometimes, yes. But you know that already, don't you?"

"Yes."

He shot her a quick glance. "And that doesn't shock you?"

"My bosses are involved in a three-way relationship. Why would it shock me?"

"It's unusual."

"True but that doesn't make it wrong. Why should I condemn you and Jesse for the same thing?"

"So open-minded for such a good girl."

"Is that what you think?" She refused to allow him to goad her into losing her temper, but damn, he knew exactly where to strike. "You don't know *me* well enough to know what I'm like."

His haughty expression never changed. "I've done my homework, Mary Alice. I know enough—"

"No, you really don't."

"Then why did you agree to this arrangement? Are you really that committed to your friends that you're willing to sacrifice your reputation—"

She laughed, cutting him off. "Oh please. You sound like the reputation police are going to show up and drag me away to prison."

"Then what the hell are you doing here?"

Could the man really be that clueless?

Maybe you're the one without a clue.

The thought made her heart pound a little harder.

Had she misread him?

"Do you really need me to spell it out for you, Max? You're supposed to be so smart. You tell me why I'm here."

He didn't answer, just continued to drive in silence. She was about to goad him again when he slowed then stopped. They'd reached his home and she hadn't realized, she'd been so focused on him.

With a few quick movements, he hit the brakes, slammed the car into park but left it running. Then he turned to her, a challenge on his hard expression. "You still want to come in?"

"I haven't changed my mind in the past ten minutes."

Turning off the engine, he shoved his door open and got out. By the time she'd grabbed her purse and her pashmina, he'd opened her door and held out his hand to her.

She took it and had to work to suppress a shiver when his much larger hand curved around hers then held tight as she stood. He didn't move away and now they stood, only an inch or so separating them.

The heat of his body pressed against her skin, teasing her senses and making her breath catch in her throat. She wanted him to lean down and kiss her. He had to be able to read her thoughts on her face but his expression never changed.

A long second later, he turned toward the house, keeping hold of her hand as he walked. She liked having his hand wrapped around hers. She tightened her fingers, keeping close to his side.

She had to step quickly to keep up with him, his long legs covering much more ground than she could. Looking up, she saw an intensity in his expression that made her shiver.

He must have felt her hand shake because he glanced at her, just a quick look that made her thighs clench.

Could he see how much she wanted him? Did he know? Or was she going to make a complete fool of herself?

She'd thought he wanted her, thought there was a mutual attraction. Maybe she'd just been fooling herself because right now, he didn't look like a man who wanted to get her into bed. He looked annoyed.

A few people walking along the street gave them looks, but Max didn't acknowledge anyone. He walked up to the entrance, pressed a few buttons on the concealed panel then walked inside when the door opened.

He released her the second the door closed behind them and, in the next second, she found herself pinned against the door by his body.

Her breath left in a rush and she barely restrained herself from moaning at the feel of his hard body pressed against hers. For days, she'd been dreaming about having him this close and now that he was...

She wanted so much more.

Now she saw emotion in his expression. Lust, pure and hot and definitely directed at her.

His hands flattened on the door just above her shoulders and his head tilted down toward hers.

"Be very sure you know what you're doing right now, sweetheart. Because once we—"

Putting her hand on his cheek, she rose onto her toes and pressed her lips against his, cutting off his words. Hard enough to show him she meant exactly what she wasn't saying.

For several seconds, he let her kiss him. And she took full advantage.

Tilting her head, she slanted her lips over his and tasted him, let her tongue run along the seam of his lips and tease him into opening for her. His lungs labored and he tensed, but he didn't move away and she didn't let up.

She kissed him, rubbing her lips against his until he finally started to kiss her back. When he took over, she wrapped her arms around his shoulders and pressed her body against him.

God yes. She'd wanted this all night. Standing beside him, letting herself get worked up whenever he brushed against her.

Her nipples peaked and her pussy clenched, aching for something to fill it. Aching for him. She had been for days. Weeks, if she were honest.

Vaguely, she heard him groan and his kiss became more insistent. Her fingers scraped into his hair, along his scalp then tugged on the not-quite-long-enough strands. A little coarse, just enough to give it thickness. He always had it combed so perfect. She wanted to mess it up a little. Wanted to know what it looked like first thing in the morning, all mussed and sexy.

Getting ahead of yourself.

She gasped as he nipped her bottom lip, as if he'd realized her mind had drifted. He took the opportunity to open her lips and slip his tongue into her mouth.

Electricity zinged through her, making her breasts ache to be flattened against his hard chest but she couldn't—

Max broke away with a growl, startling her into releasing him. Her eyes flew open and she looked up into his. And nearly moaned at the heat there.

"Be sure, Mally. Be very sure."

Her eyes widened even more at the pet name only her family and close friends used. A frisson of lust made her breath rush out of her lungs. She loved hearing it coming from his mouth.

Where had he heard it? Or had he simply come up with it himself?

She wanted to hear him whisper it in her ear while he stripped her naked and filled her with his cock and made her come.

Holy crap.

His gaze narrowed and he lifted one hand to cup her jaw. His hold wasn't controlling but it made every nerve ending in her body come to attention. She squeezed her thighs together to relieve some of the pressure building between them.

Then he stepped closer and pressed his body full length against hers.

Yes. This.

His erection pressed into her lower stomach but she was too short for them to align properly so she could get that hardness where she needed it.

"I wouldn't be here if I wasn't sure."

Her voice sounded breathy but not weak. And definitely

not unsure. She knew what she wanted and she couldn't believe he was being such a Boy Scout about this.

On one hand, it confirmed her suspicion that the man wasn't as ruthless as he wanted to appear. On the other, she had to wonder why he seemed so determined to scare her off.

She didn't have time to wonder anymore because he grabbed her waist and lifted her until her feet didn't touch the ground. Completely at his mercy.

And loving it.

She had a split second to draw in a breath before his mouth descended again and this time, she realized just how much he'd been leashing himself.

Now he demanded she kiss him instead of letting her take the lead. His lip moved over hers with an unspoken command that she give him what he wanted. His hips pinned hers to the wall and his cock pressed against the vee of her thighs, the hard ridge grinding against her mound, almost perfectly aligned with her clit. She just needed—

Wrapping her arms around his neck, she lifted her legs and wrapped them around her waist, praising herself for wearing this dress because of the split that allowed her so much movement.

With his lips still pressed against hers, he tilted his head to the side and kissed her deeper. The groan rumbling in his chest vibrated into her body, making her blood respond as if he'd doused her in gasoline and lit a match.

Pressing herself closer, she arched her back and smiled against his lips when he groaned again.

Suddenly, he turned, still holding her tight, and began to

walk. She moved her lips from his mouth to his jaw, pressing kisses along the strong line straight up to his ear.

The only light in the room came from the back of the house but he obviously knew his way around in the dark. Seconds later, he sat, arranging her over his lap with her knees on either side of his thighs.

He barely gave her a chance to catch her breath when he put a hand on the back of her head and held her in place for his mouth to devour hers again.

His other hand pressed against the small of her back, urging her forward, crushing her mound against his cock. She wanted to purr at the sensation, but his kiss scrambled all of her faculties.

She could only respond and react, especially when he wound her hair through his fingers and tugged.

Her head fell back as his mouth left hers to burn kisses along her throat, open-mouthed and hot against her skin. The sensation was so drugging, she didn't realize his hand on her back had moved and now cupped her left breast in a firm hold.

He kneaded her, hard. Pinched the nipple between his thumb and forefinger and sent lightning streaking through her body, making her sex clench and her fingers dig into his shoulders.

He seemed to know exactly what she wanted and how. The tight hold, the slight pinch of pain. No other man had given it to her. And she'd been unwilling or unable to ask for it.

Max just knew that she wanted him to squeeze her breast until she panted, roll the tip into a tight point until the sensation almost hurt. Until she couldn't breathe without needing more.

The hand in her hair released at that second and she almost complained until he used that hand to push her dress out of the way of his mouth. He bared her breast, yanking down her bra until it formed a shelf to hold her breast out for him.

Then his lips latched on to the nipple and he drew the tip inside, sucking hard and causing her sheath to tighten and go wet. Squirming, she tried to get closer but he clamped one hand on her ass and forced her to stay still.

He said nothing but he expressed himself perfectly without words. And she was willing to give him what he wanted as long as he continued to give her what she needed.

At the moment, he was.

And it was so much better than she'd dared to dream about. And she'd been doing a hell of a lot of dreaming lately. About Max. And Jesse—

No.

The hand on her ass squeezed tight then he released her only to tap her ass a second later.

Oh god, she hoped the neighbors didn't hear her moan.

Her head tilted forward and she sank her fingers into his hair again. She wanted him to continue to play at her breasts but she wanted him to tear his pants open and let her sink down onto his cock. She wanted to ride him but first she wanted to suck him into her mouth and taste him.

All the dreams she'd been having lately had featured taking him in her mouth. She hadn't had much opportunity to have that with other guys, but she wanted it with Max.

Hell, she wanted whatever she could get from him. Hard and fast and a little dirty.

Why did he do this to her? Why him?

"Max."

He didn't answer. He couldn't. He was stringing a line of kisses between her breasts so he could work his magic on the one he'd neglected so far. Teasing and tormenting her with his mouth while his hand kneaded her ass, his fingers inching closer to the soft skin between her legs.

God yes. Please.

The air around them grew heated, drugging her senses. Something had changed. Something... She tried to blink her eyes back into focus but then he slipped his hand under her skirt and wrapped it around her thigh, giving her a squeeze before moving up to cup her pussy in his palm.

Her eyes closing, she moaned as he pressed the heel of his hand against her clit, ground it against her in small circles until she hovered right on the verge of orgasm. An orgasm he seemed determined to deny her.

She strained forward, trying to make him make her come, but he held off just enough, even as he pulled off her breast, scraping his teeth along the nipple and making her cry out.

His head shot up and his hand between her legs stilled as she sucked in a ragged breath.

"Don't you dare stop now."

The look he gave her made her shiver.

"I have no fucking intention of stopping. And I plan to hear that scream again. Take the dress off."

Swallowing hard, she held his gaze as her hands dropped to the bow at her side holding the dress closed. His gaze glittered as she tugged the bow open then shrugged the dress off her shoulders.

It fell to the floor without a whisper and now his gaze dropped. Hers followed and she caught a quick glimpse of his throat convulsing as he swallowed hard.

Nice to know he wasn't as cool as he tried to pretend. Hell, she couldn't even pretend. She was burning up.

She sat on his lap, basically naked with the exception of her bra pushed under her breasts and the tiny silk panties.

The way he looked at her made her lungs burn for air.

When he leaned forward again and drew her closer, she expected him to go for her breasts. Instead, he pressed an almost sweet kiss against her neck. Shivering, she reached for his shoulders and felt the muscles flex beneath her hands.

She wanted to feel his skin against hers. Wanted him naked and—

He nipped at her breast at the same time he twisted his hand against her clit and made her gasp.

Her hands slid under his jacket and she tried to push it off.

He smacked her ass again, this time a little harder. This one stung. And she liked it. Her moan had to make that obvious.

"I'll have to take my hands off you to take off the jacket." He twisted his hand on her clit then let his fingers press back along her slit. "And I don't want to do that."

"Do you always get what you want?"

When he didn't answer right away, she looked into his eyes. And blinked at the darkness she saw there.

"No. But I will tonight."

This time, his kiss held a harder edge. With another man,

she might've balked. But for this one, she'd give him what he wanted. Because she knew he would give her what she wanted. He already was.

"On your feet, Mally."

He didn't wait for her to comply, just wrapped his hands around her waist and lifted her, as if she weighed nothing at all.

The show of strength shouldn't have made her quiver. It did.

"Take your panties off."

His voice dropped an octave, stroking her deep inside. She sucked in a breath but her hands rose to her hips, her fingers sliding beneath the lace that matched her bra then pushing her panties down.

Holding his gaze, she shrugged out of her bra as well. She left the shoes. For one thing, she'd have to bend over to loosen the straps. For another... well, they made her legs look great. Which Max affirmed when his gaze finally dropped from hers to rake down her body.

He let his gaze linger for several seconds, until she thought she wouldn't be able to continue standing.

Then his hands went to his belt.

And she took a step forward.

"No." She waved a finger at him. "I'll do that."

His eyes narrowed but he moved his hands to the cushions on either side of him.

She smiled and took a step closer. "Now don't move."

9

Jesse heard the front door open and knew Max was home.

But when he heard Mary Alice's voice, he stopped in the second-floor hallway. And then he didn't hear anything.

Goddammit.

He told himself he wasn't going downstairs. He'd told Max he wasn't going to—

Fuck.

Shoving a hand through his hair, he turned to go back to his room. But he couldn't force himself to go in and close the door behind him.

He stood in the doorway, hands on the doorjamb.

Just go inside and close the door.

He knew he should.

He couldn't.

Turning, he headed toward the stairs, deliberately making no sound as he walked.

The stairway led into the kitchen, where the light over

the stove cast the rest of the room into shadow. He knew their home like the back of his hand so he knew exactly where to stand to get the best view of the living room.

When he finally came to a stop, he had a full view of the action.

His jaw locked as he caught sight of Mary Alice, her arms curved behind her as she unhooked her bra then let it drop to the ground.

He barely heard her say "Now don't move" before she went to her knees in front of Max and Jesse lost sight of her.

God damn, he should go back upstairs right now. Before—

He heard the unmistakable sound of a zipper being pulled down and his cock throbbed and swelled.

Sonovabitch.

"I don't want you on the floor."

Max reached down and lifted her onto the couch next to him.

Jesus, she looked like an angel, her pale skin luminous in the dark.

Then Max leaned closer and whispered in her ear and her head shot around until she stared straight at Jesse.

He could barely see her face in the dark but he didn't think he imagined the shock in her expression.

"Jesse."

He was halfway turned around when he heard her call out to him.

"Don't go."

Lust blazed through him at the warmth in her voice, stealing his breath. He couldn't have heard her right. No way had she asked him to stay. Did she want him to watch? He couldn't imagine she wanted him to join in. Could she?

No fucking way.

He turned and took a few steps back toward the living room. She sat on the couch, facing the back, her arms lying along the top of the cushions, hiding her nudity, though he didn't think that's why she did it. She didn't seem embarrassed by or ashamed of her body and she had no reason to be.

Slim. Sleek. Perfect. Beautiful.

What the fuck was she doing here?

"Why?"

His voice sounded like five miles of gravel road but she didn't back off.

"Because I asked you to."

His gaze narrowed. "And what is it exactly you want to do while I'm here?"

Now she did look a little uncertain. "Join us."

His jaw locked against the immediate instinct to say yes. But if he did, he knew they'd open a can of worms they'd never be able to close.

But he couldn't make his feet move.

Then she held out her hand.

He couldn't deny he wanted to take it. But he didn't have to. He shouldn't stay.

Even if he wanted to.

"You have no idea what you're asking for."

She continued to stare straight into his eyes. "I know what I want. If it's not what you want... I'll understand."

No, she wouldn't. She'd think he was rejecting her and he didn't want that.

Maybe it'd be for the best.

Best for who?

He glanced at Max, who watched him with a steady gaze. No condemnation, no encouragement.

But then he knew what Max wanted. He wanted everything. And sometimes, you couldn't have everything.

Tonight, though, they could have her. She was giving herself to them on a platter.

And yeah, he wanted her.

He walked to the couch, stopping just out of reach.

"And what if I want more than you're willing to give?"

Her head cocked to the side. "How will I know if you don't ask?"

His arms crossed over his chest. "And if I want to watch Max fuck you until you come, you're gonna be okay with that?"

Did he see relief flash through her eyes?

"Yes."

"And if I want to fuck you when he's done?"

She swallowed hard and her cheeks flushed a brighter red. "Yes."

Fuck.

Instead of closing those last few inches between them, he shook his head. "Why?"

"Because this is my part of our arrangement."

Jesse exchanged a look with Max, who looked as confused as Jesse felt.

"What the hell are you talking about?"

"I told you I had my own conditions. That I wanted something out of this arrangement. This is what I want."

Jesse shook his head but Max took her chin in his hand and turned her to look at him.

"You have to spell it out, Mally. We don't want any confusion."

She took a breath but didn't break his stare. "I want to be with both of you. Now. Tonight."

A surge of lust made Jesse's hands curl into fists as Max leaned closer.

"Be very sure you know what you're asking." Max's tone was deadly serious. "Because I don't want you to come back at us later and say we coerced you."

Her eyes narrowed as she shook her head, making him release her chin. "I wouldn't do that."

Jesse wanted to believe that. His cock swelled with blood and throbbed behind the zipper of his pants.

Max released her chin with a stroke. "Then show us what you want, Mally."

The nickname sounded right to Jesse and he noticed her slight shiver. Then he saw her gaze shift down Max's body. Her shoulders moved but he couldn't see her hands.

He wanted to see what she was doing.

Jesse was halfway around the couch before he realized his feet were moving. When he finally had a full view, he saw Mally pulling Max's pants and underwear down around his hips, freeing Max's cock.

She immediately reached for him, wrapping a hand around him while she leaned in to press her lips against his.

Max met her halfway as Jesse slid into the chair opposite the couch, his own cock stiff and ready. He had the almost overpowering urge to unzip his own pants and stroke himself while he watched but that felt almost like he'd be intruding on her fantasy. And he had no intention of hijacking her control.

Max was having a hard time with that as he cupped her head in his hands and sank deeper into her kiss, turning her head to get a better angle. She didn't protest. Instead she started to stroke Max. Tentatively at first, then harder as Max began to thrust into her hands.

With Mally on her knees beside Max, the angle of their heads made for an awkward kiss but Max took care of that by grabbing her hips and repositioning her across his lap.

Naked, she straddled him, her pussy brushing against his cock. She moaned at the contact and arched her back, rubbing herself over his erection. The sleek length of her back made Jesse want to pet her then smack the round curve of her ass. He had to force himself to stay in his chair.

Max kissed her with single-minded intensity, his hands taking the same journey Jesse wanted to, but when he reached her ass, he cupped her instead of smacking her.

Jesse heard Mally moan, watched a shiver run through her then nearly lost it when he saw Max lift her to position her over the tip of his cock.

Her head fell back as Max eased her down his shaft, his gaze now laser-focused on her face. Her long hair fell down her back, brushing against Max's thighs as she took him in completely.

But Max wasn't going to be content with slow. He fucked like he did everything, hard and fast.

Mally didn't seem to have any objections. She followed his every unspoken command, her hands on his shoulders to steady herself as she rode him.

Jesse couldn't see her face but he heard her soft moan

every time Max thrust deep. Jesse's cock hardened to stone, his lungs laboring for air.

Max was having a hard time holding it together. Jesse couldn't blame the guy.

Christ, he hoped when it was his turn to have her, he could hold on at least long enough to get her off.

Which was probably what Max was waiting for. One of Max's hands had moved around to Mally's front, where Jesse couldn't see, but the cry she gave made it clear she liked whatever he was doing.

In the next second, she shuddered, slamming down onto his thighs and holding there, arms wrapped around Max's shoulders, her forehead buried in his neck.

In the next second, Max groaned on one last thrust.

The only sound now filling the silence in the room was the sound of their heavy breathing.

Mally couldn't catch her breath.

She couldn't stop her racing heart either. And even though she'd just come so hard she swore her teeth were loose, her lust was already rising.

Because she felt Jesse's intent stare on her back. Every breath she took was laced with Max's scent, so utterly male it defied an easy label. She couldn't help but wonder how Jesse would smell. And feel. And taste.

But she didn't want to move, not now that Max had his arms wrapped around her, cradling her like he truly cared about her and not just an object of his lust.

Isn't that how you see him?

She wasn't going to answer that, not even to herself.

Then she felt Max press a kiss against the top of her head, so damn softly, she almost thought she'd imagined it. Then he did it again and she knew he hadn't.

In the next heartbeat, he lifted her off his lap and set her on the cushion next to him. So she faced Jesse.

The blazing-hot desire in his eyes made her pussy clench and, though she couldn't really believe it, she was ready to go again.

She must've made a move to rise but Jesse shook his head and stood. Her gaze dropped to his waist, to the bulge behind his zipper. Just as big as Max, if not bigger.

She'd never been the kind of girl who compared. If a guy knew how to use his equipment, size really didn't matter. Not that she was an expert but she had enough experience to know.

But Max was one of the biggest guys she'd ever had sex with. And holy hell, that had been amazing.

Add Jesse into the mix...

Closing the distance between them, Jesse stopped in front of her, staring. As if trying to figure her out.

Or maybe simply watching to see what she'd do.

She reached for him, hooked her fingers into his belt loops, and tugged him closer.

But Jesse had his own agenda. Like she'd done before, he went to his knees in front of her, holding her gaze as he spread her legs then used his shoulders to spread her open even farther.

Leaning forward, he put his mouth on her pussy with no more hesitation and her head fell back as her eyes closed. She felt movement beside her but Jesse ate at her with so much fierce intent, she could do nothing but let him have her.

Unlike with Max, who'd basically let her fuck him, Jesse took her. His tongue flicked over her clit then lapped between her labia, making her squirm as he worked her over-sensitized flesh.

Grabbing her hips, he held her down when she wanted to move, pinning her to the couch, completely at his mercy.

Another orgasm began to rise. She knew this one would be stronger than the first. But she wanted Jesse fucking her when she came.

So she held back, enjoying the sensation but not letting herself fall over the edge, no matter what he did. It was touch and go for a few seconds but she managed to hold on until finally Jesse growled and rocked back on his heels.

"Stubborn."

Her eyes opened, the hint of amusement in his tone curving her lips. "Always have been."

Then she realized Max was no longer by her side. Her gaze darted around but Jesse reached and grabbed her chin, forcing her to look at him.

"He didn't go far. Trust me, he'll be back in a minute. He won't want to miss this."

Jesse rose to his feet again, hands on the button of his jeans and then the zipper, pulling it down and shoving his jeans below his hips, releasing his cock.

"Lay out, Mally."

She loved hearing her nickname from Jesse just as much as she had from Max and she obeyed without a second thought.

That's when she saw Max return, his pants zipped but not buttoned and his shirt still untucked and mostly unbuttoned. Just looking at him made her heart pound. Then Jesse grabbed her legs, pulled her closer and hiked her up to just the right height. And impaled her on his sheathed cock.

She had a second to wonder if they kept condoms hidden in the couch before Jesse's cock stretched her wide.

Moaning, she couldn't process the sensations flooding her. There were too damn many.

Jesse's pace was different than Max's. Slower, more deliberate. Max had had an urgency that had heightened every feeling. Jesse seemed determined to make her so damn frustrated she screamed.

She gripped the cushion beneath her as he lifted her ass off the couch with his hands around her ankles. The angle of penetration hit a different spot inside that lit her up. Moaning, she closed her eyes, letting Jesse hold her high and fuck her hard.

"She likes that, Jesse. You can tell by the way her lips move."

Max's voice came from above, making her stomach clench at the sheer sexiness. He hadn't said much when she'd been with him but now it seemed he had a lot to say. And he could talk all night for her.

Moaning, she arched a little higher as Jesse worked his cock back inside on a slow push. She hadn't expected Jesse's deliberate attempt to make her lose control. She'd thought Max—

Jesse thrust in hard, making her breath hitch.

"Open your eyes, Mally." Max didn't suggest, he demanded. Her eyes flew open, looking into Jesse's as Max continued. "Jesse wants to see your eyes when you come. He wants to see how fucking responsive you are."

She didn't know why she continued to resist. Maybe

because this felt so amazing. Maybe because she worried she'd never have this again. Maybe—

Her orgasm hit her hard, every muscle in her body tensing as she tried to tighten around Jesse's cock even more. He continued to pump into her until she could barely breathe. Then finally, he thrust once more with a hard grunt and she felt his cock twitch and flex inside her.

For several long seconds he held her gaze in an intimate stare until finally his cock stopped pulsing.

Gently, Jesse disengaged and laid her back out on the couch. Dropping onto the cushion beside her, he reached for her immediately and pulled her onto his lap.

Beside her, she felt Max sit. Turning her head, she found him watching her carefully. His slightly mussed hair made her smile and his gaze narrowed.

Reaching for him, she dragged her fingers along his jaw, feeling the muscles jump under fingers.

Raising an eyebrow, he held up her clothing.

And a shiver of apprehension ran through her.

Was he telling her it was time to leave? Or simply being considerate?

Jesse's arms loosened and finally fell away as she leaned back and reached for her dress and underwear.

Deliberately holding Max's gaze, she stood, dropping her dress on Jesse's lap and shimmying into her bra and panties. Both men watched her every move as she grabbed her dress and shrugged into it, tying the bow at her side.

She waited for either man to say something then realized they were waiting for her to make the first move. And the silence was starting to get awkward.

Should she say thank you? She certainly wasn't waiting

for them to declare their undying love. Why was this so hard?

Maybe it was best to stick to business.

She turned to Max. "Are you going to need me for other events this week?"

If she'd surprised him, he didn't show it. Instead, he stood. "It's possible. I'll look at my schedule and let you know tomorrow."

Behind her, Jesse stood. "I'll drive you home."

No way. That would be even more awkward than this was already becoming.

She glanced over her shoulder. "No. If you don't mind, I'll take a taxi."

"And if I do mind?"

She thought she heard irritation in Jesse's question but he didn't get to be pissy. Not now. If anyone had the right to be pissed, it was her. What the hell was with these two?

"I'll tell you I'm a grown woman who's decided she wants to take a taxi home."

"A woman who just came around both of our cocks."

A blush burned her cheeks at Max's dry statement but she refused to be intimidated now. If she was going to dictate any terms in this relationship, she had to start now.

"Yes, I did. And I plan to again another night. But tonight, I'm going home."

Behind her, she heard Jesse on his phone, ordering a taxi, but she couldn't drag herself away from the gleam in Max's eyes.

"So this...arrangement of ours will continue."

She nodded. "I agreed to the terms. Six months as your date."

"And the sex?"

She would *not* let him intimidate her. "Will continue as long as all partners are willing during the same six-month period."

Was he smiling? She couldn't tell.

Out of the corner of her eye, she saw Jesse tilt his head back, eyes glued to the ceiling.

Max glanced at Jesse then with a raised eyebrow. Jesse's only answer was a muted sigh.

"We accept."

10

"Fuck."

Jesse's low curse drew Max's attention away from the door as it closed behind Mary Alice.

Max wanted to follow her, throw her over his shoulder, and take her up to his bedroom where he and Jesse could take their time with her. Play with her until they'd wrung every ounce of pleasure they could from her then let her rest for a few hours before starting all over.

Tonight had been good. But it definitely hadn't been enough. He wanted more.

How much more? Not a question he was prepared to answer right now. Especially not with Jesse ready to go nuclear.

"Jesus, Max, what the fuck did we do?"

Taking a deep breath, Max turned to face his best friend.

Jesse's face was set in hard lines and his dark eyes glittered like obsidian. "Pissed off" wasn't strong enough to describe Jesse's mood right now but Max wasn't about to coddle him.

"Nothing she didn't want."

No, she'd been a more-than-willing participant. Hell, she'd practically begged Jesse to fuck her. Just the thought made Max's cock throb.

Jesse's gaze narrowed even more. "That's not what I'm saying and you know it."

Yeah, he knew that but he knew Jesse needed to get this out. "Then what are you saying? Are you telling me you didn't want her? Because we both know that's not true."

Running a hand through his dark hair, Jesse shook his head. "I'm saying this is gonna be way more complicated than you bargained for."

Max knew that, too. He just didn't fucking care. He'd had her and now he wasn't going to be satisfied until he'd had his fill. But six months wouldn't be enough. That was only the start.

"Isn't everything?"

Jesse's frustration continued to build as he paced until Max thought Jesse would explode. Jesse never exploded, at least not like other people. He didn't yell and scream or throw punches. He imploded. Silently. Until he disappeared one night and returned the next morning with bruises covering most of his body.

"Goddammit, Max." Jesse couldn't seem to stop shaking his head. "This is the wrong fucking time."

"No." Max was sure about this. "This is the *only* fucking time."

Jesse held his gaze and Max silently willed his best friend to get on the same page. How could Jesse not see that they needed this? Needed *her*? Deserved her.

Everything they'd worked for, everything they wanted... they were so damn close to getting it.

They just needed to hold steady and hold together. Bringing Mary Alice into their relationship would fill the gaps between them, not push them apart.

And, goddammit, they both wanted her. Why the fuck were they not entitled to go after what—and who—they wanted, just like everyone else?

With a rough growl, Jesse stopped to glare at him. "And what happens when someone comes at us? Because, sure as shit, someone will eventually. This week, next month, next year. Are you really willing to risk her? You weren't a couple of days ago. What the hell changed?"

Max's gut tightened but he shook his head and willed back the fear. "I'm not willing to risk her. We'll keep her safe. We've had enough damn practice."

Jesse's gaze narrowed even more. "You painted a huge fucking target on her back tonight at that damn mixer."

Boiling heat began to build in Max's chest at Jesse's absolute stubbornness. He wanted to rage and snap, but he was determined to keep his cool. He knew that was the only way to get through to Jesse. "That's bullshit and you know it. No one will dare touch her."

Jesse sliced a hand through the air. "We can't count on that. Not anymore. David and Mickey are gone. They can't watch our backs from fucking halfway across the world."

Max knew that better than Jesse would ever know. Every day, he had a reminder thrown in his face, whether it was a "friendly" email from a former acquaintance or an anonymous phone call threatening him with destruction. He hadn't told Jesse about the phone calls yet. Hadn't wanted to set him off, not when they had other shit to worry about.

"Christ, Jesse. Calm the fuck down. She gave herself to us tonight. Obviously, she trusts us enough to fuck her. She'll trust us enough to protect her."

Jesse grimaced. "She's curious. That's all. Eventually she'll realize she doesn't want to be associated with low-life criminals—"

"Fuck that." God damn it, Max hated when Jesse started down that road. "We're not criminals. That's not our life anymore."

Jesse glared at him. "You're right, it's not. But you're not that stupid. No one is going to trust us. They may do business with us, but they're not going to invite us into their homes like old friends. We're always going to be outsiders."

Every word Jesse said hit Max in the gut. It wasn't anything he hadn't thought of himself, but he'd made the decision not to dwell on the negative. Maybe he was delusional. He chose to believe he was moving forward. Leaving the crime and the violence and the constant rage behind them.

"Or maybe we can prove them all wrong." Max held Jesse's gaze, willing Jesse to believe him. "Maybe we build our own world and invite only the people we want into it."

With a sigh, Jesse stopped pacing and just stared at Max. "You honestly believe that, don't you?"

Max had to. It was the only way he knew to move forward. "You know I do. What I don't know is why you don't."

Jesse didn't answer right away. Max could tell he wanted to say something. He just had no idea what that could be.

Max's gut twisted at Jesse's continued silence. He and Jesse had never been farther apart on anything than they were now, and Max knew that wasn't going to change tonight.

So before they went at each other with their fists, Max decided to withdraw.

Turning, he headed for the stairs to the second floor. Jesse needed to process what had happened tonight in his own way and come to his own conclusions. The fact that they usually always came to the same conclusion was the only thing that kept Max moving.

"I'm going to get some sleep. You should, too. We'll hash this out tomorrow."

"Sleeping on the problem isn't gonna make it go away," Jesse called from the bottom of the stairs.

Max gritted his teeth, thankful Jesse couldn't see him do it. "No, but maybe it'll help you realize how fucking wrong you are."

The shakes didn't hit until Mary Alice pushed through the door into her apartment.

Leaning back against the solid wood, she closed her eyes and pulled in a deep breath. Jesus, she felt like she hadn't been able to breathe for hours.

Probably because her entire body continued to tingle with remnants of the orgasms Max and Jesse had wrung from her.

Holy shit.

She'd done it. She'd really done it. She'd asked for what

she'd wanted and gotten a whole hell of a lot more than she'd bargained for.

Not that that was a bad thing. Oh God no, it wasn't bad at all.

But...holy shit, what happened now?

"Hey, you're back. Where've you been all night? I was getting ready to text you."

Mary Alice caught back a scream just before it escaped.

"Izzy! Holy crap, I didn't know you were here."

Isabella DeMarco stared at her, eyes wide. "Yeah, I kinda get that. What happened? Is something wrong? Where've you been?"

Having sex with two amazing guys. "I, ah, had a date."

Pushing away from the door, she headed for her room but Izzy followed on her heels, a pint of rocky road ice cream in one hand and a spoon in the other.

"Really? You had a date?"

Looking over her shoulder, Mary Alice wrinkled her nose at Izzy as she reached her room, Izzy hot on her heels. "What does that mean?"

"It means, you didn't tell anyone you had a date and you haven't even mentioned a guy in ages. So..."

Hopping onto the bed, Izzy watched Mary Alice take off her jewelry, licking ice cream off her spoon. Obviously not going anywhere until Mary Alice said something.

"So what?"

Izzy let her head drop back, black hair falling in long waves to the bed. "Ugh. You're so not fooling me. So who's the guy?"

Jewelry off, Mary Alice grabbed her pajamas and headed for the bathroom. "No one you know."

"And…" Izzy drew the word out to about five syllables. "Spit it out."

Closing the bathroom door behind her, Mary Alice stripped, trying to decide if she should spill her guts or not. She had no idea how Izzy would respond.

But she couldn't process this by herself. She needed someone to talk to.

"Can you keep a secret?" she yelled through the door.

"Well, duh," Izzy yelled back. "Who didn't tell anyone when you smoked that weed you found in your brother's truck? Or the time we drank that entire bottle of tequila and you nearly missed your brother's graduation puking in the bathroom?"

Good points. And now their neighbors probably knew her secrets as well.

"Promise not to freak out."

"Oh please," Izzy scoffed. "When do I ever freak out?"

Both sets of Izzy's grandparents had emigrated from Italy, which meant Izzy had a double dose of high-intensity freak-out potential.

"Seriously?" Mary Alice opened the door and headed back across the hall to her bedroom where Izzy practically bounced on the mattress. "Iz, you have two speeds, freak out and asleep."

Izzy made a face. "Okay, fine. But you know I won't tell a soul if you don't want me to."

Since she was dying to talk to someone, Mary Alice dropped onto the bed, grabbed her pillow, and hugged it to her chest.

"I went to a chamber mixer with Max Burdanov."

Izzy's nose wrinkled. "I know I know that name…"

"He used to work for the Oleksy family."

Now Izzy's forehead wrinkled. "He works for Ada—" Her friend's eyes went wide. "Oh wait. What the *fuck*? Mally! Are you fucking serious?"

Mary Alice smiled at the South Philly accent that popped out of her friend's mouth. Usually, Izzy managed to smooth it out.

"And that's not all."

Izzy's mouth dropped open for a full second. "Okay, you just told me you had a date with a Russian mobster. What the hell else can you possibly—"

"He's not a mobster." She wanted to bite her tongue at the immediate need to defend Max but she had a feeling she'd be doing it a lot. "And I had sex with him."

Izzy's eyes couldn't get any wider. "You had sex with a Russian gang member—"

"And then I had sex with his best friend, Jesse Kanatawa. While Max watched."

Her friend's mouth opened, closed, opened, closed. She blinked. Then she shook her head. "Wha— Wait. Just... Did I seriously just hear you say you had sex? With two guys? Tonight?"

Mary Alice refused to blush. If she couldn't get through a conversation with Izzy about dating—okay, having sex with two men, how the hell was she supposed to face the firing squad, otherwise known as her family?

At the moment, she couldn't even think about facing Tristan and Adam Monday morning. She knew they'd hear about her date with Max sometime this weekend. Then they'd put two and one together and get the right amount of information to make them crazy. And possibly lock her in her office until they could fill in her brothers, who would take her out of her office and lock her in her parents' house.

"Yes, you did."

Mary Alice seriously thought she might have to reboot her friend with a smack on the head. Izzy just continued to sit there, staring at her, her lips parted as if she were going to speak. But nothing ever came out until finally, Izzy swallowed, took a deep breath and shook her head.

"No fucking way."

Mary Alice just nodded.

"No *fucking* way." Izzy's eyes kept getting bigger. "Did you take something? Did they give you something? Force you to take— Wait, are you tripping? Do I have to take you to the hospital to get your stomach pumped?"

Mary Alice rolled her eyes, anger and a healthy dose of righteous indignation setting in. "No. I'm stone cold sober. And Max and Jesse would never do *anything* to hurt me. They're not like that. You don't know them."

Izzy's head continued to shake as if it were on a spring. "Then...what the *fuck*, Mally?"

Mary Alice grimaced at the genuine shock in her friend's voice. She'd known her friends would think it was weird, strange, odd. Totally out of character. But she'd thought—

"Holy shit. Was it good?" Izzy asked.

Oh thank God. Finally.

Breathing a sigh of relief, Mary Alice felt tears sting the corners of her eyes.

Mary Alice grabbed for Izzy's hand and her friend gripped hers tight. "Will you be freaked out again if I say yes? Like...oh my God, it was amazing."

That glint in Izzy's eyes meant her friend's wicked side

had started to rise. "Well, damn, girl, I hope it was. Otherwise, I might have to sic your brothers on them."

Which made Mary Alice bite her lip. "I know people are going to find out but you have to promise not to say anything to anybody. At least not for a little while."

"What about Maris?" Their other roommate.

Mary Alice bit her lip. "Let me tell her myself, okay? Where is she, anyway?"

Izzy rolled her eyes. "Out with that douchebag she's been seeing for the past few weeks. Have you met him yet? Total creep. No idea what she sees in him."

"No, I haven't. And Max and Jesse are so *not* creeps. I like them, Iz."

Izzy shook her head, her expression still dazed. "I guess you better 'cause not everyone's gonna understand. I mean, Jesus, I get it. I think. But I still think you're gonna be dealing with a lot of shit from a whole lot of people. And I know you, Mally. You don't like to be the center of attention. This is gonna put a lot of eyes on you. I mean, okay, if you say you like them and they're not really criminals anymore, but most people are still gonna look at them and see 'Russian mob,' even if they're wearing thousand-dollar suits."

Trust Izzy to hit on every single one of Mary Alice's fears. "But I don't, Iz. And shouldn't that count for something?"

Izzy's expression went soft and sympathetic as she reached across the bed to grab Mary Alice's hand. "Aw, babe. Of course it does. Yeah, yours is the only opinion that should count. But that's not how the world works and I don't want to see you get totally depressed because of a bunch of assholes who should keep their noses out of other people's business but don't."

"Well, I'm not gonna stop seeing them." She'd made a bargain with Max. For the next six months, she was his companion. She'd fulfill her end of the bargain. And in return, she'd have them both in bed. "And if I want to have sex with both of them, I'm going to. Is that fucked up?"

Izzy shrugged, her expression incredulous as she shook her head. "I don't have the first damn clue. But you know I'll never judge. I just don't wanna see you hurt."

Mary Alice had a feeling that was going to be the toughest part.

11

"Are you saying the line was intentionally damaged?"

Thursday morning, Jesse had a knot in his chest so tight he felt as if he was being suffocated. And even though he knew from experience that actual suffocation was entirely different, he still couldn't shake the feeling.

He could barely hear the electrician, who had his head stuffed into the ceiling in the building that'd had the fire last week. But he heard enough to confirm his suspicion.

"...lines nicked...a clean cut...no other wear...not mice... probably switchblade...don't see any more...should be replaced..."

The guy went on for another minute before climbing back down the ladder and looking Jesse square in the eyes.

"Put me on the spot, I'm gonna tell you different but between you and me, yeah, it's intentional."

Since Jesse had known Victor Finucci since he was five years old and was the only person Jesse trusted not to fuck with him about this shit, Jesse shook his head and started to swear.

Victor nodded his head in commiseration. "Yep. Hate to be the bearer of bad news, kid. Know that wasn't what you wanted to hear. I can fix it, no problem. But you're gonna hafta fix the rat problem or you're gonna have a lotta other problems. Know what I mean?"

Yeah, Jesse knew what he meant. He just hadn't wanted to believe it. Now, faced with proof, he had too many other considerations to keep track of.

"Thanks, Vic. When do you think you can get to it?"

"For you, kid, I can have Jimmy out tomorrow."

Jimmy was Vic's oldest son, about five years older than Jesse and with much more of an attitude problem than Vic. Jimmy didn't like Jesse. And he really didn't like Max. But if Vic said jump, Jimmy jumped, even if it was over the side of the Ben Franklin Bridge. Or he fixed Max's plumbing. Jimmy probably thought the two were equally as painful.

"I'd appreciate it, Vic."

Vic nodded and grabbed his toolbox then headed for the door. Vic was a man of surprisingly few words for being from South Philly and Italian. "No problem. I'll call ya."

Alone in the building now, Jesse released the breath he'd been holding and restrained the urge to kick the nearest solid object. Or put his fist through the wall. But then he'd be hiring someone else to fix it and he didn't want to give anyone else the opportunity to screw with them.

They were already screwed enough.

Max was at Shivers, having the entire electrical system checked out. Jesse knew what they'd find without having to be told. Someone had tampered with the wiring there. He'd bet his left nut.

And the mechanical problems at the brewery meant they'd have to check every single property they owned. Including the house.

Where they'd fucked Mary Alice Monday night.

His jaw clenched so tight, it cracked.

Christ. At least he could admit to himself that it'd been more than a quick fuck. It'd meant more. At least to him. Max... Hell, he knew what it meant to Max. Max almost had himself convinced he had real feelings for her.

And maybe he did. Maybe this was the girl for Max.

Maybe she was the girl for both of them.

Jesse couldn't let himself think about that. Not now. Not when someone was trying to take them down.

Jesse had known this problem was man-made. Vic had merely confirmed it.

And even though it made him want to punch something, he needed Max to see that this damn arrangement with Mally wasn't going to work. Not now.

She needed to be far away from them.

Or maybe you just need to keep her really, really close.

That insidious voice in his head had been speaking up a hell of a lot more in the past three days. Taunting him with visions of Mally in their lives for more than a six-month fucked-up affair that was sure to end in heartbreak and broken bones. Not hers. Neither he nor Max would ever lay a hand on her in anger. Jesse would cut his off before he did that.

No, the broken bones would be theirs when Mally's

parents, brothers, and bosses found out she was spending time with them.

Adam and Tristan would know immediately what was going on between the three of them. They had the kind of relationship Max wanted. A relationship Jesse couldn't believe would actually work. A relationship that would horrify her parents and her brothers. And when they got over their initial shock and picked themselves off the floor, they'd ship her away. Somewhere Max and Jesse would never find her.

And damn, wasn't he just fucking melodramatic today.

Pulling out his phone with a sigh, Jesse punched in Max's number.

"I don't wanna hear it. Whatever you're gonna say, just fucking keep it to your goddamn self."

Max must've talked to the electrician. Who must have told him the same thing Vic had told Jesse.

Jesse closed his eyes and rubbed them with his thumbs. "Shit."

"Yeah. I'm heading to the nightclub now. The electrician's gonna meet us there in half an hour but I already know what he's gonna say. I need you to set up inspections for the other properties. Quietly. Find out what else has been fucked with."

"And you're gonna do…what?"

"Try to figure out who's screwing with us and shut them down."

"And how the hell are you going to do that? Legally?"

The line went silent and Jesse knew Max was grinding his teeth together.

Jesse sighed. "I'll handle it."

"Fuck you. Fuck that. Just...don't. I'm not in the fucking mood."

"Then don't go off half-cocked. We'll handle this together. Just like we have everything else."

Another silence before he heard Max sigh. "I know. Shit. I know. I just thought..."

Yeah, Jesse knew what Max had thought. He'd thought maybe they'd actually be able to get away from the lives they'd been living. To not have to look over their shoulders every day.

Right.

"Why don't we meet at the brewery tonight? We can eat, have a few beers, and go over the place after hours with Rick. No one will think twice about us being there."

Another pause. "I was going to call Mary Alice tonight."

Jesse knew Max had no business function tonight. So there was only one reason for him to call her. But Jesse asked the question anyway. "Why?"

He heard Max's sigh through the phone. "You know exactly why."

"Max—"

"No. Don't start in on me again. I'm going to call her. I'm going to ask her out for tomorrow night. Somewhere high-end. Somewhere we'll be noticed."

"Jesus fucki—"

"Come with us."

Yes. "No."

"We're safer together. You know that." Max paused when Jesse said nothing else. "Now's the time to take what we want. To show no fear. Because if we flinch now... If we show any weakness, we might as well just raise a white fucking flag and surrender."

"You keep saying that, Max."

"Because it's fucking true."

Jesse heard the stone-cold resolution in Max's voice and knew Max had reached the end of his rope with this conversation. They'd had the same argument before Max had taken her to the mixer. Jesse knew it was time to either get on board or cut and run.

"I'll see you at the brewery at seven."

"Jess—"

"I'll see you tonight."

Then he hung up and dropped his phone on the nearest table before he threw it across the room.

About two o'clock Thursday afternoon, Mary Alice looked up to find Adam standing in the doorway to her office.

Gasping, she caught herself before she threw her pen at him. "Jesus, Adam. What the hell? Are you part ninja? Seriously, don't do that."

"Mally."

Uh-oh.

He stood with his arms crossed over his chest, his expression relaxed and his eyes hard.

Shit.

Damn it. He knew.

And, damn it, she refused to feel guilty. She had no reason to be. He wasn't her father or her brother. He was her boss.

She raised her eyebrows and stared straight at him. "Do you need something?"

"An explanation would be nice."

"For what?"

His gaze narrowed ever so slightly. "I'm pretty sure you know what for."

"No, I really don't." She sat back in her desk chair and crossed her arms over her chest. "Why don't you give me a clue?"

"You sure you want to play it like this?"

Her chin went up before she could stop herself. "I don't know what you're talking about."

"Fine." Adam walked into her office and closed the door behind him. Then he sat in the chair opposite her desk and settled in, looking completely at ease. "Do you want me to start with all the reasons it's a bad idea?"

She opened her mouth to protest.

"Or," he continued, "do you want to hear why I think you should tell me to go to hell?"

And shut her mouth with a snap.

Adam's lips quirked into a self-deprecating grimace. "Nothing to say yet?"

She shouldn't. But she couldn't help herself. "Other than I'm a grown woman and you're not my father or my brother?"

Adam's laughter surprised her. He didn't do it often and then usually only with Kat, who shared the same dry sense of humor. Even so, he didn't often just burst into laughter.

She sighed as he wound down, shaking his head and continuing to grin at her.

"Oh, just spit it out." She knew she sounded grumpy but

she didn't care. "You're going to anyway. How'd you find out?"

He shrugged. "Eyes and ears everywhere. Something you should remember. And yeah, I am gonna talk. So…bad idea. They've got a history they'd can't change or outrun. And eventually they're gonna have to meet it head-on. I pity anyone who thinks they can take something from Max and Jesse because obviously they don't know them well enough to beat them. But there's always going to be someone out there who thinks they can."

Spoken so plainly, the words packed more of a punch than she'd expected. Because they were totally true. She swallowed hard and nodded, more to herself than to Adam. "And the good?"

Adam's mouth curved into a hard smile, one she was sure made grown men quake. "I've known Max and Jesse since I was a kid. I used to think I was a hard-ass…until I met them. Even back then, they were a unit. Always together. Always looking out for one another. I'd thought—" He shook his head and huffed out a laugh but he didn't finish his sentence. "Max is one of the smartest people I know. Maybe *the* smartest. And Jesse is one of the most loyal. Together, they're a force of nature. They can pretty much do anything. Together. They draw you behind that wall, they'll die before they let anything happen to you. I admire the hell out of that."

She sensed a "but" coming and braced for it. There had to be a "but."

Adam didn't disappoint. "I know you didn't ask for it but I'm gonna give you the best advice my dad ever gave me."

Since his dad had once run the criminal organization

Max and Jesse had recently left, she figured this was the "but."

"Never be afraid to take what you want and never listen to anyone tell you you shouldn't want it. But never forget to look over your shoulder because, sure as shit, something will come up to bite you on the ass if you don't."

A little shocked that he hadn't come right out and said she shouldn't see Max and Jesse, she gave herself a few seconds to think about what he'd said. "That sounds...sad."

Adam shook his head. "It's not. It's just life on the streets. Something you really don't know anything about. But if you're going to...associate with Max and Jesse, you need to be prepared to get bit."

Because the first thing that jumped into her head at the thought of being bit was probably not what Adam had meant, she had to bite her lip against the smile that wanted to break loose.

But she must not have been fast enough because Adam actually rolled his eyes at her before standing and heading for the door.

"And that's my cue to leave." He shook his head before he turned back to look at her. "You know if you need anything, Mally, you only have to ask, right? If you're in trouble or... hell, anything at all. Even if you just need to talk. You know I'll be there, right?"

Tears sprang into the corners of her eyes at the sincerity in his voice. Adam was always such a hard-ass. The only time she saw him soften was with Kat or his nieces and nephew. "Yeah."

Adam nodded. "Okay. And I'll try to keep Tris off your back, but I don't know for how long."

She grimaced. "Does he know?"

Sighing, Adam shook his head. "Not yet. I haven't said anything and I won't. But take pity on me. Tell him before he finds out from anyone else. You know Tris. He gets pissy."

From the hall behind Adam, she heard Tristan say, "What the hell? I don't get pissy. What the hell are you talking about?"

Adam's eyebrows rose and she sighed before nodding. Might as well get it over with all at once.

"Hey, Tristan," she called out, "do you have a minute?"

By the time three o'clock in the afternoon rolled around, Max finally had a few minutes to take a breath. And make a phone call.

After his talk with Jesse this morning, he hadn't been in the mood to talk to anyone. Especially not the woman he wanted to ask out to dinner. They way he'd felt earlier, he would've fucked up that conversation completely.

Of course, after dealing with about ten tons of shit all day, he probably should wait until tomorrow to attempt this.

Fuck that. I'm sick of waiting.

Picking up his desk phone, he rang the outer office. "Delia, hold all my calls until I get back to you."

"Of course, Mr. Burdanov. Do you need anything else?"

Max caught back a sigh at her use of "Mr." "No, thank you, Delia."

"Then I'll wait to hear from you."

As the connection ended, Max released that sigh.

They'd brought Delia Kincaid with them from the Oleksy

organization. At twenty-nine, she had ten years of experience as Mickey Oleksy's office assistant, a job she'd taken after nearly dying from a knife wound in a drug deal gone bad.

Streetwise and more cynical than Jesse, Delia had been friends with Max since seventh grade, when she'd offered Max her virginity in exchange for protection. Her uncle had been taking bids, and as soon as he'd found the highest buyer, she was to be drugged and given to some old pervert to be raped.

She'd told Max, at least if it was him, she wouldn't puke or end up beaten or dead. They'd been each other's first and when her uncle had beaten her senseless afterward, Max had gotten her into the Oleksy organization, where David Oleksy had set her up as a ward of the ancient aunt of one of his captains. She'd taken care of the old woman until she'd died three years later then Delia had hit the streets with Max and Jesse.

Now, she managed their office like she'd dealt with the street—no bullshit and no tolerance for it. And total loyalty. He had no doubt she could handle anything thrown at her.

Mary Alice...didn't have the same life experience. And that was a complete understatement.

Pushing that thought out of his mind, he picked up his cell and punched in her number.

It rang four times before she answered. And he couldn't help but wonder if she'd seen the number and had to decide whether she wanted to pick it up.

"Hello, Max. How are you?"

"I'm good, Mal—Mary Alice. How are you?"

"I'm fine."

And silence. Christ almighty, he sucked at this. "I'd like to take you to dinner tomorrow night."

A slight pause. "Is this for a function?"

"No." But it wasn't merely a date either, was it? His jaw clenched.

"Sooo…this is an actual date?"

Was she going to say no? "I need to make appearances at places other than our own. I have to be seen around town."

"Ah."

What the hell did that mean? And did it really matter? She'd made the bargain. She'd stick to it. "I'll pick you up at 6:45."

"Will Jesse be with us?"

"Do you want him there?"

Say yes.

"Not if he doesn't want to be there."

Which sounded exactly like something Jesse would say.

Be careful what you wish for. "He'll be there if that's what you want."

"And what do *you* want, Max?"

He smiled at the exasperation in her voice. And told her exactly what came to mind. "I thought I made that perfectly clear the other night. I want you in bed between me and Jesse. Or on the couch or on the floor or in the damn car. I don't really care as long as I get to be inside you."

Her sharp, indrawn breath was either arousal or shock. Considering what she'd demanded of them the other night, he was going with arousal.

"And if I want to skip dinner and simply go to your house?"

Was she trying to avoid being seen with them? "Then I'd remind you of the terms of our arrangement."

A very short pause. "Fair enough." And did he hear amusement in her voice? "But, Max, it's customary to at least call a woman after you've had sex with her. And I don't mean three days later. I'll see you tomorrow."

When she hung up, he was smiling.

And when he met Jesse at the brewery that night, he continued to be amused by her dig. He'd deserved it. Hell, he liked that she had sharp claws. Any woman they took on would need to be sharp.

He and Jesse and Rick Kerr, who'd started the brewery, had gone over every inch of the brewery together and found no signs of tampering. And since Rick had built every piece of equipment himself, he'd know if anything had been tampered with.

By the time Jesse and Max got home, Max was ready to decompress before bed.

"You want another beer?"

They'd brought two growlers home with them and Max was in process of opening one.

When Jesse didn't answer his question, Max looked over his shoulder to find Jesse leaning against the counter on the other side of the kitchen, arms crossed over his chest as he stared at Max.

"Why the hell do you keep smiling?" Jesse asked.

That wiped the smile away and Max glared over his shoulder. "Did you seriously just ask me that question? What bug crawled up your ass and died?"

"I don't find any humor in the fact that someone's fucking with us. Yeah, the brewery's clean but that doesn't mean everything else is. We need to have all the buildings examined then we need to figure out who the hell—"

"I talked to Mally today. We're having dinner tomorrow night."

Jesse's eyes narrowed. "Dinner. As in a date."

Since Jesse didn't seem to want a beer, Max poured one. "She wants you there."

Jesse's face expressed extreme disbelief. "Did she actually say that?"

"She asked for you."

"She wants me there? For dinner?"

"I believe that's what I said."

Jesse paused before releasing a huge sigh. "And you still think this is a good idea?"

"I think someone's fucking with our business. Not with our lives."

"Maybe they just haven't gotten to that point yet."

Frustration twisted in Max's gut. "Christ, Jesse—"

"No. Wait." Jesse held up one hand. "I don't want to start this fight again." After a brief sigh, he nodded. "I'm in."

Max's breath caught for a brief second before he started to grin. "Glad to hear it. What changed your mind?"

Jesse's gaze narrowed. "Maybe I just enjoyed the sex."

Bullshit.

If Jesse was looking to get a rise out of him, Max wasn't going to give him the satisfaction. "Then I have to say I don't blame you. The sex was fucking amazing. And it'll only get better."

A pause. "So we're handling her like any other woman we've fucked?"

No fucking way. "Why wouldn't we?"

Jesse nodded. "So she's just a bed partner."

No. "Of course. What did you think she'd be?"

"I just want to make sure I've got the rules clear going in."

"There are no rules. It's just sex. Just like it's always been."

Jesse refused to release Max's gaze. "And when the six months are up? It's over?"

Max's jaw tried to clench but he loosened it before it could. "Of course."

Except that was total bullshit. But if it made Jesse feel better about getting Mally in their bed, then he'd lie through his teeth. Hell, Max had no idea what was going to happen in six months. But for right now, she would be theirs. And they'd more than make it worth her while.

* * *

Mary Alice's day went to shit by noon.

It started with a phone call from her second-oldest brother, Jason.

"Jesus, Mal, did you think we wouldn't find out? What the hell were you thinking?"

"Hello to you, too, Jase. And how are you today?"

"I'm pretty pissed off at the moment, little sister. And I'm pretty sure you know why."

Not bothering to hide her sigh, she pushed back from her desk, where she'd been trying to translate Tristan's shorthand into a report for the client. Today, her mind just wasn't on her job and it frustrated the hell out of her.

And now this.

"I don't have the first frigging clue," she lied. "Why don't you spell it out for me?"

"Max. Burdanov."

Yep. That sealed the deal. Today was going to suck.

She didn't want to have to deal with her brother. She wanted to leave now. She wanted to meet Max and Jesse. She wanted to strip them naked and gorge herself on them. She'd never wanted to do that in her life. And now that she did…

"What about him?"

"Don't. Just don't. What the hell are you playing at?"

She sighed, not bothering to hide it from her brother. "I'm not playing at anything. It was a date. Do you even know what that is anymore?"

Jason practically growled in frustration. "I know perfectly well what a date is. And there's no way you should be anywhere near that lowlife."

If she were in a Bugs Bunny cartoon, Mary Alice swore she'd have a lit fuse coming out of her head.

"Jason. You need to think very carefully about the next words that come out of your mouth."

"And why is that?"

"Because I'm going out with Max Burdanov again tonight."

The silence on the other end of the line nearly scalded. Jason might not be a redhead but he had the temper of one.

"What?" she taunted, because she couldn't help herself. "Nothing else to say?"

"Jesus Christ, Mary Alice."

The fear in her brother's voice rocked through her like an earthquake. "Jase—"

"Sweetheart, what's going on? Are you in trouble? Do you need help with something? Do you...need money?"

Her mouth dropped open and her brain stuttered for a second. "You think I'm seeing him because I need *money*?"

"Fuck." Jason's voice sounded like five miles of bad road. "No, goddammit. That's not what I meant."

Shaking her head, she closed her eyes and took a deep breath. "Then what do you mean? Exactly."

"He's not someone you need in your life."

"And how do you know that? Do you know him? Have you met him? Have you ever talked to him?"

"I don't need to. Everyone knows—"

"Who's everyone?"

"Every damn cop in the city knows who Max Burdanov is. And that's enough for me to know you should stay the hell away from him."

Well, she couldn't argue with him about that. All the cops did know Max's name. He'd never been convicted of anything but he was a well-known member of the Oleksy organization.

Damn it, she'd known this was coming. Had known sooner or later one of her brothers would find out and confront her. Hell, she'd even thought she had something remotely rational to say in reply. And here she was, practically stomping her feet like a teenager.

"Jase. I love you. But I'm a grown woman with a brain. And I'm telling you, you're wrong about Max." She wanted to add "and Jesse" but, oh my God, that might actually make Jason's head explode. "He's not the man you think he is."

"So you're telling me he's not the same man who worked for the Russian mob for most of his life?"

"No. What I'm telling you is that he's changing his life. He's a legitimate businessman, one who works eighteen hours a day to make it happen. But he *is* making it, with no help from anyone because all people see is the man they *think* he is. I'm dating the man he actually is."

Silence from the other end.

Then finally, a big sigh. "Damn it, the guy's not right for you."

She knew that wasn't true. She was pretty sure he was just right for her. Him *and* Jesse.

How she knew that after only one night together was a mystery. Didn't make it any less true.

And Jesus, she couldn't even imagine how this conversation was going to go with her brothers, much less her parents.

Cross that hurdle when you come to it.

God, she hoped she didn't fall flat on her face when she did.

"No, he's not right for *you*," she finally said. "But you're not the one dating th—him."

"Christ, Mally. If anything happens to you…"

"Do you trust me?"

Jason huffed. "Of course I trust you. That's not the issue."

"Yeah, it pretty much is. You have to trust me to make my own decisions. And who I date is definitely my decision."

"You're making a mistake."

"And you're entitled to your opinion. You just don't get to make me feel bad about mine."

Another pause where she could hear Jason trying to get himself under control. "You need anything, you call me, little girl."

"You're first on my favorites list." That hadn't always been the case but her older brother was gone now. He'd been first on all their favorite lists.

"You know Mom and Dad are going to find out sooner or later."

She winced. "I know. I planned to tell them this weekend."

"I wouldn't let it wait too long. Dad owns a weapon and he knows how to use it."

Rolling her eyes, she sighed. "Yeah. Thanks for making me feel better."

"Yeah, well, consider it payback for making me crazy."

A smile curved her lips. "I love you, Jase. I gotta get back to work."

"Love you too, brat. Just...be careful. All right?"

"I'm always careful."

Jase snorted. "Yeah right. Talk to you soon."

He hung up before she could respond to his last dig. Damn him, she was one of the most careful people she knew. She often wished she could be less careful and more carefree. Not worry so much about every damn little thing.

Is that why you agreed to Max's arrangement?

No, this wasn't her being rebellious or even careless. She wanted Max. She wanted Jesse. And, damn it, that's the only reason she was going out with them. Danny's gambling debt had been a convenient way for her to initiate contact. Which probably made her an awful friend for using Bethann and Danny's troubles to her advantage.

"Shit."

She huffed out a sigh and shook her head. Maybe she hadn't thought this through as well as she should have. But

Jason was right about one thing. She needed to tell her parents and soon.

She didn't want Max to wind up on the wrong end of her dad's temper.

Punching in her mom's number, she glanced at the time on her computer. She still had that report to finish and another one to start and billing to complete—

"Hi, sweetheart. It's been a while since we talked. Busy?"

"Hey, Mom. Yeah, I've been busy. Work's been crazy."

"I know the feeling. Your dad's got more work than he can handle right now and I've been looking for another installer to help him but we just haven't found anyone yet."

Mary Alice let her mom carry the conversation for the next few minutes, let her complain about her dad's stubbornness and her brothers' perpetual state of bachelorhood and the fact that her sisters all had grandchildren.

Well, she didn't actually complain. Her mom never whined or bitched.

No, she was much more subtle. She explained how her dad was always tired because he had more work than he could handle for his carpet-laying business. And how her brothers needed to get housekeepers because their houses and apartments were pigsties. And how adorable Mary Alice's cousin's newborn daughter was.

Not that Mary Alice didn't think her cousin Tiff's baby was cute. She totally was. It's just that her mom wanted to have her own grandchildren to fuss over.

"So now that I've exhausted the family gossip, why don't you tell me why you called?"

"Do I have to have a reason?"

"Of course not. But you have something on your mind. Come on. Out with it."

Mary Alice took a deep breath. "I've got a date tonight."

Her mom laughed. "You make it sound like it's a punishment. I swear, I'll never have grandchildren. So who are you going out with?"

"I don't think you know him. His name's Max Burdanov."

"Hmm, the name sounds familiar. Is he a local boy?"

Only guys who'd grown up in their neighborhood got to be called local. Anyone not from an eight-square-block area was practically a foreigner.

"He's from Bustleton."

"Okay. So what does he do?"

He's a former Russian gang member, Mom. And the other night, I had sex with him and his friend. How about I bring them for dinner tomorrow?

"He owns a couple of clubs in town."

"That's sounds good."

"And a restaurant. And a couple of buildings."

"Sounds like he's successful."

"And he used to work for David and Mickey Oleksy."

"Who— Oh."

Her mom's quiet tone made her flinch. "Yeah. I figured I should let you know before someone else spilled the beans."

Her mom fell silent for several seconds. "Well, that's... interesting."

"Mom, before you say anything else, just— I like him. And I think you will too. He's smart and intense and fascinating. He's not..."

"A former gang member? Dangerous? Someone I

wouldn't want my daughter to *know* much less date? Oh, Mary Alice. I don't even know where to start."

"How about we start with the fact that I'm an adult and can make my own decisions."

Her mom huffed. "Then why did you call me? Do you want me to tell you it's okay? That I approve? Of course I don't approve of you going out with a gang member, former or otherwise."

Mary Alice took a deep breath before she started screeching like a banshee. She needed to keep her composure, didn't want to stamp her foot and whine like a teenager.

"I called you so you wouldn't be blindsided when one of your friends or one of my brothers decides to tattle on me."

"Your brothers care about you. They only want you to be happy. And safe."

And confined to the safe little world she'd always lived in, surrounded by family and the friends she'd known since high school and the very few people her family drew into the circle who hadn't grown up with them or lived in that eight-block radius. A circle that'd grown smaller after they'd lost John Matthew.

She took another deep breath. "I know that. I also know I'm a damn good judge of character. And if you don't trust me to pick the men I want to date, then I'm going to stop telling you about the men I date."

They both fell silent. Mary Alice figured her mom was wondering why she'd pushed her luck and tried for that girl after four boys.

"You're right. I'm sorry."

Mary Alice blinked and her mouth dropped open but she

had no idea what to say. She couldn't actually believe her mom had said that.

"Thanks for giving me a heads-up," her mom continued. "We do trust you, Mally." Her mom's soft huff of laughter came through the line perfectly clear. "It's just... We don't want you to be hurt."

"We're just dating." *And having sex. And, oh yeah, I'm having sex with his friend too.* "It's nothing more serious than that."

"Okay, honey. I'm glad you called. I'll, ah, talk to your dad, though how I'm going to bring this up... Maybe you can come for dinner one day next week. It'd be nice to see you."

Mary Alice wanted to sigh in relief. Her mom had decided to give her a pass. But probably only until Mary Alice showed up for dinner or her parents caught up to her at Tommy's bar, where she usually spent her weekends. Then they'd give her the third degree.

"Sure. I'll talk to you soon. Love you."

"Love you too. Just...be safe."

"Always."

She really hoped she wasn't lying.

12

Max could tell something was wrong the second Mary Alice opened the door to her apartment.

Yes, she smiled up at him as she waved him through the door and into her small apartment, but it didn't reach her eyes and she turned immediately and headed toward the back of the apartment.

"Hi, sorry. I just need to put on my jewelry and my shoes. I was a little late getting home."

"Busy day?"

"Yeah, you could say that."

Even though she'd disappeared down a short hall to the left of the kitchen area, he could hear the sarcastic tone of her voice. It made him smile, even though he didn't have much to smile about.

They'd found indications of sabotage in four of their five properties. Nothing major but nothing they could overlook. If they hadn't caught the one, the entire building could have gone up in flames, the electrician had said.

Not exactly the way he'd wanted to start his day.

Tonight, he just wanted to enjoy this time with Mally and Jesse.

He had a feeling it wasn't going to be that easy.

"Is everything okay?" He raised his voice to be sure she heard him, figuring if any of her roommates were home, she would've said something. "Did something happen?"

"Everything's fine. Just...busy."

He was about to add something but his brain blanked when she walked into the room again.

Damn, he hadn't really gotten a good look at her when she'd opened the door because she'd immediately turned and headed in the other direction. Now...

Holy shit.

She looked edible.

He knew what the term "little black dress" meant and he'd seen his share recently at cocktail parties. But Mary Alice showed him why women had made them a thing.

Her little black dress wasn't little in terms of fabric. This one covered her from neck to knee. But it covered her like a second skin, so close, he couldn't help but wonder if she had anything at all on under the damn thing.

The neckline was practically Puritan but he'd noticed that it dipped down in back when she'd walked away. The way the dress was made, though, drew attention to her breasts and her hips.

She'd rolled her hair up in some kind of bun at her nape, which left her neck bare so all he wanted to do was brush aside the dangling, sparkling earrings hanging from her lobes and bite her.

Then he'd put his hands on her hips and pull that dress up until he found out whether she was wearing underwear.

"Max?"

He blinked and met her eyes. He was absolutely not going to feel guilty for staring. She had to know what she looked like. And he hoped like hell she'd dressed just so he'd react like this.

"You look beautiful."

"Thank you." Her smile peeked out for a brief second and he felt the black cloud that'd been hanging over his head lift a bit. "You don't look so bad yourself."

He was wearing a suit. A boring suit, actually. Hell, he wore suits every day. He was pretty sure no one wanted to strip him out of it and kiss the hell out of him.

Except the way she was looking at him now…

Acting on instinct, he wrapped an arm around her shoulders and put his other hand on one hip and drew her closer. He gave her plenty of time to pull away, though he didn't know why. She'd practically begged him and Jesse to fuck her the other night.

Still, this was different. She wasn't some socialite with more notches on her bedpost than he had. She was sugar-sweet Mally, who melted on his tongue like cotton candy and made him want to strip her naked and take her against the nearest wall.

He leaned closer and, when he finally had his lips on hers, he forced himself to simply press their lips together and give her the most chaste kiss he could manage.

Which was hell.

Her lips were soft under his, and when he drew in a breath, her scent made a groan build in his chest. He pulled away before he could give in to the urge to part her lips and slide his tongue inside her. Kiss her harder and press his burgeoning erection between her thighs—

"We'd better go."

She blinked and took a step back when he finally released her.

"Sure." Shaking her head, she turned to grab her purse from a nearby chair. "I'm ready whenever you are."

"I told Jesse we'd meet him at the restaurant in fifteen minutes. With traffic, we should just about make it."

Minutes later in the car, Max continued to try to rein in his libido. Or at least level out his breathing. Christ, he felt like a fucking teenager.

Shouldn't've kissed her.

Now he wouldn't be able to think of anything else all night. Except maybe the fact that, if she agreed to come home with them tonight, she wouldn't be leaving until tomorrow morning.

And there were a lot of hours between now and then.

"So what did your busy day include?" she asked.

They'd been driving in silence for a few minutes, Max trying to settle on a topic of conversation. This definitely wasn't what he'd wanted to talk about, but he wasn't going to ignore her. He also didn't want to scare her away by telling her the truth.

Bad idea.

"We had several site visits and two meetings this afternoon. And your day?"

"Oh, just a few phone calls from family." Sarcasm oozed from her voice. "That always manages to make my day a little more interesting."

He shot her a glance. "Interesting doesn't sound very good."

"Not today, no."

When she didn't continue, he pressed forward, wanting more from her.

"What did they want?"

He had a feeling he knew, but he wanted her to talk to him about it. Wanted her to feel like she could open up to him.

"I told them we were dating."

His back stiffened though he immediately forced himself to relax. "I take it that didn't go over well."

"Actually, it went better than I thought it would."

He couldn't hide his surprise. "Who did you talk to?"

"My mom and my brother Jason. The cop."

Shit. "And neither of them tried to talk you out of dating...me?"

"Oh, they did. I got them to change their minds."

He was sure that had taken a miracle. "And how did you do that?'

She sat a little straighter. "By telling them I was a grown woman who could make her own decisions and that you wouldn't hurt me."

Was that a subtle warning? Or had she given him the gift of her trust? He wanted to believe it was the latter.

"Should I expect a visit from your father or your brothers? And will I need medical attention afterward?"

She laughed, which was what he'd wanted. God, she had a great laugh. It made his dick hard.

"No, I don't think so but I guess it wouldn't hurt to be on guard."

He was always on guard so that wouldn't be a problem. "What about you, Mally?"

Her head cocked to the side, her eyes on his profile. "Are you asking me if I trust you?"

Do you really want to know? "Do you?"

She didn't answer right away and he refused to believe he was holding his breath.

Finally, the corners of her mouth curved up. "I wouldn't be here if I didn't."

He felt her gaze like a physical caress. "Why?"

Her shrug held a slight haughtiness. "Because I believe in my ability to read people. And I trust you not to hurt me."

No, he didn't want to hurt her. He only wanted to give her pleasure. It was a primal need he couldn't explain. And one he didn't want to examine too closely.

He'd never had such an overwhelming desire before, at least not one that wasn't fueled by rage or frustration. What he felt for her was a constant ache, one he couldn't explain. And yes, that made his teeth grind. But he wasn't about to give her up because of it. Not now that he'd had his cock lodged inside her and felt her come around him.

Shit. Probably shouldn't think about that too much. He wouldn't be able to walk into the restaurant without embarrassing himself.

"I definitely don't want to hurt you, Mally." But he couldn't tell her with any certainty that she wouldn't get hurt. But he could make damn sure she knew that he and Jesse would stand between her and anything that came near her.

As long as she allows you to.

"What's wrong?"

Mally's question made him realize his expression had hardened into a scowl, and he relaxed it immediately.

"Nothing." Relief flooded through him as he pulled into the parking lot. Thank God Jesse would be here because Max didn't want to fuck up the conversation all night. At least with Jesse as a buffer, he had a fighting chance of not saying something stupid.

"So why this restaurant?"

He'd helped her out of the car but released her as they started to walk. He wanted to put his hand on her arm, on her back, somewhere to show any other man that she was his, but he restrained himself.

Except… She slipped her hand around his bicep and kept it there as they walked. Maybe she didn't want to risk falling on those heels, though she looked pretty steady in them.

And maybe she actually isn't embarrassed to be seen with you.

That would be nice. Could also be wishful thinking.

They walked into Fond on Passyunk Avenue and were immediately taken to a table. Max wasn't surprised to see Jesse. He'd stood as they walked to the table, his gaze connecting with Max's for a brief second before switching to Mally. Max figured he'd had the same look on his face when he'd seen her.

Jesse, however, let his smile linger as he pulled out the chair next to him for her. Which meant Max would sit across from her and get to stare at her all night. And Jesse would get to sit close enough to her to touch.

He didn't know which of them had the better seat.

Max couldn't help but hope they'd all be winners by the end of the night.

. . .

Jesse thought he managed to hide it well, but he felt like someone had smacked him with a two-by-four.

Christ, she was fucking beautiful. With her hair up and that damn dress plastered to her body... Fuck, just shoot him now. He wanted to throw her over his shoulder and head for the nearest exit. Instead, he'd be forced to sit next to her for at least an hour and a half before they could leave. By then, he'd be so damn turned on, he wouldn't be able to make small talk much less do more than stare at her.

When they'd all been seated, Jesse looked across the table to find Max grinning at him. Probably because he hadn't been able to hide his reaction. And probably because Max had had the same reaction when he'd first seen her.

Bastard.

"So how was your day, Jesse?"

The waitress had just left after taking their drink orders and leaving them with menus, and a short silence had fallen.

"Busy."

It was the first thing that came to mind that didn't hint at their problems. He figured short and sweet was the way then he'd turn the conversation back to her and let her talk.

But when she started to laugh, he frowned at her.

"Why is that funny?"

"Because it's exactly what Max said." Shaking her head, she glanced first at Max over the top of her menu and then sideways at him. "Do you two coordinate your answers ahead of time? Or do you really communicate telepathically?"

Jesse glanced up to find a half-assed smile on Max's face, amazing considering the way they'd spent their day. The tension in Jesse's shoulders eased, made the hot anger seething in his stomach fade.

Until that moment, he hadn't been sure he was going to be decent company tonight. At least, not decent enough for Mally's company. Now, the night was looking up.

"I can tell you exactly what Jesse's thinking right now." Max's deadpan delivery drew Mally's attention back to him.

Her smile widened. "And what's that?"

Max looked up from the menu. "Exactly what I'm thinking."

Her head cocked to the side, her smile never wavering. "Are you going to let me in on the secret?"

Max exchanged another glance with Jesse, who knew exactly what Max was thinking.

"I don't think it's much of a secret how we feel about you. Neither of us can wait to get you home."

Jesse knew there was more Max could've said. Like, "and get you out of that dress and spread out on a bed."

Luckily, Max didn't add that. And Mally continued to smile.

"Then I guess we'd better order fast. Because that's exactly what I'm expecting for dessert."

Neither Jesse nor Max said anything in response. Frankly, Jesse wasn't sure what the hell to say.

Mally continued to confuse him. She seemed comfortable saying whatever came into her mind. Not that he didn't appreciate her candor, but he was surprised that it included her attraction to them.

She didn't seem at all embarrassed to be seen in public with them. Other women they'd had relationships with had made it clear they'd be happy to spend time between them in bed. But if they were ever together outside of the bedroom, then they didn't want anyone else to know the three of them shared a bed.

Usually that meant Max was her official date. Jesse faded into the background as Max's bodyguard.

And maybe that's how those other women had viewed him, simply as a third body and not a second man in the relationship. Then again, they really hadn't had any relationships with those women.

Fuck.

"We could get dinner to go."

Max had finally answered, and good thing too, because Jesse wasn't sure he could've responded to her flirty response with anything other than a caveman-like grunt of approval.

She pouted at Max, and Jesse's cock throbbed with lust. Tonight was going to be absolute torture. Until they got back to their place.

"Then why did I bother to get all dressed up? I don't get to wear this dress often and I like it."

"Most of the men in this room like it a little too much," Jesse muttered and was rewarded with another bright smile.

"Trust me, the women are looking at you the same way." She picked up her menu and transferred her gaze to it. "We call it suit porn."

Max set his menu aside and Jesse figured the guy had seen chicken and stopped there because nothing said steak.

"Seriously?" Max sounded genuinely shocked. "That's actually a thing?"

"Oh, yeah." Mary Alice nodded. "And trust me, you two qualify for a few fantasies tonight."

Christ, he hoped so. He hoped like hell those fantasies were all hers.

Since Max seemed to be having a hard time coming up with a response to that, Jesse changed the subject to something much more boring. He asked about her day and for the next hour, while they ate food he could barely pronounce and drank a bottle of decent wine, they managed to hold a conversation that didn't make him want to throw a couple hundred dollars on the table and drag her back to their place.

Mally fascinated both of them so he and Max kept the spotlight on her. It helped that she could talk about anything and everything. And he didn't mean that in a bad way. He only meant she had no problem keeping a conversation going.

Jesse let Max do most of the heavy conversational lifting, though Jesse was careful to contribute occasionally. Didn't want her to think he wasn't listening.

Truth was, he could listen to her talk all night. The sound of her voice mesmerized. Which meant he had to keep reminding himself not to fall too deeply under her spell. He hadn't forgotten that someone was trying to sabotage their livelihood.

And Jesse wasn't convinced he and Max weren't in danger as well. Which meant Mally potentially could be.

By the time dessert rolled around, Jesse had started seeing threats everywhere, and Max and Mally had noticed. They keep sneaking glances at him whenever his attention would veer away to check out the room.

So he was the first one to see the older woman approach across the room. Her tentative smile and the way her eyes kept flashing between him and Mary Alice and Max made his back stiffen.

He tried to hide it but Max's gaze narrowed on him and it wasn't long before Mary Alice turned to him as well.

He didn't have a chance to say anything because the woman stepped up to their table.

"Mary Alice, sweetheart. I thought that was you. How are you?"

Mally stiffened for a millisecond before turning a bright smile on the woman and rising, prompting Jesse and Max to do the same.

"Hi, Aunt Viv. I'm fine. And you?"

"Oh, as well as can be expected these days. We're celebrating your uncle's birthday with friends so I can't stay but I just wanted to see...if you were all right."

Now, Jesse could be completely off base here but he didn't think he was. He was pretty sure Mally's aunt was asking if she felt right in the head because clearly she couldn't be if she was having dinner with him and Max.

Jesse shot a quick glance at Max, who had a charming smile on his face. Max could do charming when he wanted to. Jesse had to work much harder at it. The best he could hope for was slightly warmer than stone face.

"I'm doing well. Work's been busy but that's better than not. Aunt Viv, these are my friends Jesse Kanatawa and Max Burdanov."

He and Max nodded and tried not to appear like they were looming over the women. Though that proved hard to do when they both had at least half a foot on them.

Mally's aunt barely held her smile, though she didn't

outright dismiss or ignore them. She didn't offer her hand either.

"Nice to meet you both."

The woman turned back to Mally immediately. "Well, I don't want to interrupt your...evening. If you get a chance, stop by and say hello on your way out. I'm sure your uncle would love to see you."

"I will, Aunt Viv." Mally smiled brightly and gave the older woman a hug, which her aunt returned. "Thanks for letting me know you're here."

The older woman nodded and walked away, though Jesse saw her glance back at them from the other side of the room, worry plain on her face.

When Jesse sat, he turned to find Mary Alice shaking her head. "Sorry about that. Aunt Viv's...kind of..."

Surprisingly, Max said exactly what Jesse was thinking. "Prejudiced?"

Mary Alice's head popped up immediately. "No. No, it's not that. I think it...probably has to do with your history. Aunt Viv's married to a city judge. I think she or Uncle Simon recognized you. I'm sorry. She was rude and—"

"Actually, no. She wasn't. She was more polite than some people we've met."

Unfortunately, that was true. Some people looked straight through them like they weren't there. Jesse had learned to ignore it better than Max, who'd sometimes deliberately antagonize them for kicks.

"Seriously?" Mally shook her head. "You deal with that a lot?"

Max shrugged, like it was no big deal, but Jesse saw the coldness brewing beneath his calm expression. "More than you'd imagine. You'd think if people believe you're criminals, they'd be more careful how they treat you. Hell, we could pull out a semiautomatic and blow away the entire room."

Damn it. Max was gearing up for a full-blown sarcasm attack, something Mally hadn't seen from him yet. Her gaze narrowed and her lips pursed, as if trying to figure out Max's mood.

Then she shook her head and the look she flashed both of them was pure exasperation. Which was a hell of a lot better than anger or fear.

"I can't imagine either of you own a semiautomatic."

Jesse had to bite his tongue because, yeah, he did own a semiautomatic. Had for years. As well as five other legally registered firearms. And two not as legal. Max had his own legal pieces. Which meant they had ten weapons in various places throughout the city. And Jesse hadn't included the blades.

"Do you want me to respond to that truthfully?"

Max's quiet question took Mally and Jesse off guard, and they both turned their full attention on Max, who caught and held Mally's gaze.

"Of course I do." Mally huffed out a sigh, shaking her head, never breaking Max's gaze. "I'm not stupid and I'm definitely not unaware of the life you've led. I know who you worked for. I know what you did—"

"No, you don't." Max's voice had dropped another level in volume but the intensity had ratcheted up. "You might think you do but I can assure you, you don't know the half of it. And you don't want to."

Her gaze narrowed. "Isn't it a little late to try to scare me away? Maybe you should've tried that *before* we had sex."

And there was the Mally Jesse knew lurked under that sweet exterior. The woman who didn't hesitate to say what was on her mind.

Jesse wondered if Max realized how close he was to getting reamed out by a very pissed-off woman. Sometimes the guy could be a little dense, particularly when it came to females.

"I'm not trying to scare you away but I'm starting to think you don't have a clue what you're getting into with us."

Jesus Christ. Jesse wanted to smack Max on the back of the head, but he'd never draw attention to them like that. Max was being a dick, and if he didn't watch it, Mally would soon tell him to stuff his attitude and storm away. That's not how he wanted this night to end. And he knew that's not what Max wanted either.

But Mally's aunt's visit had triggered something in Max.

"I knew exactly what I was getting into when I made this arrangement, Max. Don't patronize me. I get enough of that from my older brothers."

Max opened his mouth to say something, probably something stupid, and Jesse kicked him in the shin before he got the words out.

Max's mouth shut and his gaze snapped to Jesse's for one brief, furious second before Max took a breath and dialed back his attitude.

"You're right. I'm sorry. Would you like dessert?"

Mally shook her head. "No. I think... I'm finished."

Jesse was pretty sure that meant she was finished with them for the night, as well.

"Are we going back to your place?" she asked. "I think we need to talk."

Shocked, Jesse answered before Max could stick his foot in his mouth again. "We can if that's what you want."

She turned to give him a rueful smile. "It is."

"Then let's go." Max managed not to sound too pissed off as he said it.

"I need to stop by my aunt's table and say happy birthday."

Jesse rose. "No problem. I'll get the car and meet you out front."

"I'll wait for you at the door," Max added.

For a second, Jesse thought Mally would object but then she nodded.

"I'll just be a minute."

As she walked away, Jesse and Max walked to the front door. They got a few looks but nothing like they would have if they were in one of their own places. People knew them there. This was neutral ground.

Max and Jesse exchanged a glance before Jesse left to get the car. Max knew to stay inside until he pulled up to the door.

By the time he got back, Max and Mally stood just inside the entrance. At least a foot of space between them, staring in opposite directions.

Oh yeah, this was gonna be fun.

As soon as he pulled up to the curb, Max opened the door and stepped out, looking around before reaching for her and leading her to the car. He opened the front passenger door for her and let her slide in before he closed the door and got in behind her.

"Where to?" Jesse figured he'd better double-check.

She turned to him with a steady expression. "I thought we were going back to your place."

"Just wanted to make sure."

He pulled out into traffic and glanced at Mally again, but she was staring out the front window. Glancing in the rearview, he saw Max staring out the side window.

Silence prevailed for the rest of the way home, a silence so heavy Jesse turned on the radio for background noise.

By the time he parked in the garage, Jesse figured there was no way he wouldn't be taking her home in fifteen minutes, tops. Max had barely managed to keep his mouth shut but Jesse knew he wouldn't for long.

Walking into the house with Mally between them, Max led them into the living room. Jesse stopped in the doorway, waiting. Knowing Max was gearing up for something. But Mally turned to face Jesse first.

"Are you planning to keep your distance for the entire length of this arrangement?"

Jesse's eyes widened in surprise before he could control the impulse.

What the hell? "Excuse me?"

Her arms crossed over her chest and she gave him that look, the one that let him know she wasn't taking any shit. But he honestly had no idea what the hell he was talking about. He'd expected her to go after Max, not him.

"I believe you heard me correctly. Is this how you're going to act for the rest of this arrangement? As if nothing matters and you're not involved?"

Yeah, that's exactly— "I don't have the first clue what the hell you're talking about."

"Yes, you do. You're just not going to man up and admit it."

"And what about you, Mally?" Max jumped in with both feet. "Are you going to cringe every time someone you know approaches you when you're with us? You think I didn't notice how you acted when your aunt approached. You were terrified she'd say something."

She turned on Max, hands on hips. "I was worried she'd say something to offend you."

Max shook his head. "But don't you see? That's exactly what's going to happen every time we go out together. The three of us. Are you really telling me you can handle it?"

God damn Max. He'd gone on the offensive, which is how he typically handled all problems. But Mally wasn't a problem. And she wasn't about to back down.

Her chin went out and her back straightened. "I'm not afraid of a little gossip. And if I hadn't been willing to pay the debt, I never would've asked you for help in the first place."

"Oh, we're not talking about a little gossip." Max's voice had dropped another octave. He was well and truly pissed. "We're talking Greek-tragedy-level gossip. You got a tiny taste of it tonight. Jesus, your aunt looked like she wanted to grab you and run for the nearest exit. I have no idea what the hell you told your mom or your brother but you can damn well be sure they're not going to let this go."

"And again I say, I'm a grown woman who can make her own damn decisions. My parents trust my judgment—"

"It might seem that way now but once word gets around that you've been seen out with Jesse and me, how long do you think that's going to last? How long until your brothers and your dad show up at our door to beat the shit out of us?"

Her gaze narrowed. "Are you trying to tell me you're afraid of my family? Seriously?"

"Goddammit, Mally!" Max's restraint finally broke. "Are you always this stubborn? Whatever it is you're expecting to happen, if you think people are going to magically accept us into decent society, it's not gonna happen. You're living in a fantasy world. You may be the princess but we're no Prince Charmings."

"Is that seriously what you think?" Her tone held so much mocking disbelief, Jesse couldn't help but smile.

As foreplay, this worked for him. Whether he got laid tonight or not, watching Mally face down Max made him hard. Sue him. She was fucking hot.

"It's exactly what I think." Max drew in a deep breath and crossed his arms over his chest. "You're playing this situation like it's straight out of some fucking movie."

"And you're deliberately making me furious. Why is that, Max?"

Jesse knew the answer to her question, but he wasn't stupid enough to stick his two cents in now. Max was taking the brunt of her anger. And the bastard deserved it. He was deliberately baiting her.

Which didn't make any fucking sense because Max was the one who kept telling Jesse he wasn't going to give Mally up.

So he stayed silent. When he thought Mally had taken enough of Max's shit, he'd step in, but, for right now, he was going to enjoy the show.

"I just don't want you to have expectations we aren't going to be able to fulfill."

"And what expectations do you think I have?"

"That this is some sort of fairy tale where the beasts become the princes."

She snorted. "Oh, trust me, Max." She shook her head very slowly. "Right now, you're very far from my idea of a prince."

"Then tell me what the fuck you're doing here."

And that was Jesse's cue to step in, because when Max started to swear, he'd reached his breaking point. But he could only think of two ways to separate them and one involved taking her home. Which he didn't want to do.

The other... That one he really did want to do.

Jesse pushed away from the door frame he'd been holding up and started walking toward Mally. "Max, shut the fuck up."

Mally's gaze immediately shot to him, and by the time Jesse stopped in front of her, she'd lost a little of the fire in her eyes.

But only a little.

She still continued to breathe hard, and the resulting rise and fall of her breasts made his cock harden even more. And it'd been pretty damn hard to begin with.

"You're not here to fight, are you, babe?"

He deliberately used the endearment because he knew it'd throw her off track. And it worked like a charm. She blinked up at him and her lips parted as if she wanted to say something but nothing came out.

"You're here to get laid. That was the arrangement, wasn't it?"

The blush that burned her cheeks made him grin. She constantly charmed him. She'd made a deal with them to help out a friend and then maneuvered them until she got what she wanted, which was both of them for sex.

Max had jumped at the opportunity, but now he was on the verge of fucking it up completely. It was up to Jesse to put them back on track. Because tonight he'd realized a few things.

First, Mally had no fear. She went after what she wanted and, for some reason, she'd set her sights on him and Max. For whatever reason, she wanted *them*.

And second, Max was starting to have cold feet. Whether that was because he'd finally realized how much shit Mally was going to take from almost everyone she knew for being seen with them or because he'd realized how much danger she could be in, Jesse didn't know.

And third... Well, that was all on him. He'd had a taste and he wasn't going to be satisfied until he had more.

How much will be enough?

Jesse had no idea. But he knew it wasn't once.

He'd been deliberately crude to get her attention but now he had it. Completely. Her gaze narrowed and her hands went to her hips. She stared up at him and opened her mouth to blast him.

Before she could, he wrapped one hand around her neck and clamped the other to her hip and yanked her forward. He took her off guard and she stumbled against him, stiffening when he bent to put his mouth over hers.

He kissed her hard, gave her no time to back away. She didn't struggle or try to escape, but she didn't respond right away either. She stood there and let him kiss her, let him coax her lips open so he could slide his tongue inside to stroke against hers.

God damn, he loved the taste of her. Hot and so fucking sweet. Christ, his teeth should ache. But it wasn't his teeth that ached. No, just the rest of his body.

Pulling her closer, their lips still locked, he plastered her body against his and let the hand resting on her hip slide down to cup her ass. The material of her dress felt like silk against his skin as he tilted her hips against his and pressed his erection into the soft flesh of her belly.

Fuck yeah.

Groaning, he released her neck so he could put both hands on her ass and grind his aching cock against her. Fuck, all he needed to do was hold her against him and he swore he could come.

But that's not how he wanted this to go. He wanted to be buried inside her tight little ass when he came this time, preferably while Max filled her pussy with his cock.

Now, she gasped and he had a second to wonder if he'd hurt her before she wrapped her arms around his neck and moved even closer. Her breasts flattened against his chest and her head tilted to the side, deepening their kiss.

Her body softened against his, melted into his until he felt every breath she took. Her scent made him light-headed, and the remembered feel of her bare skin under his hands had his fingers clenching around the soft curves of her ass.

He wanted her naked, but this time they weren't doing some rush job in the fucking living room. This time, he was taking control.

Lifting his head, he broke the kiss, opening his eyes to find her blinking up at him. She tried to pull him back down and he allowed her to do it for a second, just a brief chance for her to brush her lips against his.

Then he swung her into his arms and headed for the first-floor bedroom. Before he left the living room, he stopped and looked back over his shoulder at Max.

Max stood, arms crossed over his chest, stone-faced and unmoving. Until Mary Alice looked over Jesse's shoulder. She didn't say anything but whatever look she gave Max, it made his feet move. Or maybe Max just realized what he'd be missing if he remained behind.

Jesse was finished with waiting and hesitating where Mally was concerned. She was prepared to go to battle for them. What did it say about him if he didn't have the guts to do the same?

With Max now in tow, Jesse continued down the hall. He saw Mally taking in the surroundings, her head on a swivel.

They'd have to give her a tour one of these days. When they weren't half-crazy with lust. Which seemed to be never. Something they'd have to keep an eye on. They still needed to be on guard. But not tonight. Not here.

The light from the hall illuminated the room enough that he didn't have to flip the light switch. He knew exactly where he was going. But he wasn't surprised when Max turned it on anyway.

Max liked to watch, wanted to be able to see everything. And Jesse had a feeling Max would be watching at first. He'd still be pissed and he wouldn't trust himself until it'd dissipated completely.

And that would mean watching Jesse take her first this time. Jesse certainly didn't have a problem with it. But he knew he and Max were working up to the day they took her together. He just hoped like hell they didn't spook her before that.

Not that Mary Alice seemed spooked.

Especially not when he set her on the bed and she popped back up onto her knees to reach for him.

He hadn't worn a tie tonight so she went straight for the buttons of his shirt, shoving them through the holes with furious fingers. He let her mess with those while he carefully found each of the long pins holding up her hair. He wanted that shiny mass of red curls spread out over the dark sheets, wanted to wrap it around his hands, bury his nose in it while he fucked her hard and fast this first time. And then again when he took her slower the second time.

When he had the last one in hand, he watched her curls fall around her shoulders and brush the top curves of her breasts.

Against her pale skin, her hair looked almost blood-red and he reached for her to wind it around his fingers. If his fingertips stroked over her beaded nipples, well, that was just a bonus.

And then it was the sole reason.

But she halted his progress when she shoved his now-unbuttoned shirt down his arms, effectively limiting his movement unless he let his hands hang for a moment to let the shirt fall. He didn't want to do that. Not now when he pinched her nipples between his thumb and forefinger and pulled on the little nub until he felt her shudder.

"Jesse."

"Yeah?"

"Harder."

She practically moaned the word, her head falling backward as he did what she asked. Lifting his other hand to her free breast, he played with her nipples, taking his cues from her. She appeared to like that tiny bit of pain when he squeezed just a little harder and tugged.

"Oh god."

"Like that, do you?" Jesse could barely get the words out through his clenched jaw. He was trying hard not to let the full force of his lust off the leash at once. If he did, he wasn't sure she wouldn't run.

"Yes." Her hands gripped his waist, digging into the flesh before scrambling to undo his belt. But he grabbed her hands before she could get his pants unbuttoned.

Leaning down, he fused their mouths together again and quickly got rid of his shirt before reaching behind her for the zipper to her dress.

"Let me."

Max's voice came from behind Mally. Jesse hadn't heard him move. Mally broke the kiss with a gasp and let her head fall forward onto Jesse's shoulder as Max released the zipper at her side and pulled the dress down.

She wasn't wearing a bra so when Jesse reached for her again, his hands met warm, naked skin.

With her dress caught at her hips, Jesse could only stroke his fingertips from her waist to her breasts. But for now, that was enough to keep him occupied for hours.

Wrapping one hand in her hair, he tugged her head back and kissed her again, sliding his tongue into her mouth to play with hers while he gave his fingers free rein to touch her.

Cupping her breasts, he molded them to his palms and massaged them until she panted into his mouth. She gripped his waist again, fingers digging into the muscle before sliding around to the front of his pants to fumble with the button.

She brushed against his cock, straining against the zipper, and made it throb even harder. He let her open the button but stopped her before she released the zipper.

"Not yet, sweetheart." He eased her fingers away and drew her arms around his waist, where she spread her hands over his back.

His eyes snapped closed as she raked her nails up and back down, scoring his flesh and making him groan.

Her head lowered and she settled her mouth on his neck, parting her lips and sucking the sensitive skin between her teeth.

Fuck. His blood heated, pumping through his veins like lava. His hands flattened on her back but quickly slid to her hips to grip her dress. He yanked it down, managing not to rip it. When he had it down to her knees, he lifted her and laid her out on the bed.

Fuck yes. Her hair spilled over the pillow, practically glowing against her pale skin. But it was her blue eyes staring up at him that hit him hardest. She looked at him like she wanted him to devour her. And since that's exactly what he wanted to do, he had to restrain himself from tearing off his pants and falling on her.

Instead, he let his gaze travel down her body. Slim and toned, she curved in all the right places. He wanted to put his mouth on her breasts and suck on her nipples then kiss his way down her stomach to her mound, covered now by the tiniest triangle of black silk.

He reached for the strings on her hips and considered ripping the thong off her body. But he reconsidered when he saw her smile. So soft and sweet.

Instead, he hooked his index fingers into those strings and tugged. She let him work them down for long seconds before lifting her hips so he could pull the scrap of fabric down her thighs and off her legs before tossing them to the end of the bed.

Her gaze stayed with him as he moved between her legs. Then motion to their left caught her attention and she looked away. Toward Max, who looked much more stable than he'd been in the living room. Lust had taken the edge off the anger.

But he still did nothing more than walk to the chair on the other side of the bed and sprawl into it.

Mally's distraction gave Jesse the chance to take her off guard.

Bending down, he slipped his hands under her ass to lift her off the bed...and straight to his mouth. Her cry of surprise quickly changed to a moan as he pressed his lips to her sex and licked her labia.

God damn, she tasted like heaven. Playing his tongue along her folds, he worked to drive her into a frenzy. He had to brace her thighs open with his shoulders because she immediately tried to tighten them around him. Whether to cut him off or keep him there, he wasn't sure.

Until she reached down to slide her fingers through his hair and grip him tight.

Yes.

Then he got to serious business. He loved going down on a woman. Loved the taste, the way they moved and moaned and danced to his tune. At his mercy.

But it was different with Mally. He wanted to pleasure her, just as he had the other women. But he also wanted

Mally to want more from him. To demand more. Just as he was starting to want so much more from her.

The thought made him push her harder. Slicking his tongue through her folds, he bared his teeth and nipped at her tiny clit. As soon as he made contact, she shuddered, her hand pulling at his hair. Yes, it hurt but, damn, he wanted more. Wanted to feel her come around his tongue before she came around his cock a second time.

Each of her panting breaths made her body tremble but he knew the exact moment she broke. Her body tightened and froze for a second before she cried out.

With one last nip at her clit, he speared his tongue into her sex as she clenched around it.

His lungs struggled for air as he held her while she writhed. His cock ached with the need to be inside her while she clenched around it but he strung her orgasm out as long as he could with his tongue.

And when she finally went limp in his hands, he set her back on the bed and sat back on his heels between her legs, staring down at her.

Beautiful. Absolutely fucking beautiful. And he wasn't finished with her yet.

Neither of them were finished with her.

He glanced at Max, who was having the same trouble with his breathing. He'd leaned forward in the chair and now watched with his elbows on his knees and his hands laced together in front of him. The same hunger Jesse felt could be seen in Max's eyes.

Slowly, Jesse leaned forward and sucked one of Mally's tightly pebbled nipples into his mouth, knowing Max watched his every move. Without opening her eyes, she moaned, one hand reaching up to the top of the bed to anchor her.

"Oh God. Jesse."

He switched to the other side, his hands stroking from the sides of her breasts to her hips. He couldn't not touch her. It felt like a compulsion. And he was okay with that.

But the ache to have her intensified with each second. And still Max didn't make a move.

Fuck him.

He slid Max a glance, raised his eyebrow, and then pointedly looked at the bedside table. Finally, Max moved. He knew what Jesse wanted.

Max leaned forward to open the drawer and Mally's eyes opened, staring straight at Max. He held her gaze as he withdrew a condom. But he didn't hand it over right away.

He stood by the bed, never breaking the connection with her. Jesse could tell Max had finally worked through his anger and was holding on to his control by a bare thread. Max was ceding the dominant position to Jesse this time, knowing his time to have her would come.

But not until Jesse had her first. And not until they got her primed.

With a flick of his wrist, Max tossed the condom to Jesse, never taking his eyes away from Mally. Who drew in an audible breath when Max shrugged off his suit jacket.

While Mally was preoccupied watching Max strip, Jesse got rid of his pants and underwear and rolled on the condom. By the time he was finished, Max had stripped off his shirt and was standing after shoving his pants to the ground.

Mally had started to breathe through her mouth,

drawing in shuddering gulps of air that made her entire body shake. And when Jesse grabbed her hips and dragged her down the bed, she gasped but didn't struggle. And her submission, whether it was inherent or simply a result of being startled, made him want to push his cock into her to the hilt and fuck her until they both couldn't breathe.

He was sick of slow. Time to show her exactly what they wanted from her. And how much pleasure they could give her.

She blinked, her gaze shifting between Jesse and Max before sticking with Jesse as he sank lower onto his heels and drew her ass up his thighs.

Thighs spread wide, she attempted to reach for Jesse but Max slid onto the bed above her head and grabbed her hands before she could.

As Jesse took his cock in hand, Max pulled her arms over her head and held them there with one hand. The other went to her chin, tilting her head back so he could bend and kiss her.

Her body arched and Jesse seized the opportunity. Lodging his cock at her entrance, he pressed inside at a steady pace, spreading her wide. And torturing himself in the process.

Fuck, she was tight. And hot.

Jesse felt sweat bead on his forehead as he pushed farther, sinking his cock inside her by increments. Each inch made her eyes narrow until they were almost closed and he had his balls pressed against her ass.

His cock throbbed, the tightness of her sex rippling around him and increasing his need to move.

"Jesse, oh my god. Move."

Mally's barely audible plea made Jesse's entire body tighten. But he'd be damned if he let her goad him into rushing this.

"Keep still, sweetheart." Max leaned down to speak directly into her ear, making her sex grip Jesse's cock even tighter. "If you don't, we may have to resort to other... methods of restraint."

The expression of lust on her face made Jesse bite back a groan.

Goddammit, if she was any more responsive, he might come right now without moving a muscle.

He barely managed to restrain the urge to fall over her and nail her to the bed. Barely. Because he knew what Max had in store. Jesse knew they couldn't just throw her straight into a full-on threeway. They both realized they couldn't simply put her between them and expect her to take them both at the same time.

They had to ease her into it.

All right, maybe ease was a little too tame for what they had planned for her. But it wouldn't be hardcore. And hopefully next time—

She shimmied against him as Max bit her earlobe and used his free hand to play with her breasts and Jesse practically bit through his tongue to remain still.

Fuck, she felt amazing.

Jesse tried to detach his emotions from the visual stimulation but every sound she made and every time she moved fueled his lust.

The way she bit her lip as Max squeezed her nipple hard,

leaving it tight and pointed before moving to the next, made Jesse want to lean down and bite her, make her cry out and squirm a little farther onto his cock.

He wanted her to want him to fuck her hard. But first she needed more encouragement from Max.

That didn't mean Jesse was going to sit here twiddling his thumbs. No, he'd put those thumbs to better use.

Flattening his palms on her thighs, he dragged his hands to her hips then down again as Max continued to tease her breasts and moved his mouth to her neck until he reached her lips.

When Max finally put his mouth on hers and kissed her, Jesse started to move. He barely heard Mally's moan but he swore he felt it quiver through her body and into his as he pulled his cock out slowly, until only the tip remained inside her. Her thighs tightened on his hips, her legs curling around him, trying to get him to move.

When that didn't work, she arched her back and tried to draw him back in that way.

He let her work herself on his cock for as long as he could take it before he shoved back in. Jesse heard her sharp cry, even stifled by Max's mouth. The sound made Jesse want to growl with triumph. Instead, he moved his hands to her hips and put his thumbs on either side of her clit.

Spreading her folds, he watched his cock disappear inside her then reemerge, glistening with her wetness.

The sight made him grit his teeth as savage pleasure shot through him. He pulled back and hammered home again. And again.

He found a rhythm and stuck to it, watching her respond Max's kisses while he fucked her.

Max ground their mouths together and molded her breast in his hand with an almost punishing grip. And then Max shifted, pulling his mouth away from hers. She tried to follow him but couldn't lift her head high enough. Her eyes opened and fluttered shut immediately as Jesse thrust forward, hard.

When he stopped and held deep inside her, she looked up at Max then shifted her gaze to his cock, only inches from her lips.

Jesse watched her lick her lips then lean forward and wrap those lips around Max's cock. Max sucked in a breath as she took him in, her eyes closing as her mouth worked around his length.

Holy fuck. Watching her suck Max brought out the fierce need to feel her come around his cock. Jesse pulled out slowly, enjoying the drag on his sensitized skin, watching her face contort with pleasure and hearing Max groan as she sucked him harder.

Yes. There you go, sweetheart.

With one hand wrapped around the base of Max's cock, she reached for Jesse with the other. He took her outstretched hand, lacing their fingers together as he fucked her as slowly as he could. Watching her every response, soaking them in and letting them burn him to the core.

The telltale throb in his balls told him he was close. And the way Mally had started to clench around him let him know she was almost to the breaking point as well.

Increasing his thrusts, he let instinct take over. The only sounds in the room were his and Max's heavy breathing and the soft moans coming from Mally. Those moans made

Jesse's hand tighten around hers as he slid his other hand from her hip to her mound, seeking her clit.

Her skin felt like velvet beneath his, the slick flesh between her legs warm. If he let himself, he could get lost in the sensations and that was a sure path to destruction.

He found the tiny nub, his thumb brushing over it and making her shudder. The need to make her come was a raging force of nature eating him from the inside. His entire being focused on bringing her to orgasm.

His hips slammed forward, trapping his thumb against her clit. She shuddered.

He did it again, even harder this time, needing to be deep inside her.

He felt the second she broke. He didn't need her throaty moan to tell him. Her sheath clamped down around him as she came, her fingers tightening around his until he thought she might break them.

Would've been a small price to pay for the fiery pleasure that washed over him with his own orgasm.

He groaned, the sound echoing through the room as he pulsed his release into her.

And through the haze of pleasure, he heard Max's answering groan. Jesse opened his eyes just in time to see Mally's cheeks hollow as she sucked Max deep while he came.

Mally woke with a warm, male body on either side of her.

She also woke with a smile.

Jesse faced away from her, stretched out on his back, with her curled into his side, her head resting on his outstretched arm.

Turning her head, she saw Max on her other side, lying on his side facing her.

In the dim light seeping around the curtains, he looked so damn adorable in sleep, completely relaxed, as if he didn't have a care in the world. Except for the hand he had clenched on her waist. He gripped her so tightly, she wouldn't be able to move without waking him.

Which, apparently, she'd already done.

His eyes opened and he stared straight into hers. They lay in silence for several seconds before he spoke.

"Good morning."

The tone of his voice made her shiver. Husky and deep. And the look in his dark eyes… She could barely catch her breath. She wanted him to lean over and kiss her but when he didn't move, she figured what-the-hell and closed the distance between them, pressing her lips against his for several seconds before drawing back.

"Good morning."

A little of his ever-present intensity toned down and his lips curved in a slight smile as the hand on her hip began to move in slow, steady circles.

"Are you hungry?"

For food? "Not really."

No, that hand made her crave something else entirely. How the hell did he do that?

His gaze narrowed. "Is there somewhere you need to be this morning?"

Was he trying to get rid of her? "No. Is there somewhere *you* need to be?"

His mouth moved in a slight, self-deprecating grin. "No, actually, I don't. At least, not for a few hours."

The tone in his voice made her lungs tighten with lust because he was apparently on her same wavelength.

Her teeth lodged in her bottom lip. "So, you have a little free time?"

He blinked and his feature tightened. "More than enough for what I want to do with you."

The corners of her mouth curved up. "And what's that?"

"Why don't you let me show you?"

He didn't wait for her to answer. Curving a hand around her neck, he brought her close again for another kiss, and when he had his mouth on hers, he grabbed her around the waist and lifted her over him. Her legs naturally fell on either side of his hips, and since she was naked, she felt his cock lodge against her sex.

With a quick twist, Max grabbed a condom off the bedside table and handed it to her.

Shit. She'd almost forgotten. Taking care of it, she moved back into position in record time and—

God, yes, that's exactly what she wanted.

Scrambling to get her knees under her, she pushed up onto her hands then reached between them to angle his hot, hard cock directly where she needed it. Without waiting, knowing she was already wet and ready, she wiggled her hips until the tip spread her labia, seeking entrance.

Which she granted him in one downward push.

Gasping at the slight burn, still a little sore from last night, she immediately wanted more.

"Mally, are you—"

"I'm absolutely fine."

Pulling herself up to a sitting position, she sat on Max's lap with his cock lodged deep inside. The look on his face was pure aphrodisiac. Male demand mixed with longing. All for her.

She couldn't *not* move. Hell, she swore her body was under his telepathic command.

Hands planted on his chest, she didn't bother with slow. She went straight for all-out. Every nerve ending shot to almost-painful longing as she rode him. Every time he spread her wide, she moaned. Every time she rose almost far enough for him to slip free, she sighed.

Max watched her through slitted eyes the entire time. She'd realized last night that visual stimulation was almost as important to him as tactile stimulation. Jesse got off on touch, being stroked and fondled. Max did too. But he also got off watching her every move. Watching her splinter. His concentration focused so intently on her, it heightened her sensation to an almost unbearable level.

She wanted to break that concentration.

The fact that his chest rose and fell so fast beneath her hands helped her to focus. Even though she was so highly sensitized and every motion made her muscles tingle in reaction, she slowed until she could feel every inch of his cock dragging against her internal walls.

Her body responded with a demand, her pussy clenching, begging to be filled. Still, she didn't rush. She was beginning to see the appeal he found in watching. Because watching him lit her libido like a match to gasoline.

Her fingers dug into the strong muscles of his chest, her short nails cutting tiny half-moons into his flesh.

Damn, she'd have to watch that. She didn't want to hurt him. Then again, he didn't seem to mind.

Maybe, like her, he liked that little bit of pain. She never had before. Had never considered she would. And yet, with them...

With them, anything was possible.

She opened her eyes, which she hadn't realized she'd closed, just as his closed and she felt his cock jerk and twitch inside her. Grabbing her hips, he pulled her down hard, seating her fully on his cock as he came with a rough groan.

It was that sound that triggered her orgasm, one that ripped through her body with enough force to make her curl forward. If he hadn't been holding on to her, she might've fallen off.

As it was, he held her tight and didn't allow her to move, which only heightened her pleasure.

She was still shuddering when she felt Max shift her off his body and to the side.

Strong arms caught her before she hit the bed. Jesse pulled her into the curve of his body, her back to his front.

Twisting her head, she was able to turn enough for him to lock their lips together. And as she continued to shake from her first climax, Jesse thrusting into her from behind shot her straight into another.

She could barely moan, barely breathe as Jesse folded her into his body and took her hard and fast.

His cock hit at a different angle, different sensations creating a vortex of lust that pushed her past any limit she'd ever been at before.

When she couldn't breathe anymore, she ripped her mouth away from Jesse's so she could gulp in air, only to lose it again when Max leaned forward to suck one nipple into his mouth and bite the tip.

Caught between them, she could only let herself be sucked down into the sensation and hope she came out on the other side.

13

"So who's going to feed me? Because I don't think I can move."

Max smiled as Mally spoke against his shoulder. After that last round, they'd all fallen back onto the bed and slept for another hour but he'd heard Mally's stomach rumbling a few minutes ago and couldn't help but grin.

"That's Jesse's job." Max reached over her to shove at Jesse's shoulder. "You probably don't want me to cook for you unless there's no other choice."

"Trust me." Jesse's muffled voice came from the other side of the bed. "You don't want him to cook. Ever."

"Good to know."

She yawned and stretched, her sleek skin moving against Max's, making him contemplate rolling over and sliding into her from behind. She was warm and soft against him, and his cock was ready.

But that would show a distinct lack of self-control, wouldn't it?

With that thought in mind, he rolled off the bed and

headed for the bathroom. Though not before pressing an open-mouth kiss to her exposed neck and adding a bite at the end. When she shivered, he felt a little more in control.

By the time he got back, wearing a pair of loose gym shorts, Jesse was gone and Mally was slipping a three-sizes-too-big t-shirt over her head. Her back was to the door, so she probably didn't know he was there. He watched her tug the shirt down, covering the pale skin of her back. But not before he caught sight of the tattoo on her right shoulder that he'd noticed last night. Three tears and a date. The date her oldest brother had died.

When the shirt fell to her waist, she slid her hands beneath her hair to release it from the neck and let it fall down her back.

He could barely breathe by the time she was finished. That something so mundane had the power to make him want to go to his knees was...frightening.

Shutting his eyes for a second, he forced his pounding heart to calm. When he opened them again, he found her standing on the opposite side of the bed, staring at him.

"Jesse gave me this." She plucked at the shirt with her fingers. "He said it's yours. Hope you don't mind."

"Of course not. Did he go to start breakfast?"

She didn't answer immediately. Her head cocked to the side, watching him. Then she nodded. "Yeah. Is this going to be weird now?"

He blinked, confused. "What are you talking about?"

She waved her hand between them. "This. Us. The three of us. Is it going to be weird?"

"I don't understand your concern."

Her nose wrinkled with consternation as she huffed out a sigh. "I mean, I've never done this before."

"I assume you mean sleep with two men."

She gave him a haughty glare. "Yeah. You assume correctly. So I'm not quite sure of the etiquette. I just want to know if there are any rules I'm supposed to follow. I mean, am I supposed to treat you both equally? Or if you piss me off, am I allowed to be pissed at you but still able to be affectionate with Jesse? Or do you both share the same punishment?"

He wanted to smile but forced himself to contain it because she was absolutely serious. "We're not the same men. If you're angry at one, by all means, be angry just at that one. We're big boys. We can handle a little feminine displeasure."

In fact, he actually thought he might thrive on it, if it came from her. But he had the feeling he wasn't giving her the answer she needed because she huffed out another sigh.

"This isn't coming out right."

"No, I'm sorry." He held his hands out in front of him. "I'm baiting you and that's not fair."

"Why are you baiting me?"

Good question. "Truthfully? I enjoy riling you."

Her lips curled. "Well, you're pretty damn good at it."

"I don't mean to be. But you're definitely up to the challenge of handling me."

"Is it always going to be like this between us? This constant bickering?"

"I don't think we bickered at all for several hours last night and this morning."

She shook her head as she walked around the bed. "I guess that's technically true."

Damn it. She'd started to put distance between them. He felt it like a cold void between them. He wanted to rip his own damn tongue out.

"Mally."

She stopped at the door but turned to face him, one eyebrow lifted. Totally willing to face off with him.

He'd never dated a woman before who'd been so unconcerned about pissing him off. Most women used their smiles to coerce and cajole and get their way. Mally just laid everything out.

It disconcerted the hell out of him. And he loved that she felt she could.

"For the length of our agreement, I want you to treat me however the hell you feel like treating me. If you want to express your displeasure with me, you go right ahead. If you want to kiss me, I'm all for it. If you want to kiss Jesse for any reason, you go ahead and do it. But don't be surprised if I expect the same. But I'll never take something you don't want to give."

Her haughty look was back and his cock throbbed with lust. Damn it, how the hell was he supposed to keep his emotions detached if she kept looking at him like that?

Why do you want to do that anyway?

"And how will you know I don't want to give it to you if you don't ask?"

"Hey, guys! Coffee's ready."

Max heard Jesse call from the kitchen but never turned his focus away from Mally.

"You'll know when I'm asking for something, Mally. I will make it perfectly clear."

Did he imagine the shiver that ran through her? He didn't think so.

"Fine." The haughty tone of her voice made him smile. "Just so we're clear."

"We're clear. And for the record, just because I'm not bending you over the bed right now and fucking you doesn't mean I don't want to. It just means I have a little self-control."

She blinked up at him, her lips parting as a flush painted her cheeks bright red. Bending, he kissed her, smashing their lips together until he had to let her up for air.

"Now, unless you want me to follow through on that threat, I suggest we go downstairs."

Her head tilted to the side, her eyes narrowed. And her stomach growled.

"I'm not sure I'd consider that a threat. But I think I need a little food before I do any other...strenuous activities."

Smiling, he waved his hand at the door. "Then by all means, let's eat something. I wouldn't want you to starve."

Following her down the stairs, he held onto his grin. And tried not to overanalyze every last little detail, including how happy Jesse looked this morning.

Not that the guy smiled outright or anything. Max just knew him well enough to know how Jesse felt.

And damn if breakfast wasn't the most amazing meal he'd ever eaten.

The three of them held a conversation that didn't revolve around business. They actually held a discussion about that stupid movie they'd watched when she hadn't known they were there. She'd been surprised they'd seen it. Neither he nor Jesse had enlightened her about the fact that he'd been stalking her that night.

Then she and Jesse had talked about some television show Max had never heard of, which allowed him to watch the two of them interact until Mally drew him back into the conversation with a pointed remark about how Max needed to increase his pop culture IQ.

He'd told her maybe she'd have to become more knowledgeable about local politics. She'd wrinkled her pretty nose and declared politics off the table then she'd insulted his lack of interest in sports.

He wasn't really the kind of guy to waste three or four hours sitting in front of a TV yelling at the screen. If he was going to watch a game—football, hockey, or baseball—he was going to have damn good seats at the actual game. Football and baseball were okay but they went too slow and the games could last for hours. At least hockey kept moving.

Of course, Mally was a die-hard Eagles fan. He made a mental note to get tickets for a game this fall.

If she's still in your life this fall.

Considering it was only June, the answer to that should be yes. Which didn't mean a damn thing. Yes, they had an arrangement but—

"Max? Earth to Max? You went away."

He blinked and found her giving him that look. The one with the raised eyebrows.

"No. I didn't. I'm right here."

He barely gave a thought to his answer, but Mally's expression made him bite back a grimace. She was right.

He'd been gone when he should be right here. With her and Jesse. Because this wouldn't happen every day. It couldn't.

Hell, he didn't want this every day. He'd never considered having a woman in his life full-time. Not with the life he lived.

The life you're trying to leave behind. So why are you fighting so hard?

Damn good question. One he didn't want to examine too hard.

"Are you planning to stay for the day?"

She blinked at him and her lips parted but nothing came out.

He'd taken her off guard. Nice to know he still had the power to do that. He felt like he'd lost some footing in this relationship. Which wasn't a relationship. It was a business deal.

Yeah, right.

Then her head tilted to the side. "Do you want me to stay?"

He and Jesse should spend the day trying to figure out who was sabotaging them. He had two sets of books for one of the clubs to continue to go through and he had a meeting early tonight with a couple of other business owners to discuss collaborative ventures.

"Yes."

She smiled. "Okay."

He smiled back.

His day was looking up.

"Jesus Christ, Jesse. Are you sure?"

"Yeah, I'm pretty fucking sure. Someone got into Shivers sometime this week and messed with the gas lines. If we hadn't been keeping an eye on things, the whole damn building could've gone up."

"Sonuvabitch. When can we get it fixed and how long will the club be closed?"

"At least until tomorrow. Maybe longer if we can't get an inspector to come out and okay the fix."

"We're going to have to double-check every goddamn building again."

"I know. Already on it. I'll call you if we find anything else."

Max nearly threw his phone across the room after hanging up with Jesse. For the first time since Sunday, four days ago, he'd woken up in a decent mood. He and Jesse were supposed to see Mally tonight. He hated to admit he'd been looking forward to their date but just the thought of it had kept him from tearing out his hair a few times.

This week had been a bitch. He felt he hadn't had a spare second to breathe while he and Jesse tried to put out one fire after another.

One of their chefs had handed in his two-week notice Monday. Max had known it was coming. The guy hadn't liked the fact that Max and Jesse now owned the restaurant and he hadn't been quiet about it. Max wasn't upset the guy was leaving, just the fact that they only had two weeks to fill the position.

On top of that, one of the managers at Ivy Brown, another of their clubs, had turned in her notice Tuesday. Max hadn't seen that one coming. She'd seemed excited to continue working for them when they'd talked after he and Jesse had taken over. Hell, they'd even talked about her future with the club and some of her plans, which had been good. So he had to wonder if something or someone had deliberately poached her.

And now this.

Max wanted to put his fucking fist through the wall. He should call Mally and tell her they had to cancel tonight. He should join Jesse and go through the buildings with him. Then they needed to figure out who had it in for them.

That list was long and it'd take them awhile to go through it, and until then they shouldn't—

Fuck.

Fuck, fuck, fuck.

Last weekend had been amazing. He'd been hoping they could spend this coming weekend the same way. But even as he'd thought about it, he'd known it wasn't going to happen.

Because Jesse had been right. Back before they'd made this agreement with her, Jesse had said this wasn't the right time.

Max had just been too fucking arrogant to listen.

Sucking in a deep breath, he picked up his phone and punched in her number.

"Sorry, can't talk right now but leave me a message and I'll call back."

He considered hanging up but she'd know he called. And he wasn't fourteen, for Christ's sake.

"It's Max. I believe we're going to have to cancel for tonight. Something's come up. I'll call you later."

He hung up before he could add anything or babble. That'd just be pathetic.

Then he got off his ass and headed for Delia's desk in the front room.

Her head swiveled away from her monitor as he stopped behind her. Long, silky brown hair rippled down her back as she turned to stare at him. Her eye color matched her hair almost perfectly but he could barely see them now because they narrowed when she saw his face.

"What's wrong?"

Somehow, she always knew. He didn't know whether it was because they'd known each other for so long or because she actually did have a little bit of the "gift." She claimed to have a little Romany in her blood and had a sixth sense about things. Max thought she was just that good at reading people.

"Another incident at Shivers. Jesse and I need to go back through the other buildings, see if we missed something or if someone got in and fucked us over again."

"Damn. Someone's actually coming after you."

Delia shook her head, though she didn't look surprised. She looked resigned, as if she'd expected this.

He probably should have. But, goddammit, even though he was the most pessimistic person he knew, he'd hoped—

"So what are you going to do?"

Delia's question made him snap back to attention. "We're going to figure out who's behind it and put a stop to it."

"And how do you plan to do that?"

With her eyebrows raised like that, Max knew exactly what she wasn't saying. That was the blessing and curse of knowing someone so well.

With a sigh, he walked around to the front of her desk and fell into the chair across from it.

"With whatever means necessary."

She didn't look surprised. Delia had grown up on the same streets as Max and Jesse. "Do you want me to call my cousin?"

Delia's cousin, Mike, fixed things. Not like broken pipes or cars or people. Mike fixed problems. Usually with his fists and a whole shitload of intimidation.

"I'm trying to avoid that solution."

"And how's that working for you?"

He let his lips quirk into a sarcastic smile. "Not so great, apparently."

"Aww. Did someone kick your puppy?"

Now he gave her mocking reply a suitable response. He shot her the finger.

She smiled. "Now there's the Max I grew up with. Suck it up. You knew this wasn't going to be easy."

"True. I just thought..." Hell, he'd been an idiot. "Yeah, well, that doesn't matter. Guess it's time to get my hands dirty again."

"Or it's time to let someone else handle the dirty work."

For years, he and Jesse had been the ones to handle the dirty work. Together. Always. To think about handing over control of even a small part of their operation made this teeth clench.

"Then again," Delia said when he didn't reply, "maybe not."

"Do *you* think that's how we should handle this?"

Delia looked so surprised, he couldn't contain his grin. "Are you seriously asking me for advice?"

"It's not like it's the first time."

She shrugged. "Actually, it pretty much is."

Seriously? He leaned forward. "Well, shit. I guess I'm an asshole."

Delia laughed, something he didn't hear from her often enough. Christ, they were all fucked up, weren't they? "No, well... Okay, sometimes you can be an asshole but never to me. And you already know what I'm going to tell you. If you really need help, let me call Mike. The man knows how to keep his mouth shut. He also knows I'll take him out if he says anything."

She'd do it too. Delia wasn't afraid of anything. And they might just need the help.

"I'll let you know, okay?"

Delia nodded, as if that was the exact answer she'd expected. "Wanna tell me what else has got you looking like you wanna do murder?"

"What? Someone trying to sabotage our businesses isn't enough?"

"Yeah, that's more than enough. But I know there's something else and I figure it has to do with the woman who spent the weekend at your house."

Max huffed. He should've known she'd find out. But Delia wasn't the problem. "Does anyone else know?"

Delia shrugged. "I didn't actually know until you just confirmed it. But it wasn't that hard to figure out. You guys didn't exactly try to hide the fact that you went out Friday night."

"True. And I'm regretting it now."

"Regretting the date? Or regretting the fact that people saw you?"

He couldn't answer that because he wasn't sure he had an answer.

"So it's like that?" Delia's grin softened. "You really like her, don't you?"

He didn't have to answer. Nothing in the world could compel him to answer anything he didn't want to. But Delia was one of four people in his life he considered a friend, which was pretty pathetic, if he stopped to think about it. Jesse, Delia, and Alisa, who'd probably be surprised to find herself included in that group...and now Mally.

Christ, now he felt sorry for himself.

"Yeah, I like her. But I have a feeling Jesse and I are going to be bad for her."

Delia snorted. "I don't think I've met a man yet who isn't bad for some woman. That doesn't mean she wants you to make that choice for her."

Since that's just about exactly what Mally had said, he shook his head. "So you're telling me I shouldn't stop seeing her?"

"I'm telling you you should do what you want. Just make damn sure you can keep her safe when the shit hits the fan."

And the shit would hit the fan. No doubt about that.

Possibly sooner than later.

"You think too much sometimes, Max. Sometimes, you just gotta let go and enjoy yourself."

But at what cost?

14

When her phone rang, the number on the screen surprised her.

She'd gotten Max's earlier message and had spent most of the day talking herself out of calling him back. Now Jesse's number made her heart stutter a little.

"Hi."

"Hey, Mary Alice. How are you?"

"I'm fine. And you?"

He didn't answer right away and her stomach clenched. Was this how it would always be? Would she always be worried about them? Worried about them being hurt?

"I'm fine. We're fine. Look, I know Max called you earlier to cancel tonight and I know he didn't get a chance to talk to you. But I thought you should know what's going on."

Her stomach twisted. "Did something happen? Are you okay?"

"Are you still at work?"

"Yes. Jesse—"

"Are Tristan and Adam there?"

"No. What's going on?"

"Good. I don't want them involved in this. And honestly, I don't want you involved either but..."

Her throat had tightened with each word. "Jesse, what's going on?"

She heard him blow out a harsh breath. "Someone's sabotaging our businesses."

"What?"

The list Jesse laid out for her chilled her blood. The latest event especially made her shudder. "People could've been killed. You and Max could've been killed."

"We weren't. And we're going to figure out who did this, but Max told me he hadn't said anything to you about why he canceled and I figured you'd want to know."

"Do you think I'm in danger?"

"Honestly, I don't know. But I do know I don't want to risk you getting hurt."

She melted a little at his concern but she didn't want to give up her time with them. "So what if I come to your place tonight? We can get pizza or we can order in or whatever. I... want to see you tonight."

Another short pause. "And we want to see you too. I just want you to have all the facts before you make a decision."

"I want to see you. Both of you."

"Then how about tonight around seven? Do you want me to pick you up?"

"No, I'll drive. That way you won't need to drive me home—"

"So bring a bag and stay."

Yes. She wanted to say. It was on the tip of her tongue. And the intensity in Jesse's voice made all of her girly parts clench with desire. "Okay. I can do that."

"Good. We'll see you tonight."

She hung up, excited for that night. But fear began to bite into her stomach. Not for herself but for Jesse and Max.

If anything happened to them...

She tried to shake the thought out of her head but it followed her all afternoon.

"Did you honestly steal the mayor's car and get away with it?"

"We had no idea it was the mayor's car at the time. We were, what? Fifteen?"

Jesse looked at Max and the smile on Jesse's face made Max's tight muscles relax a fraction more.

"Yeah." Max nodded, trying to rid himself of the black mood hanging over him. "I think I was still fourteen. That damn Cadillac drove like a dream."

Sitting on the couch in their living room, Jesse, Mally and Max had been talking for two hours as they sat on the couch while the Phillies game played on the TV. Mally and Jesse had been keeping the conversation going as they ate pizza and drank beer and wine.

He'd been shocked as hell when Mally had arrived a little after seven with a bottle in her hand and a smile on her face.

Jesse hadn't told him she was coming. Probably because Max would've told her not to.

But she'd walked in like she did it every day. Like they were old friends. Or comfortable lovers. Nothing felt awkward with her. And he realized that's why he was drawn to her.

She didn't treat them any differently than she would anyone else. He had no idea why. For so many years, anyone they'd come into contact with treated them like they were bugs under a microscope or dangerous animals who should be behind thick glass.

Why didn't she?

"So you just took the statue and ran?" Mally laughed again, covering her mouth with her hand. "How did you carry it all that way?"

Jesse must be telling her about the time they stole the St. Francis statue from the church. They'd been even younger then, maybe eight or nine. They'd gotten caught that time, but instead of handing them over to the police, the priest had conscripted them for the summer. They'd repainted the church's living quarters and completely redone the extensive gardens where they'd stolen the statue.

Though he and Jesse never went to church, they did that summer in exchange for Father Gregory not turning them in to the police. They'd absolutely hated Sunday morning mass but they'd actually enjoyed the labor.

"Yeah, I kinda think Father Gregory expected us to turn the corner and lead upstanding, crime-free lives after that," Jesse said to Mally, leading Max to wonder if Jesse was reading his mind. "He was pretty old at that point and he died when we were..." Jesse looked at Max, "twelve, I think."

Max nodded, a grin kicking up the corners of his mouth. "Yeah. But that old man was sharp. I swear he was psychic. If you even thought about doing something wrong, he'd give you a lecture about eternal damnation until you were too intimidated to even think about screwing up."

Damn, when she smiled at him like she was now, he felt that pit in his stomach open. The one that made his world fold in at the corners.

How the hell did she do that?

Jesse said something that Max didn't catch but that made her smile, making her even more beautiful.

"Does the fact that we were criminals not bother you at all?"

The question had been circling Max's brain for days, especially since her aunt had stopped at their table on their date the other night. He was surprised Jesse hadn't asked it already. He knew Jesse had to be thinking the same.

But Jesse probably hadn't asked because it was a surefire way to kill the conversation.

Silence descended as Mally and Jesse looked at him. But he only had eyes for her. He watched as so many emotions crossed her face. He knew he didn't catch them all. But one he was sure of.

Pure stubborn will.

Tonight had absolutely nothing to do with their arrangement. No one knew she was here. No one would know she was here unless she told them or they saw her car, which she'd had to park a block away.

So what were they doing? What was *she* doing?

"You do realize you said 'were criminals,' right?"

She raised her eyebrows at him and waited.

Yes, he'd deliberately used the past tense because that's

how he thought about their time working for the Oleksy family. In the past.

"And," she continued, "have you considered the fact that maybe I enjoy your company?"

Yes, he had. But he couldn't quite bring himself to believe that. For a second, Max let his gaze snap to Jesse, whose attention was solely focused on Mally. Jesse had that air of expectant stillness. He wanted that to be true just as badly as Max did.

"Can you blame us for being skeptical?"

Mally's chin went up, but that stubbornness eased a little and morphed into something Max recognized as compassion.

Did she feel sorry for them? Did she pity them? He'd accused her of looking at them as fairy tales beasts who transform through the power of love. Was that how she really saw them and he was just too blinded by lust to see it?

Finally, she sighed and shook her head. "No, I guess I can't blame you for doubting me. You don't really trust anyone, do you?"

"We trust each other." Max didn't bother to look at Jesse for confirmation. He knew he had it. His unspoken "And that's it" was implied. And understood if her short nod was any indication.

"Then whatever I say, you won't really believe me."

Max took a deep breath. "You are the only person I've met in years that I've considered trusting."

She sucked her bottom lip between her teeth and bit on it. Max let his gaze drop to watch, wanting to lean over and lick away the hurt. Not wanting to stop there.

"And if I told you I've wanted you since the first moment

I met you, would you believe me?" Her head tilted to the side as she spoke, those beautiful blue eyes watching his every movement. "That I knew about you and Jesse and how you share women. How the idea made me wet every time I thought about it. I've seen how Adam and Tristan treat Kat, how much they love her, and maybe I thought, wouldn't that be amazing? To have two men who care about you so deeply. I knew how other people would react. I knew how my parents and my brothers would react. And I still decided to go after what I want." She paused, checking each of their expressions in turn. "So what do you think now?"

Lust hit him hard, like a swift kick to the balls, taking his breath. And maybe finally breaking through the shield he'd built around his heart years ago. The one only Jesse got through.

"I think we have to make damn certain we live up to your expectations."

Jesse's rough growl barely made it through his teeth before he shot across the cushion separating him from Mally, wrapped her in his arms, and took her horizontal.

Max figured they were lucky she didn't have a glass or a plate in her hand. Then again, he wouldn't have cared if they painted the walls with wine or stomped pizza into the carpet. They could repaint and replace anything in the room.

Except her.

She hadn't exactly been ready to be pounced on by Jesse, but after her initial gasp of surprise, she wound her arms around his neck and kissed him back.

Jesse kissed her with a ferocity Max would've taken exception to...except Mally appeared to love it.

She kissed him back just as fiercely, with the same sweet

intensity she did everything, her fingers sinking into his dark hair to hold him close.

Still reeling a little from the realization that he might care more for her than he wanted to admit, Max leaned back into the couch and prepared to enjoy the show, content for now to watch. He'd already been half hard all night but now he stiffened completely as Jesse reversed their positions on the couch, pulling her on top of him and letting his hands mold against her back before sliding down to her ass so he could pull her even more tightly against him.

Her deep moan made Max's blood heat as Jesse grabbed her long, loose skirt and pulled it to her hips so she could spread her legs, and straddle his lap.

Bracing her hands against Jesse's chest, she pushed up until she broke their lip-lock and could look into his eyes.

Then she smiled, a slow, seductive grin, and wriggled her hips, making Jesse groan as his hips lifted to grind into hers.

"I'm here, now, because I want to be. Because when I'm with you," she flashed a look at Max, still on the other side of the sectional, "*both* of you, you make me want things I've never wanted before."

"And what's that?"

Jesse's question held so much desire, so much naked *want*, Max felt a response deep in his own body.

"To be taken. By both of you."

Jesse sucked in a breath but Max got out the question first. "Are you telling us you want both of us to make love to you? At the same time? And be very sure of your answer, Mally. Because we'll stop if you ask but I'm not sure my heart will be able to take the strain."

Her smile softened, just a little. "I know what it means and I know what I want."

When had sweet Mally become the one with all the power? How had that happened? And why wasn't he more freaked out by that realization?

"Then we're all yours." Max spoke for both of them. He knew Jesse would've said the same. "You tell us what you want and we'll provide. But remember…at some point, we're going to want you to reciprocate. At some point, we're going to demand and you're going to give."

She swallowed hard and shuddered but she nodded. And, while she was somewhat distracted, Jesse took the opportunity to shove his hands beneath the thin t-shirt she wore and cup her breasts.

As her eyes closed on a moan, she let her head fall back while Jesse caressed her for several seconds before stripping off her shirt and getting rid of her bra. Naked from the waist up now, she bent to kiss Jesse again but he intercepted her, curling up to put his mouth on her breasts.

Her head fell forward, her hair falling around them, momentarily blocking Max's view of them until Jesse pushed her hair over her shoulder. Now Max could watch Jesse suckle her breasts then bite her and make her moan.

Watching her get off gave Max a satisfaction he'd never felt before. Knowing he'd touch her soon only added to the excitement.

Jesse suddenly shifted on the couch, throwing his legs over the side and standing, lifting her with him and wrapping her legs around his waist. Kissing her hard, Jesse headed for the first-floor bedroom, not bothering to look at Max. Jesse knew he'd follow.

Max made a side trip to the kitchen, dropping off the half-eaten pizza and grabbing another bottle of wine. For later.

By the time he got to the bedroom, Jesse had her naked and spread out across the bed and was kissing his way down her body. As he went, she pulled his shirt up his back until he obliged her and lifted his arms so she could pull it over his head.

As soon as his head was free, Jesse put his mouth over her sex, eliciting a moan from her that had Max stripping off his clothes in record time and dropping them to the floor. Jesse licked and sucked until she writhed on the bed, eyes tightly closed and her arms thrown above her head to hold onto the comforter.

Sliding onto the bed beside her, Max gathered her hands in one of his and held them captive while he kissed her. She groaned into his mouth and rolled into his body. Jesse had released her to remove his pants, and her warm skin molded to every available inch of his. Already erect and aching, Max pressed his cock into the cradle of her hips and let her squirm against him. Her body radiated heat, making his body temperature rise, as well.

With his mouth over hers, Max slid his tongue between her lips, kissing her harder and longer. Keeping them both on the edge.

The bed dipped as Jesse stretched out behind her, his hands going to her hips to pull her ass against his groin.

As she moaned, Max used the distraction to roll to the side and open the drawer for condoms and lube. When he rolled back, Jesse's dark head was bent over her shoulder, his mouth latched on to the soft skin of her neck.

Mally's head was tilted back, eyes closed, the pale column of her neck exposed. A flush spread across her entire body. Absolutely beautiful.

Max lay there, head propped on his hand, watching Jesse make her forget everything but them. His pulse pounded and his lungs felt like they were encased in concrete. His fingers itched to touch her but he wanted to postpone the pleasure. Drag it out as long as he could.

And he was worried that if he touched her now, he'd pull her out of the moment.

But then her eyes opened and she stared directly into his. And she reached for the condom in his hand.

He watched her open it carefully then reach for his cock. She pulled his stiff flesh away from his body then rolled it down. Trying to control his body's response so he didn't come in her hand, Max seriously considered counting down by sevens from one hundred.

Instead, he watched her chest rise and fall faster and faster as Jesse reached for the lube and other condom.

She knew what was coming. She'd asked for it.

Fuck, he couldn't wait.

Grabbing her, he rolled onto his back, bringing her with him to lie on top of him. Her legs fell on either side and she rubbed her mound against his erection, now trapped between them. Pushing herself up just enough to move her hips, she got his cock where it needed to be. He didn't even need to use his hands. She tilted her pelvis until his tip parted her lips.

Max plunged inside as far as he could go, wringing a moan from her and making his every muscle tense with pleasure. Then he fucked her, hard and steady. She held on but didn't complain. In fact, she urged him to go faster by biting his earlobe and neck.

When she broke apart, she did without warning. Just tightened around him and came with a cry that hit Max right in the balls.

Fuck, he wanted to come but he reined in the urge.

And Jesse made his move. They'd done this many times before but this didn't feel like any of those. Max caught Jesse's gaze for a few brief seconds and he knew they were thinking the exact same thing.

Ours.

Then Jesse looked down, his hands moving to her hips while Max's arms wrapped around her back, holding her tight to his chest.

He heard her draw in a sharp breath but Jesse had already breached her and she barely had a chance to stiffen before Jesse slowly invaded her ass.

"Oh my god. That's…"

"Are you okay?"

She turned her face into Max's neck and he felt her lips move against his neck, "It's— Oh wow. It's almost too much."

"Mally, are you sure—"

"One of you has to move. Right now or I'm going to—"

Max pulled out while Jesse stayed deep. They knew how to do this to give her more pleasure than she'd ever had.

And her arms tightened around his neck as she moaned, her pleasure audible.

They fell into the perfect rhythm, in perfect sync. Max could barely catch his breath. Jesse sounded like a freight engine. Mally... God, Mally bit into his neck with those perfect little teeth and made him shudder.

Jesus Christ, he couldn't—

Max came hard, buried deep inside her, his arms so tight around her.

Jesse followed him seconds later as Mally shook between them.

And Max knew this was way more complicated than any of them had bet on.

15

Jesse sat up in bed, the silent alarm triggered and buzzing through the wristband he wore at night.

On other side of the bed, Max stirred then sat up as well. Neither of them woke Mally, still sound asleep between them.

Sonuvabitch. He really fucking hoped this was a false alarm.

He knew it wasn't.

Nodding at Max, Jesse slid from the bed, the Berretta he kept between the mattress and the box spring already in his hand.

Motioning for Max to stay behind with Mally, he headed for the door. Max would already have retrieved the Glock in the bedside table.

In the hall, Jesse checked the security pad, which said the breach had come from the kitchen. There was only one window there but it was a big one. And it didn't open.

He hadn't heard glass breaking so that meant someone

might have deliberately tripped the kitchen sensor to throw them off.

Closing the door to the room behind him, he knew Max wouldn't be content to be left behind for long. He'd take Mally out the secret exit and stash her in the safe room in the garage, then he'd come back for Jesse.

Jesse wanted to have the threat neutralized before that happened.

Crouching just outside the door, he listened for any noise out of the ordinary and heard something almost immediately. The faint sound of rubber soles against carpet.

Not in the kitchen. The living room or the dining room. Possibly Max's study.

Fuck. The sound was too faint to get a read on it.

He couldn't wait here. He needed to clear the house.

Since Max's office was closest, he headed there first.

And knew immediately that he'd picked wrong.

The intruder ran at him from the living room, giving Jesse just enough time to turn and meet the guy head on.

Smaller and slimmer than Jesse, the guy was fast and he had the element of surprise on his side.

Jesse tried to wrap his arms around the guy and use brute strength to take him down fast but the intruder kept evading him, moving just out of reach every time. Not trying to run. Jesse couldn't figure out why.

Until the guy feinted to his left, as if to get around him. And when Jesse moved to intercept him, he felt the knife sink deep into his side, all the way to the hilt.

Jesse reacted with a burst of strength as he shoved the attacker away. He heard the guy hit the opposite wall with enough force to break the drywall, but the motion made the knife tear something inside that hurt like ever-loving hell.

He didn't have time to catch his breath, though, because his attacker bounced off the wall and came back at him. The guy grabbed the knife and twisted it, sending agony pouring through Jesse like hot lava before his assailant pulled it out.

Jesse couldn't keep silent and a pained grunt escaped but he managed to grab the other guy's arm as he brought the knife down again.

With a twist of his wrist, Jesse heard the guy's arm break.

"Jesse! Oh my god."

Through the ringing in his ears, he heard Mally's voice. What the hell was she doing in the goddamn hall? Why the fuck hadn't Max got her out of here?

Then he realized his assailant was no longer near him.

Blinking the blurriness from his eyes, he saw Max toss the guy across the room then go after him with a speed Jesse had forgotten Max possessed. But their intruder was smart and good. He evaded Max, getting in a few punches before Max finally got him in a headlock and slammed his head into the wall hard enough to put a hole in it.

The guy slumped into a ball against the wall.

And Max pulled his gun.

"Max! No."

Max held the gun straight at the man's head as he walked to the wall to flip the switch for the light in the hall. Not bright enough to blind anyone, even momentarily.

Max ripped off the balaclava then pressed his gun to the guy's temple.

And even through the pain clouding his thoughts, Jesse knew Max was about to do something really stupid.

"Max," Mally pleaded. "Don't do it. Please."

Max ignored her, his focus laser-point sharp on the man who'd dared to break into their home. "Did you think I wouldn't know who you were?"

Their intruder said nothing, staring back at Max with an impassive gaze.

"Not willing to talk, huh?" Max shrugged. "Doesn't matter. You know I can't let you leave."

"And you can't shoot him." Mally's voice shook. "Max. Put the gun down."

Max ignored her, keeping the gun pointed at the man as he took a few steps away.

Jesse felt the world spinning, felt Mally pressing something against his wound, making it hurt like fuck, while trying to talk Max out of killing the man on their floor.

A man both he and Max recognized.

"Go ahead," the guy finally said. "Just do it. But I'm pretty sure you don't have the—"

Max pulled the trigger.

16

Mary Alice had expected the gunshot to be much louder.

She'd turned away when Max had pulled the trigger, flinching even though the sound was a muted pop instead of a blast.

"It's okay. Trust him."

Her eyes opened as Jesse whispered in her ear. Jesse... who was bleeding and possibly dying on the floor in front of her.

Swallowing hard, she pulled back to look down at him. Pain made tiny lines appear at the corners of his eyes but otherwise, he looked fine.

Except for all that blood.

Deep breath. And another. She focused on slowing her galloping heart and drawing in much-needed air as she stared into Jesse's steady eyes. How could he be so calm? He'd been shot.

"Gonna be okay. Trust him."

Who? Max? Who'd just shot the man who'd tried to kill

Jesse.

"...sent you?" Max said. "Just for curiosity's sake because I already know the answer. I want to hear you say it."

Her gaze connected with Jesse's, his expression calm. Much calmer than she felt.

"Breathe."

She obeyed him immediately, realizing she'd been holding her breath. Her lungs burned and she blinked hard to clear sudden tears. Adrenaline burned through her body, fear and anger creating a toxic stew in her stomach.

Behind her, she heard Max continue to question the intruder. She figured he was trying to get information before the guy died.

"Jess—"

"Have her call Haverstick."

Max's voice stunned her like an electric shock. He sounded deadly calm. Unemotional. And so very cold.

The urge to scream rose up in her throat. She wanted to turn on Max and tear into him but Jesse grabbed her arm and squeezed.

"Phone. In my pocket."

Okay, now that seemed like a plan. Call for an ambulance. Get Jesse to a hospital.

She reached for his pants but froze because the pocket where Jesse had his phone was right below the wound. The still-bleeding wound.

Her gaze snapped back to Jesse's. He watched her every move with laser focus.

Probably because he was afraid she was going to pass out. And she hadn't been shot.

"I..."

She swallowed the rest of her words because she'd been going to say she couldn't do it. Couldn't get his phone because she was weak. Jesse couldn't afford for her to be weak now.

Taking a deep breath, she stuck her hand in his pocket, and, as gently as she could, withdrew his phone. He didn't move but she saw the way the skin around his eyes tightened.

"Jesse."

Her voice was barely a whisper though he must have heard her.

"I'm okay." But his voice sounded just a tiny bit weaker. "I have to open it and then you need to make the call."

When she held out the phone to him, her hands shook so hard, she almost dropped it. After he used his thumb to unlock the screen, he handed it back. Carefully. Not moving more than he had to.

"Contacts. Haverstick."

Vaguely, she realized Max continued to interrogate the intruder. But, even though she wanted to listen, she forced herself to make the call.

"Just say the address," Jesse said. "No names. Nothing else. They'll recognize...the number."

Jesse had lost his breath by the end of his sentence and he had to stop to suck in air. Fear wrapped around her lungs. With a shaky finger, she found the name in his list and punched it.

Taking a deep breath, she waited. One ring. Two. Three.

"Yes."

The voice on the other end of the phone was female. And young. Mally hadn't expected that.

Then she remembered what Jesse had told her. She recited the address. The only response was the click to end the call.

She looked back at Jesse and opened her mouth to speak but stopped when he shook his head. Just once and very slowly.

She closed her mouth.

"I need you to say that again. Slower this time."

Behind her, she plainly heard Max. No mistaking that hard tone.

Swallowing down her fear, she turned, bracing herself for another gruesome sight.

But...the intruder didn't appear to have a gunshot wound anywhere on his body. At least none that she could see on his all-black clothing. No blood seeped from his body, except from the cuts on his face, probably caused by his fight with Jesse.

Then she looked a little closer and realized there was a hole just to the left of his head in the wall.

Max hadn't shot him.

Relief literally made her thighs shake. Good thing she wasn't standing.

And if he had shot the guy?

She glanced at Jesse, bleeding onto the floor. If anything happened to him...

I'd shoot him myself.

She turned back just in time to see Max cock the gun and, instead of aiming at the guy's head, he aimed directly between his legs.

"You don't have to talk but if you don't," Max said,

"you'll leave here with fewer body parts than when you arrived. Now...who sent you?"

When the man didn't answer, Max pulled the trigger. She flinched but didn't look away this time.

The bullet lodged in the floor between his legs.

"Next one goes in your thigh and you'll bleed out before the doctor gets here."

Max cocked the gun again.

The intruder tilted his head back, a sneer on his lips. "No one sent me."

"Then no one will miss you when you disappear."

The guy was young, she realized. Probably younger than her. Short, dark hair. Huge, dark eyes. Wiry but not too tall. And the defiant look on his pale face made her wonder if he knew exactly who he was dealing with.

Because she couldn't believe anyone who saw Max now would believe he wouldn't follow through on his threat.

"Man," the sneer in the guy's voice made her want to smack him, "you're not gonna shoot me. You would've already. You can't afford to. You wanna be Mr. Perfect now. Mr. Executive. Never gonna happen. You're always gonna be a lowlife hood rat. And everyone's gonna know who took you down."

Max's smile made Mally shiver. "Obviously, you're not as smart as you think you are."

In the blink of an eye, Max shifted the gun and shot the intruder in the arm.

This time, she didn't even flinch.

The bullet went through the fleshy part of his arm, making the man cry out in pain. "You mother*fucker*. I'm gonna kill—"

Max cocked the gun once more and aimed at his leg. "Tell me who you're working for."

"Jesus Christ." Fear finally showed in the intruder's voice. "You fucking know who I work for. But he didn't send me. You two are fair game, asshole. You know that. You painted a huge bull's-eye on your back the second Oleksy left town. Somebody's gonna take you down. It's just a matter of time."

"No one will come after us. Not when they hear what we do to you."

The total lack of emotion in Max's voice made a chill run up her spine and she sucked in a sharp breath.

"You're not gonna do anything to me." The guy's voice really shook now. "You can't. He'll kill you and you know it."

"Your boss understands the way the game is played. He understands that some losses are acceptable. And some are out of his control. Now, I can make this quick or I can draw it out. Tell me who's responsible for the sabotage in our buildings, because you're not smart enough for it, and I'll make it quick. Stay silent and..."

Max turned the gun in his hand slightly and the intruder held up his good hand.

"I don't know who. Not exactly. But yeah, he's been fucking with you. Just to see what you'd do." Something on Max's face must have warned the guy because he tried to cover his face with both arms. "No, wait—"

With a practiced move, Max flipped the gun and slammed the butt against the guy's temple. The dull thump as it made contact caused her stomach to flip but she forced herself to swallow down the queasiness.

Max had already turned before the guy started to slump.

He closed the distance between him and Jesse in a second and fell to his knees, putting his hands on Jesse's. When he added pressure, Jesse groaned and Mary Alice felt a sob build in her chest. She quickly swallowed it down. None of them could afford for her to crumble now.

"How bad is it?"

She heard fear in Max's voice, a low undertone that made her eyes well with tears. She'd never heard that level of emotion from him before. She wanted to throw her arms around his shoulders and hold him but she wasn't sure he'd let her.

Jesse shook his head. "Didn't hit anything vital."

She hadn't realized she'd started to shake again until Max took one hand from Jesse's side and wrapped it around hers, still twined with Jesse's fingers.

He squeezed for a brief second then guided her hand down to Jesse's wound. "Press hard. I've gotta tie that fucker up and let the doctor in when she gets here." He stared into her eyes, his dark. And cold. Which didn't match the tone of his voice. She wondered if he realized how much of his fear came through in his voice. "He'll be okay, Mally."

She didn't know if he was trying to convince her or himself.

Then he got up and headed for the kitchen, where she heard him opening and closing drawers.

She alternated between watching the doorway and watching Jesse until Max returned. Jesse didn't move, just continued to breathe, slow and steady. When Max finally walked back into the room, he went straight to the intruder and zip-tied his hands and feet before coming back to them.

"Do you want to leave?"

She blinked at him, her brain taking a few seconds to work through what Max had said. And when she had, she couldn't believe she'd heard him right.

Her mouth opened and closed twice before she spoke. "Are you seriously asking me if I want to leave while Jesse's bleeding on the damn floor?"

Max's expression remained stone cold but his eyes... The wildness in his voice had started to seep through.

"Yes, I am. I'll call Adam to pick you up. I don't want you to leave by yourself. The doctor will be here in minutes and—"

"Max. Shut up. I'm not going anywhere."

His mouth tightened and she thought he might argue with her. Prepared to put up a fight, she watched as he took a breath and held it for several seconds before releasing it.

She could've sworn he was going to say something else, but he shook his head after a few seconds and turned to Jesse.

"Haverstick will be here in minutes."

Jesse nodded. "I know. I told you, he didn't hit anything vital. I'll be fine."

Max nodded but it was jittery, and Mally realized he was barely holding it together. This man, who never seemed to get rattled, was about to lose it. And she had no idea how to make it better.

She wanted to wrap her arms around him but didn't want to take the pressure off Jesse's wound.

She'd started to regain her own equilibrium, though she wasn't sure how long it would last. By focusing solely on Jesse, she'd been able to maintain, to hold off the terror.

But if Max fell apart...

"Max."

She kept her tone low and steady, as if he was one of her younger cousins having a tantrum. She'd done her share of babysitting and she'd learned how to calm a screaming toddler.

Max wasn't a toddler and he wasn't screaming, but the theory was the same. She almost expected him to snarl at her. Instead, he took another breath and, in the blink of an eye, reined himself in.

Steady, stable Max reappeared as he stood. And she breathed a sigh of relief.

"Keep the pressure on that wound. I'll be right back. Need to get a towel from the kitchen."

Then he stalked away again and she watched him until he disappeared.

"Hey. Mally."

Jesse's voice drew her attention back to him and she had to suck in air to stave off the tears that suddenly threatened. He looked pale, more now than he had earlier. And fear crept back in, threatening her composure.

Not now. Can't cry now.

"What do you need?"

Jesse's lips curved in a slight smile. "A beer."

His joke took a second to sink in but when it did, she couldn't even muster a smile. "You need to keep still."

"I'm not gonna bleed out. It hurts like a bitch, but it's not gonna kill me. But you gotta listen. Max'll think this is his fault. Hell, he thinks everything's his fault. Don't let him fall into that trap."

She shook her head. "You must've mistaken me for someone Max actually listens to."

"He does listen to you. He's just—"

Jesse cut off with a grimace and her heart stuttered in her chest, wondering why Jesse had stopped...until she realized Max had walked back into the room.

He looked as if he'd taken a few seconds to pull himself together. His expression had leveled out. While he didn't look like he was about to commit murder, he certainly looked as if he could.

"Move your hands." Squatting down beside them, Max waited for them to do what he'd said before putting a towel against the wound, which didn't seem to be bleeding as much anymore.

He didn't say anything, didn't look at either of them. Just watched as they pressed the white cloth into Jesse's side then got up and contemplated the still-unconscious intruder.

Max had his back to her but she sensed the stiffness in his body, saw the hands clenched at his sides.

And had a moment of serious panic that he was going to do something he'd regret and could never take back.

"Max."

She said his name so softly, she wasn't sure he'd heard her. Then she heard him suck in an audible breath and his hands unclenched. He turned to look over his shoulder at her, that wild emotion still in his eyes. Her breath caught in her throat.

A knock at the front door broke their connection. Max shot off to answer it and returned half a minute later with a woman who looked barely old enough to be a resident, much less a full-fledged doctor.

With a body that wouldn't look out of place on a runway

and short blonde hair as flawless as if she'd just left the salon, the woman walked with an inbred confidence. And her expression when she saw Jesse told Mally the woman's feelings for him went beyond traditional doctor-patient relationship.

Mally had the uncharacteristic and completely ridiculous urge to bare her teeth and tell her to stay the fuck away from her men.

Maybe Max isn't the only one losing it.

"You know," the woman sank onto her haunches beside Mally, her entire attention focused on Jesse, "there's a much easier way for us to spend time together. All you have to do is pick up the phone and call."

"Haven't exactly had a lot of time lately, Dorrie."

"So I hear." The woman peeled away the towel at his wound, her expression showing nothing as she began her examination.

Mally would've stayed by his side but Max touched her shoulder, making her look up.

"I have to take out the trash and I may be gone for a while. Don't leave unless it's with Adam or Tristan. I'm going to call someone to watch the house. I believe this one was working on his own but I'm not taking any chances. Are you sure you don't want to leave?"

Standing, Mally looked Max directly in the eyes, trying to see beyond the purposefully blank expression. Did he want her to go? Did he not want to have to deal with her? She wanted to ask, but she wouldn't while the doctor was here. But if Max didn't stop trying to push her away, all bets would be off.

"I'm not going anywhere. I'll be right here when you get back."

He looked like he wanted to say more, his jaw flexing as if he was biting back the words. Did he really want her to leave that badly?

"I'm calling Adam anyway. He'll be here to watch your back. And I'm calling in someone else, too. I'll wait until they get here then I have to take care of this. But you should leave with Adam."

Guess she should've seen that one coming, though it didn't change her mind in any way.

"I'm. Not. Leaving." She spoke slowly and clearly and loud enough that Jesse could hear her, too. She wanted him to know she wasn't abandoning him.

Frustration made Max's mouth tighten. "Damn it, Mally—"

"Max, maybe you could shut up for a few minutes while I make sure Jesse's guts don't spill out, okay? Thanks. And maybe you want to introduce me to your friend."

The doctor's words felt like a slap but they served their purpose.

Max's jaw flexed like he was trying to grind his molars into dust but he flipped a quick glance at the doctor. "Dorrie, Mary Alice. I'll be back as soon as I can."

Then he grabbed the intruder off the ground as if he weighed less than a bag of cat litter, threw him over his shoulder and headed for the kitchen and, she assumed, the garage.

"Mary Alice." Dorrie's voice dragged her attention away from Max. "I need you to take a few steps back or go around to Jesse's other side, please. You're in my light and I really need it to see."

The woman's matter-of-fact tone rubbed Mary Alice the wrong way but she chalked it up to nerves. One of her men had been shot.

She moved to Jesse's other side, sank down onto the ground, and put her hand on his shoulder. She needed to touch him. Had to feel the warmth of his skin. Had to tell herself over and over again that he was going to be okay.

That *they* were going to be okay.

And that Max would get his head out of his ass before he returned. Or she wouldn't be responsible for her actions.

17

Max managed not to throw the guy in the trunk of his car. Just barely.

He settled for letting the body fall, maybe from a higher distance than necessary, and refrained from slamming the hood on his foot that hadn't made it all the way inside the trunk.

What he really wanted to do was put a bullet in the guy's side. Just like he'd done to Jesse.

But he wasn't going to. Because that's not how they needed to settle this.

No, he needed to have an uncomfortable talk with this punk-ass kid's boss. Which was going to suck. And could turn ugly.

Goddammit, he wanted Jesse by his side. Only, Jesse was lying in the hall of their home having the doctor patch him up.

Shit. If he thought about that any longer, this asshole wouldn't last another five minutes.

Shoving the guy's foot inside the trunk, he slammed it closed and got in the car.

He debated for about two seconds before he picked up his phone and pulled up a number he hadn't ever had to use.

But he couldn't leave Jesse and Mally undefended. Even if their intruder was telling the truth and he was working alone, Max had to make the call.

With a sigh, he pressed the number and, when it connected, he held a short conversation that he knew would have repercussions he'd need to deal with later.

His next call was almost as bad.

"Max?" Adam sounded wide awake. "What's wrong?"

"I need your help. Jesse had an accident. Mally could use some reassurance."

Adam's short pause let Max know he understood what he hadn't said. "We'll be there in ten."

Fuck. Mally was going to hate him.

He didn't care. Not as long as she and Jesse were safe.

Maybe she needs to hate you. Maybe this will push her away and you'll finally realize this relationship will never work.

And maybe he just needed to shut the fuck up and take care of the situation at hand. They'd figure everything out later.

If you ever see her again after tonight.

The thought made his stomach roll.

Fuck that. She hadn't been willing to leave Jesse tonight. She wouldn't leave them.

And what if you know she should?

Taking several deep breaths, he leaned against the car and waited, trying to use some of the relaxation techniques the last shrink had told him would help. They never had before.

Minutes later, his phone vibrated to let him know someone had pressed the bell at the side door to the garage. Only a few people knew about that entrance.

The man standing on the other side of the door had short, light brown hair, pale blue eyes, and barely hit six foot. He was one of the most nondescript men Max had ever met. Most people barely gave him a second look. That made him very, very good at his job.

"Ian."

"Been awhile, Max."

"Jesse's hurt. Doctor's here. There's also another woman. Nothing happens to any of them."

Ian's brows raised slightly, the only indication of emotion. "How bad?"

Max's jaw clenched. "He'll be fine." He couldn't afford to think otherwise. "I've got to leave. Have to deliver a message."

Nodding, Ian walked through the door, shutting it behind him then leaning back against it. "How long?"

"Maybe an hour."

Ian nodded again before his gaze shifted to the door into the house. "Who's the doc?"

Max had turned and was headed for the car. "Haverstick. She's—"

"I know who she is."

Max glanced over his shoulder at Ian as he opened the door to his car and slid inside. "Is that a problem?"

Ian shook his head. "No. Just curious."

Something in Ian's voice made Max think it wasn't just curiosity, but it didn't matter, not now. "Adam and Tristan will be here in a few minutes. Don't shoot them."

Now a slight smile curved Ian's lips. "Arrogant assholes probably deserve it for something."

Ian and Adam had history. Max didn't give a shit. "Nothing happens to the girl or Jesse."

"Finally found one, huh?"

Max didn't have the time to answer that question completely so he didn't even bother. "I'll be back in an hour."

"I'll be here."

Max didn't look back. He had to keep moving forward or he'd do something he regretted. Like beat the shit out of the guy in his trunk.

Jesus, Jesse could've been killed. Mally could've been hurt.

If either of those situations had happened, their intruder would be dead. No questions asked.

Half an hour later, Max arrived at his destination, feeling a little steadier. Detached. And ready to confront the man who owned the piece of shit in his trunk.

Stopping at the gate of the Main Line mansion, he announced himself through the intercom and wasn't surprised when it took more than a minute for the gates to open. He waited without fidgeting. Didn't drum his fingers on the steering wheel or look around. He stared straight ahead. Patient. Unafraid. All anger and fear suppressed. He couldn't show any weakness. If he did, he and Jesse might as well pack up and leave town.

And that wasn't happening. They'd worked too damn hard. And then there was Mally...

As he drove down the lane toward the three-story monstrosity sitting on the perfectly landscaped two-acre lot, he took several deep breaths and made sure his expression held no hint of anger.

When he pulled up to the front of the house, the guard who opened the front door looked like he could bench-press a tractor-trailer and ate rocks for breakfast. Impressive scare tactic but Max didn't scare easily.

Max got out of the car and walked to the door. He had to look up at the guard but he didn't do anything other than lift an eyebrow at him.

The guy opened the door a second later and waved him through. Max clicked the remote and popped the trunk before he entered the house.

"Max. I believe you've returned something of mine that got lost in your neighborhood."

Max took the hand Karel Antonoff held out, shaking it firmly and meeting his gaze directly.

"I didn't want you to think I would keep your property any longer than necessary."

Karel's chin lifted slightly. "I understand there might have been some...incidental injury."

"Daddy, is something wrong?"

Larisa Antonoff appeared at the top of the staircase, looking every bit the princess her father believed her to be.

She gave Max the haughty look her father expected from her. The one that made her appear even more untouchable than she already did. Dressed in a long white robe that managed to expose just as much as it covered and with her unbound hair a mass of blonde curls that fell practically to her waist, she walked down the stairs like she was entering a ballroom. Of course, this foyer could probably classify as one, considering its size.

"No, sweetheart. Nothing's wrong." Karel turned to smile at his daughter, a true smile that'd always fascinated Max. The man loved his daughter. He was a cold-blooded killer but when it came to Risa... If she'd asked for her father's heart, he'd cut it out himself and hand it over. Apparently, the same had been true of his feelings for his wife. But she'd been dead before Max and Jesse had gone to work for David. "Max and I have some business to discuss."

Risa's sharp eyes checked Max out from head to toe as she arrived at the bottom of the stairs before she returned her father's smile. "Must be important. It's nearly three in the morning."

Karel's smile never faltered but then he'd been playing this game with his daughter since the moment she was born. Karel pretended he was a regular businessman and Risa pretended she didn't know what her father did to afford the mansion and the designer clothes, the car she drove and the trips she took. And the business she ran.

Even though both of them knew exactly what they weren't saying.

"Max and I need a few minutes to talk, sweetheart. Come into my office, Max, and we'll finish this in there."

As Karel turned away, Risa raised her eyebrows at Max but he shook his head quickly before following her father.

Max knew it was a temporary reprieve. She wouldn't let this go.

She might have no desire to take over her father's criminal empire, but she also knew how important it was to know what was going on. She didn't want to be blindsided if something happened to her father. With the life they led, who knew when he might be on the wrong end of a bullet.

Or a blade.

Max's jaw tightened as he thought about Jesse lying in all that blood, but he quickly shoved the thought away. Wouldn't do any good to think about it now and Jesse was going to be fine.

Max needed all this brain cells firing to deal with Karel.

When the other man closed the door to his office behind him, Max forced himself to breathe normally and take the chair Karel waved toward.

He felt compelled to remain standing, simply because that's exactly what he would've done if he'd been here with David Oleksy. And he had been. Many times. Max would've stood behind this chair while Karel and David talked. Jesse would've been behind him by the door.

Tonight, it was just Max and Karel. Max wasn't sure whether to be flattered that Karel was treating him as an equal or pissed that Karel didn't think he posed a threat.

Get out of your head.

"So, would you like to tell me what happened or should I simply write you a check for damages?"

Since Max had had time to think on his drive here, he had an answer ready. "I believe your nephew made an ill-advised decision that could've cost him more than the use of his arm for a few days. Money won't be necessary. An understanding that this won't happen again will be sufficient."

Karel leaned back in his chair, his dark gaze piercing and his lips slightly curved. "Yes, my nephew does try a little too hard sometimes. He's...enthusiastic. But I can assure you that you won't need to worry about another incident, at least not from my organization. Though this won't be the last attempt. You do know that, don't you?"

Max settled deeper into his chair. "It will be after word gets around about your nephew's failure. He'll make a good example."

Karel nodded, his lips curling slowly into a full-blown smile. "Are you so sure you want to do that?"

Max didn't smile back. "You know I have to."

Now Karel's smile disappeared in a blink. "And you know that'll create problems between us."

Max made sure to keep his expression calm. "Jesse and I have kept our end of the arrangement you made with David Oleksy. We've done nothing to compromise that. Your nephew made it clear he was acting on his own. If anyone asks, I'll make it clear we don't consider you complicit in his actions.

"But Jesse and I won't allow any attempt to take us down. You've known us for years, Karel." He deliberately used the man's given name to show Karel Max considered them equals. "We're not going to pretend we didn't take down your future prince. He came at us with the intent to do harm. We can't allow any misconceptions about our ability to defend ourselves against unprovoked attacks."

"So you're going to embarrass my nephew...and me...to prove a point?"

Careful now. "I have no intention of embarrassing you. But we can't allow our authority to be challenged. It might encourage others to try to take what's ours. We don't want to have to prove ourselves with deadly force. But we will if we need to."

Max held Karel's gaze as he threw everything on the table. He really didn't want to go to war over this, but if Karel didn't listen to reason, Max was prepared to back up his declaration with action.

He'd use deadly force if he had to. He didn't want to but he would. He and Jesse had worked too damn hard to back down now.

"I understand your position." Karel finally spoke after several seconds of tense silence. "But let me make a suggestion. Allow me to publicly chastise my nephew for his... disobedience. Before you make any other announcements. Surely that won't cause any unwanted repercussions."

Max knew Karel wanted to come out with the upper hand. He also knew fighting Karel on this wouldn't end well for him and Jesse. Karel now led the largest crime organization in Philadelphia. They needed to remember that if they were going to exist in the same city.

"I'm sure it won't."

Max rose and Karel followed suit, eyes bright as he took Max's outstretched hand.

"Then you can expect a formal apology tomorrow morning," Karel said. "I'll be sure to let our mutual business interests understand the situation."

Max followed Karel back to the front door. Risa was nowhere in sight, but he knew she'd contact him later. She didn't think much of her cousin but he was family. To the Antonoffs, that meant a hell of a lot.

"We'll talk tomorrow," Karel said as he opened the door. "You can be assured there'll be no repercussions on my end. A young man has to learn to deal with the consequences of his actions."

Max nodded, knowing there was supposed to be a lesson in there for him, as well. "I'll wait to hear from you. Please apologize to Larisa for me. I didn't mean to wake her."

Karel's mouth twisted in a wry grin. "I'm sure Risa will forgive you, Max. She's always had a sweet spot for you. We'll talk tomorrow. Please give Jesse my regards."

Max's jaw tightened but he nodded and got the hell out of there.

Now, only a few blocks from home, he sucked in a deep breath while stopped at a red light. Then he took another and another, his lungs working overtime to catch up. He wasn't sure he'd taken a breath since he'd left Antonoff's house.

Max stared at the red light, his anger building with every second. He wanted to hit something, pound it into dust. His rage was so red hot, he swore his skin burned.

No, can't lose it now.

If he did, he was afraid the car wouldn't survive. And yet, every passing second made his heart race faster and his lungs work harder.

Calm down. Stay steady. Couldn't let Mary Alice or Jesse see him like this. Hell, he couldn't let anyone see him like this.

The light turned and his foot jerked on the pedal, making the car surge forward. He didn't let up, though. He wanted to be home.

"I guess I should've known he'd call you. Don't even say it. I'm not going anywhere."

Mally turned away from the front door, allowing Adam and Tristan to follow her into the house.

"Jesus, Mally—"

"Are you okay?"

Adam cut off Tristan's tight words with his perfectly calm question. Mally spared him a glance over her shoulder as she headed back to the kitchen where the doctor was working on Jesse.

"I'm fine. I'm not the one who got stabbed."

Silence from behind her. She kept walking.

The doctor had said Jesse would be fine. She had to believe that. But she wasn't going anywhere until she was sure. Whether that was a few days or a few weeks...

"How's Jesse?"

She didn't answer Tristan. He'd see for himself soon enough. She stopped in the doorway of the kitchen, where he lay on the table. She and the doctor had helped him walk there. He'd barely leaned on them, but she'd heard his labored breathing and knew he hurt much more than he let on.

Jesse's eyes were closed but his hands were clenched into fists at his sides as the doctor stood beside him. Mally couldn't see what the doctor was doing because she was on the other side of the table.

Probably better that way.

Behind her, she felt Adam and Tristan stop. Heard Adam sigh.

"Shit." Tristan kept his voice low enough not to attract Jesse's attention. "Is he okay?"

"Yes." She refused to believe otherwise.

"Good." Adam spoke loud enough that Jesse opened his

eyes and looked their way. He caught and held her gaze for several moments before switching his attention to Adam and Tristan.

The guys spoke without words and she knew exactly what they were saying.

Protect Mally. Don't let anything happen to Mally. She's fragile. She can't take care of herself.

Now wasn't the time to get into that with them. Max had called and Adam and Tristan had come running. If it hadn't been so infuriating, it'd be endearing. And if she weren't so damn worried about Jesse...

Jesse's gaze shifted back to her and she crossed the room to take the hand he held out to her.

"I know that look."

She had the childish urge to stick her tongue out at him. "Stay still or Dr. Haverstick will make me leave."

"Damn right I will." The doctor's gaze stayed glued to Jesse's side. "You move and mess up my stitches and I will stitch your colon closed."

Jesse never looked away from Mally. "Are you gonna forgive me?"

She frowned. "For what?"

"For getting hurt."

She shook her head, bemused. "I'm not angry with you for getting hurt." He just kept staring at her until she huffed. "I'm not."

But, damn it, she realized that's exactly what she was. Pissed off.

"Now's not the time to talk about it."

"I know. But, Mally, we are gonna talk about it."

"When you're better."

"I'll be better as soon as Doc stops jabbing me."

He turned his head to glare at Dorrie, who didn't bother to acknowledge him.

"And I'll stop jabbing when I decide your insides aren't going to fall out."

"Dorrie."

"Oh, please." The doctor shot Mally a quick wink, which Jesse didn't see, and that shocked the hell out of Mally. "She's not going to pass out because I made a joke. She's not made of glass. Get a grip."

Jesse grimaced and opened his mouth but Mally spoke before he could.

"She's absolutely right. Now shut up and let her finish."

"Adam's gonna stay here." Tristan spoke behind her. "I'm gonna take a look around. Check in with Ian."

Mally had no idea who Ian was but Dorrie paused, her hands frozen in the act of pulling the thread through Jesse's skin. Mally glanced up at her but then Dorrie continued to stitch as if nothing had happened.

Finally Dorrie blew out a sigh and took a step away from the table.

"All right, Jesse. You know the drill. Don't do anything to split the stitches. If you do, my fee to redo them triples and you get to listen to me call you an idiot for as long as it takes to repair them."

Jessie grimaced. "I remember. You won't need to come back."

"I'll make sure of it," Mally added. "Can he get up now? He should be in bed."

Adam walked into the room. "Let me give you a hand."

As Adam helped Jesse sit up and get off the table, Dorrie motioned for Mally to stay behind.

Though she didn't want to leave Jesse, not even for a few seconds, she figured the doctor needed to tell her how to care for Jesse's wound.

"Jesse's going to be fine. I'll leave some antibiotics. Make sure he takes them. He's more stubborn than Max about meds."

Dorrie's sharp gray gaze made Mally feel like she was being taken apart, piece by piece. And when Dorrie sighed, Mally felt like she'd barely passed muster.

"Since we've never met, I need to give you my standard line," Dorrie continued. "Don't take it personally." Then she shrugged. "Though it doesn't really matter if you do. If we meet again, you've never met me. You have no idea who I am. You never mention to another soul that you saw me here."

Mally understood the rationale but, damn, this woman rubbed her the wrong way. She couldn't figure out if it was because she didn't like Dorrie...or because she knew the doctor had a thing for Jesse.

Mally nodded. "Of course."

Dorrie held her gaze for another few seconds and Mally thought she might say something else. Then Dorrie's gaze snapped to a point over Mally's shoulder.

When Dorrie's eyes narrowed into a death glare and her mouth tightened, Mally's curiosity got the better of her and she turned.

She'd never seen the man standing in the doorway before. Then again, she wasn't sure she'd have remembered if she had. From his brown hair and pale eyes to his not-quite-handsome face, he was nondescript in every way.

"Ian." Ice coated that one word.

"Dorothea." His tone held absolutely no inflection at all.

Okay, definitely some history here. And apparently not very good history, if the eye-daggers Dorrie was throwing the guy's way were any indication.

Ian might've smiled at her. Mally couldn't be sure. Then he nodded and turned away, disappearing back into the hallway.

Leaving Mally feeling like she'd walked into the middle of a movie she'd never heard of, had no idea what it was about, and was pretty sure it'd been made in another language.

"I need to leave," Dorrie continued as though nothing had happened, "but if Jesse needs me, call."

Dorrie held a business card in her hand, which Mally took without thought. There was a number on it and that was it.

That weird feeling of being in a movie intensified. If she wasn't careful, she'd find herself falling into a rabbit hole and never emerging.

Jesse. She had to get back to Jesse.

With a nod, Dorrie brushed past her and disappeared.

Mally turned and sprinted for the bedroom.

Max parked in the garage, turned off the car, then sat for several seconds, just breathing.

The weight he'd felt hovering over his head the entire night finally broke its tether and crashed down.

Closing his eyes, he sucked in a breath and held it,

fighting off the urge to tear the steering wheel from the column and toss it through the front window.

One minute. Just one minute to let it all settle.

He watched the digital clock on the dash while the panic and the fear ate away at his gut.

And when the number finally changed, he closed his eyes, shoved all that toxic emotion back into the hole where he kept it locked away, and got out of the car.

He hadn't seen Ian but he knew the man was still here. He wouldn't leave Jesse unprotected.

Inside the house, silence blanketed everything. He stopped inside the kitchen, knew this was where Dorrie had stitched up Jesse. He'd have to clean this up later. Couldn't leave it for the cleaning lady. The blood—

"Everything go okay?"

Ian stood just inside the door from the hall, watching him with that sharp gaze that missed nothing.

"Yes. Thanks for your help. Let me know what we owe you and I'll have the money transferred."

Ian nodded but didn't move. "Did you clear up your situation?"

He stiffened. "It's taken care of."

Ian's mouth curved into a grin. "That wasn't meant as an insult, Max. I admire what you're trying to do here. Hope it works out for you."

Yeah, so did Max. Because if it didn't... "It will."

Ian's grin actually looked bittersweet. "Good. Glad to hear it."

Then Ian turned and started to walk away.

"Wait." Max's voice was barely above a murmur but Ian heard him and stopped. "Are you going to be around long?"

"I have to leave for a job tomorrow but I should be back by the end of the week. Then I should be in the area for a few weeks. Why?"

"Because I'm not sure we won't need your help again."

Because even if Antonoff did his part, that didn't mean he and Jesse wouldn't be attacked again. And maybe next time, it wouldn't be Jesse or Max who paid the price.

Ian's expression never changed. "Then you know how to reach me."

"And if I want to put you on payroll?"

The thought was barely formed before the words came out of his mouth, but Max knew they were the right ones.

Ian blinked, the only outward sign that Max had shocked him. "You couldn't afford me."

Probably true. But Ian had been in the business as long as Max and Jesse. Hell, Ian's business was even messier than Max and Jesse's. Maybe he wanted out just as much as they had. Maybe even more.

"There are other arrangements we could work out. Other things you can be doing with your life. Think about it."

Ian didn't say anything right away but Max knew he was considering the offer.

Then he nodded. "I'll hang around 'til morning. Maybe I'll be in touch about the other thing."

Then he was gone and Max headed for the first-floor bedroom, knowing that's where Jesse and Mally would be. But he only got halfway up the hall before Adam stopped him.

Swallowing a sigh, Max turned, trying not to snarl. Adam and Tristan had come running when he'd called. Adam didn't deserve to have his head bitten off now.

"Thank you again for coming over tonight."

Adam nodded, stopping only inches away from Max. Probably so they could talk low enough that Mally wouldn't hear them.

"You know we'd do anything for Mally."

And that put Max firmly in his place. "I know. And I appreciate it."

"That doesn't mean we won't come if you call for any other reason."

Shit, was he supposed to hug him now? "I appreciate it. I guess you guys want to get home."

"We're planning to." Adam gestured to the front of the house, where Max assumed Tristan was waiting. "I'm just gonna say one thing. I figure you owe me that." He paused, obviously waiting for Max to nod, which he did. "You need to make damn sure she doesn't get hurt. I don't care how. Just make it happen. And if you need help, you damn well ask for it. You don't have to swing out here on your own."

Since it was so close to what he'd said just minutes ago to Ian, Max didn't immediately dismiss the thought. He nodded again but didn't say anything else. He couldn't think about anything but Jesse right now. Max needed to make sure he was okay. Maybe tomorrow he could think clearly enough to plan ahead. But not tonight.

"I'll...give it some thought. Thank you."

Adam looked like he wanted to say something else. Instead, he nodded then turned and walked away. Max was already on his way to the bedroom.

He stopped at closed door, taking a deep, steadying breath. Then he turned the knob silently.

Jesse and Mally lay on the bed, Jesse flat on his back,

head turned toward Mally, who lay curled on her side next to him. Not against him. Just far enough away that she wasn't touching him. Except for the hand she had on his chest.

He wanted to lie on the other side of Mally and curl around her body and sleep. But he knew he wouldn't. He needed to figure out what the fuck he would do tomorrow morning. Jesse was going to be out of commission for at least a few days, if not the week.

Anyone out there who had it in for them would realize the subtext behind Antonoff's announcement. They'd put together the fact that Antonoff's nephew had been injured and the fact that Jesse was nowhere to be seen and realize Jesse had been injured as well.

Someone might think this would be the perfect time to come after them.

At least now they knew who'd been sabotaging their businesses. They'd eliminated one problem but may have created several more.

And what if that puts Mally in even more danger?

Did they fight to hold on to her or cut her loose before she got hurt?

"Max."

His gaze shot to Mally, watching him. She looked so damn tired.

"Go back to sleep." He walked to the side of the bed, unable to resist running his fingers across her cheek and lips.

"Lie down."

He couldn't. "Soon."

She sat up slowly, not wanting to wake Jesse. "You need to rest. We can talk things through tomorrow. Tonight, you need to sleep. And you don't get to say no."

Another order and this time, he smiled.

Her gaze dropped to his lips for a brief second before popping back up again. "Did you take care of what you needed to do?"

"Yes."

She studied his expression for a few seconds, obviously seeing that he didn't want to talk about it. He loved the fact that she didn't push him.

"Then that's all you need to do tonight. Get ready for bed. You have five minutes before I come after you."

He never took orders anymore. Not from anyone. He couldn't. It'd show weakness. He couldn't afford any.

She was a weakness.

Tonight he didn't care. He nodded then headed for the bathroom. Four minutes later, he returned to find her curled on her other side, watching for him.

Lifting the covers, he slid in beside her, releasing a sigh as his head hit the pillow.

Christ, he was tired. His body barely responded when she wrapped her arm around his waist and tugged until he came even closer. A few inches still separated her from Jesse, but she remained close enough that she could feel his body heat.

Curving his arm around her chest, he pulled her even closer.

It took them a few seconds to find their spot. She finally ended up with her back plastered against his front and her ass cradled against his groin. Which made him hard. He was too tired to do anything about it, but that didn't mean he didn't want to.

Tomorrow. They'd figure it out tomorrow.

With Mally finally settled, Max reached for Jesse, putting

his hand on his shoulder and letting it lie there as he reassured himself Jesse continued to breathe.

———

Jesse woke in pain.

Disoriented, he sucked in a breath and forced his eyes open. He recognized the room. Home. He was home.

Mally.

Turning his head, he released that breath on a muffled groan as he caught sight of the other two people in the bed.

Memories of last night crowded in then, making his side throb even more and his lungs tighten.

Damn it. You're fine. Everyone's fine. Chill the fuck out.

Then he realized the secondary reason he'd woken. He had to use the bathroom and that meant he had to get out of bed. And that meant possibly waking Max and Mally.

With another rough sigh, he turned to find Max staring at him. Mally's head was tucked under Max's chin so he could see Max's face. The tired eyes, the lines on his forehead, the flatness of his lips.

"How do you feel?"

Max kept his voice low but they both knew Mally would be awake sooner rather than later.

"Like I got stabbed."

Max's gaze narrowed. "Let me get the pills Dorrie left. I saw them in the bathroom. You should've—" He stopped. "Never mind. I'll go get them now."

"No, just help me up. I gotta use the bathroom anyway."

Max didn't argue, just slid out of bed, making sure he

tucked the sheet around Mally. Then he walked to Jesse's side of the bed and helped him up.

"Doc said you're gonna be okay."

Beneath the gruff tone of Max's voice, Jesse heard the question. "Yeah. I've been stabbed before. Hell, this one didn't even hit anything vital."

Max didn't say anything else as he helped him to the bathroom, just let him close the door behind him.

When he reemerged several minutes later, after washing up and taking the antibiotic and the Vicodin Dorrie had left, his side hurt even worse. But he felt a little more like himself. He wasn't ready to run five miles or go a few rounds in the pit, but he wasn't in danger of passing out, either.

Max looked worse than Jesse felt. A problem Jesse knew he'd have to deal with sooner rather than later. But not just yet.

He let Max help him back to bed, where he tried to lie down without waking Mally. And failed.

She popped up beside him, her hair a mess of orange-red strands that glowed in the dim light shining around the sides of the curtains.

"Are you okay? What's wrong? Did something happen—"

"Nothing's wrong." Jesse smiled at her, though it turned into a grimace as he tried to find a good place to lie that didn't feel like someone was still shoving a knife in his side. "Just needed to use the bathroom."

"Did you—"

"Yes, I already took the pills."

She wrinkled her nose at him, which he found charming and arousing. And he couldn't do a damn thing about it.

"But since I can't really move without risking your wrath, why don't you make me feel better with a kiss?"

She looked torn for about two seconds before she carefully placed one hand on either side of his head and pressed her lips against his. Only seconds but enough to hold him over until later. When the pills kicked in and he was feeling no pain.

Christ, he hoped that was soon.

"Are you hungry? I can get you something to eat."

Jesse had no appetite, but he knew Max would want to talk without Mally in the room. And yeah, they needed to talk.

"Actually, I could go for some juice and maybe a piece of toast."

With a smile, Mally slid off the bed, sharing that same smile with Max, who nodded in acknowledgment.

They remained silent until they heard her open the fridge in the kitchen.

"You talked to Antonoff."

Max nodded. "Taken care of."

"He was behind the sabotage."

"Yeah, but the kid's actions weren't sanctioned. Karel will make a statement. And he's agreed to back off. But..."

"What? Just spit it out."

Max released a deep sigh. "He said we need to watch our backs. That he probably wasn't the only one coming after us."

Neither of them spoke for several seconds. Max just stared at him until Jesse sighed.

"I know." Jesse wanted to put his fist through the wall,

but he couldn't move without that shooting pain in his side. "Goddammit, I know."

Antonoff had taken his shot at them and, for some reason, had let them off the hook. Jesse was under no illusion that if the man wanted to take what was theirs, he would. But he hadn't. What that meant for the future... Fuck, Jesse had no idea. The only future Jesse wanted was one including the woman in the kitchen.

And right now, that wasn't looking good.

"Fuck."

Max nodded, his expression already set in stone-cold lines. "You knew from the beginning that this was a mistake. I should've listened."

Jesse's temples started to throb because he knew what Max was thinking. "She's gonna hate us."

Max's mouth flattened. "She'll be safe."

And away from them.

"It's the only way," Max said.

No. It wasn't. He just couldn't think of another way to keep her safe while they made sure no one else lurked in the shadows.

Damn, everything had turned on its head. In the beginning, Jesse had been the one telling Max they couldn't bring her into a relationship. Now...

Fuck.

They had to do it. And they had to present a united front. Didn't mean they had to like it. In fact, Jesse pretty much loathed the idea. And he was pretty sure Max did, too.

"Why do you two look like you're about to murder each other?"

Jesse's head whipped toward the door, where Mally walked through carrying a plate and a glass.

Max recovered immediately, glancing over his shoulder with a cool smile. "We're not. I'm sure you realize we have other, bigger problems at the moment."

If Max's cold tone affected her, she didn't show it as she set the plate and glass on the bedside table next to Jesse then propped her hands on her hips and stared back at Max.

"I guess you do. Are you going to tell me where you went last night or are you going to shut me out completely?"

"The less you know about last night, the better." Max didn't hesitate, his voice steady and his expression calm as he stared back.

Max's condescending tone made Jesse want to punch him. Mally looked like she wanted to, as well.

"I understand your reason for not wanting to tell me. And it doesn't matter because I can ask Adam. And he *will* tell me. My problem is, I don't want to have to do that. I want you to tell me."

"And if I don't?"

She shrugged, but Jesse saw hurt flash in her eyes as she turned with a tight smile to pick up the plate and hand it to him. He took it, steeling himself against the smile she gave him. When he didn't return it, hers faltered.

"So that's how it's going to be."

Too damn smart for her own good.

Fuck.

She crossed her arms over her chest and stared back at Max. "Let's see if I get this right. You're about to tell me it's been fun but now you have things you need to settle and I'll be in the way. That I need to leave, and when you've taken care of this situation, maybe you'll contact me...*if* you're still interested. You think pushing me aside is for my own good, that you wouldn't be able to live with yourselves if anything happened to me. How am I doing so far?"

Max's eyebrows rose. "I think you like hearing yourself talk."

Jesse bit his tongue against his automatic response to Max's cold statement. Even though he knew Max didn't mean it, he wanted to tell Max to go fuck himself.

Jesse didn't. Because this was exactly what they had to do. And this was the way to do it.

Because Mally was stubborn. She'd dig her feet in and entrench herself deeper into their lives, and if something happened to her...

Jesse didn't think he or Max would be able to live with themselves.

"And I think you're a fucking coward."

Max didn't flinch at her angry words. "Think what you want. You're still going to walk out the door at some point and not come back. That was the arrangement, wasn't it? Six months and then we were done."

She swallowed hard but never looked away. "Six months aren't up yet."

"We all know that doesn't matter. *We* don't want you here and you should have enough self-preservation to realize it's in your best interest to get out now."

All the color left her face. "No messy emotions. Right, Max?"

"Emotions were never part of the arrangement. Your reputation for our expertise in bed. That was the arrangement. Sorry if you didn't get enough, but I'm sure there're other men out there willing to scratch that itch for you."

Jesse practically bit through his tongue as he forced his hands to unclench. The urge to punch Max for putting that expression on her face roared up like vengeance.

Mally looked ready to pass out or puke. His stomach clenched in sympathy, which made his side ache, even with the drugs starting to kick in.

Mally did neither of those things. She stood there and stared at Max like she was waiting for him to take the words back.

Jesse wanted Max to get on his knees and beg for her forgiveness. To tell her they'd keep her safe.

And last night proved you can't.

Max remained silent and so did Jesse when she turned to look at him.

She took a deep breath. "Okay. I get it. I do." She nodded but didn't move. She looked so damn fragile, as if the slightest touch would make her shatter. But she wouldn't. She wouldn't break down, beg, or cry.

No, she just turned, grabbed her clothes and shoes from the chair along the wall and headed for the door.

Max continued to stare straight ahead, not watching her leave. Jesse couldn't help it. The bed faced the door and he couldn't look away.

So he saw her stop, watched her turn. "I'd appreciate if you wouldn't stop by the office for any reason. If you need to speak to Adam, do it somewhere else."

Then she disappeared down the hall.

Seconds later, Jesse heard Max suck in air like he'd been

holding his breath for the past five minutes. Maybe he had. Or maybe he just felt as shitty as Jesse.

"Christ, Max. That—"

"Stop." Max's gaze met his, those dark eyes blazing. Furious. Hurt. "Don't."

Jesse's throat dried at the strangled pain in Max's voice.

"I'll have Ian make sure she gets home safe. Then I'll call Adam and tell him— You just...take it easy. I'll take care of everything."

"Max... Don't do anything stupid."

Max's expression looked feral. "I already fucking did that."

18

Mary Alice made it home without incident, even though everything around her seemed hyper-real.

Too bright. Too loud. Too much.

She was afraid she'd wrap her car around a pole or side-swipe a row of parked cars. But as she drove, she realized that made her hyper-attentive. So she drove all the way home like an eighty-year-old going to church.

Sunday morning traffic in Philly wasn't as bad as rush hour, but horns still honked as she drove the speed limit along Spring Garden.

Let them honk. Let them give her the finger, yell obscenities, whatever. She didn't trust herself to go any faster. She needed to contain, to hold it in. Couldn't lose control. Not here.

By the time she got to her apartment, her entire body felt like one huge knot. She needed a shower. A scalding hot one for about an hour.

Jesus, she hoped Izzy and Damaris weren't home. She

didn't want them to see her like this. They'd know some-thing was wrong as soon as she walked in the door.

All she wanted to that shower and her bed. Wanted to sleep until her heart didn't feel like it'd been used as a punching bag.

And what did you really expect?

Not a question she wanted to ask herself now, especially not while she sat in her parked car only a block from her apartment. Frozen.

God, every muscle in her body hurt from tension. Even her bones felt brittle, like she'd crack apart at the slightest tap.

No, damn it. You're stronger than this.

Carefully, she looked in the rearview for oncoming cars before she stepped out of the car and into the street. In her current state, she wouldn't be surprised to be flattened by a truck.

The street was quiet. Grabbing her bag, she headed for her apartment. And nearly wept to find a note from her roommates, both of whom had spent the night at their boyfriends' places.

She'd told them yesterday she was doing the same.

Emotion slammed into her chest. Something she couldn't put a name to. Or maybe just refused to label.

She lifted a hand to rub at the spot but knew she couldn't do anything about the ache.

Dropping her bag in her room, she headed straight for the shower. Halfway there, she heard her phone ring. Adam's ringtone.

No way in hell.

Stripping off her clothes, she stepped into the steaming water and stood there until the water started to cool.

She heard her phone again when she got out of the shower. Tristan's ringtone this time.

Had Max told them to call her? Or were they just checking up on her? Probably the latter. Max knew Adam and Tristan would kill him if they knew how he'd treated her. The thought still made her want to curl up in a little ball and cry.

No way in hell would she do that.

In fact... Fuck them all. She'd go to her brother Tommy's bar tonight. She'd talk to the regulars, make some drinks. If she was lucky, Jason wouldn't have told Tommy—

Her phone rang again. The guys had gotten smart. That was Kat's ringtone.

With a sigh, she picked up her phone as she sat on her bed.

"Kat, I'm fine."

A short pause then a slight huff of amusement from the other end. "I'm glad to hear it. My men are understandably... perturbed."

"I take it Max called Adam."

"There was a phone call, yes. And then Adam said something about Max's balls and a knife and Tristan started swearing and then they both tried to call you. And when you didn't pick up your phone—smart choice, by the way—they figured I'd have better luck."

"I'm sure they had help making that decision. Thank you."

"I did pick up a few things in law school about mediation.

Now, I've put the guys in time-out downstairs so it's just you and me. Do you want to do this on the phone or do you want me to come to your apartment? Or do you want me to back off?"

"Honestly, I don't know what I want. Except maybe a good cry and a nap. And when I wake up, I want to rewind to yesterday. Before Jesse was hurt and Max nearly killed the man who hurt him. Before they tossed me aside."

Another pause. "Is that really what you think they did? Tossed you aside?"

"That's what it feels like."

"I get that. I do. But...you know that's not what happened. You know they're only doing this because they think they're keeping you safe."

"Now you're taking their side."

"No, I'm not taking their side. I think they're being assholes." Kat's inflection on that last word left Mally in no doubt that "asshole" was the politest word Kat could us to express her thoughts. "I think they're totally discounting your feelings. And I don't think you should let them get away with it."

Mally took the first full breath she'd managed since she'd woken that morning. Then she took another.

"I'm not sure I'm up for plotting my revenge today."

"I'm not saying you need revenge. I think you need to show them exactly what they're giving up if they let you get away."

"And how do I do that?"

"Well, that's going to require a few drinks. And the addition of the only other woman I know in the same type of relationship."

For a few seconds, Mally had no idea who Kat was

talking about. Then it came to her. "You want to have drinks with your brother's girlfriend?" Who was also involved with Kat's former fiancé, Keegan. "I didn't know you and Julianne got along that well."

"This club is pretty small. Just by the nature of the relationship, the men have us outnumbered two to one. We women have to stick together. And I like Jules. I think you will, too."

"So do you think you and Jules can meet me tonight at my brother's bar? We can drink for free and I guarantee we'll be left alone. My brother will stay far away from a table full of pissed-off women."

Kat laughed. "I'll give her a call right now. If she can't meet us tonight, I'll still be there. We can plot tonight and then refine your strategy when we talk to Jules. She can be surprisingly bloodthirsty despite how sweet she is. But sometimes that's what it takes to deal with two men."

"Are you telling me I have to toughen up?"

"Not at all. You're plenty tough already. You just need to use that toughness in a different way."

"And if I can't?"

"You will if you don't want to give them up."

"Tristan and Adam have no idea what you're telling me, do they?"

"Of course they don't. They're pissed that you're upset, but they think Max and Jesse did the right thing. Which proves that most men really are idiots."

Kat let her think about that for a few seconds.

Finally, Mally said, "How's eight o'clock?"

19

Jesse had finally fallen back to sleep a few hours after Mally left and Max breathed a sigh of relief.

He had phone calls to make and he didn't want Jesse agitated. He needed sleep to heal.

Which made Max want to do serious harm. He still couldn't believe he'd let the prick who'd stabbed Jesse live. He should've put a bullet through his head and—

And she never would've spoken to them again.

She still might never speak to you again, not after the way you treated her.

Fuck.

His hand clenched on the phone and he forced himself to release it before he crushed the damn thing. He needed it. Needed to make sure he and Jesse wouldn't have to face another attack like they had last night.

He checked his messages first. Found several. A few expected, a few not so much.

The expected ones were from members of other city crime organizations. All assured him they'd gotten

Antonoff's message and wouldn't think of breaching the contract they'd made with David Oleksy to leave Max and Jesse alone.

None of them even hinted about Jesse's injuries, and Max figured Antonoff must not have made that public knowledge. Good. Jesse didn't need anyone to know he wasn't a hundred percent. It could leave him open to another attack.

Two organizations were notably absent from the list of callers. Max would give them the benefit of the doubt for a few hours. Then he'd make some calls.

Of course, Mally hadn't called.

Did you really expect her to?

The anger he'd been trying to tamp down rose up again, threatening to choke him. He couldn't let it. He still had calls to make.

The first was to Risa. He owed her an explanation because he was sure her father hadn't given her much of one. He left a message on her burner, made sure she knew Jesse was okay and that her dad had kept his word.

The next call should've been easier.

"Make it fast."

Max paused, taken aback by the level of antagonism coming from Adam.

"I wanted to say thank you again for last night."

Adam grunted, which Max took as acknowledgment. Or maybe that was Adam's way of saying "Fuck you" without having to actually say the words.

"How's Jesse?"

"Fine. He's sleeping."

"Good to hear. Anything else?"

Yeah, there was, but he wasn't sure Adam would give him an answer if he asked the question.

"Is she okay?"

Silence.

Shit. "Adam—"

"She's fine. Is that it?'

No, not by a long shot. But what the hell else could he really say? He'd been ruthless. He'd had to be.

"Max."

"I... Yes. We appreciate your support last night."

Adam sighed. "Shit. Max—"

"Thank you."

"Christ, Max—"

He hung up before Adam could finish. He didn't need any more bullshit today. Didn't need anyone else to make him feel worse.

Adam cared for Mally. He got that.

And Max had hurt her. But honestly, Max had figured Adam would be happy Max had broken off their arrangement.

His jaw clenched so tightly, he was afraid he'd crack his damn teeth.

Christ almighty, why the fuck did this suck so fucking much?

Because you didn't want to give her up.

But he couldn't see his way clear of all the bullshit crowding his life right now.

And he'd do anything to keep her safe. Even give her up for good.

Her brother's bar sat on a quiet corner on Frankford Avenue in Fishtown.

Still mostly a local crowd. The kind of place where everyone knew your name, your parents, your parents' parents, and had either taught you in Sunday school, coached your peewee team, or worked with a close relative.

Almost everyone over the age of fifty had a blue collar and sat on a barstool that held an impression of their ass.

Mally had been working for Tommy since he'd bought the bar five years ago. She'd waited tables, served, even cooked if Tommy needed help in the kitchen, which was typically his domain. She was the only one her prickly brother allowed in his kitchen beside him. He didn't even allow their mom back there.

Tonight was even slower than usual for Sunday. Only four regulars sat at the bar and another two couples had separate tables.

"Hey, little girl. How goes it?"

She dredged up a smile for Tommy, leaning against the bar and watching the game with the regulars nursing beers.

"Hey, old man. It's going."

Nodding his head to the deserted end of the bar, he met her there, sharp gaze locked onto her like a laser beam.

She caught back a sigh and tried not to let her smile falter. But Tommy had always been the one who knew her almost better than she knew herself. He was the one she'd confided in when she'd had trouble with friends or boyfriends. He didn't immediately try to fix her problem for her, like her two oldest brothers, or harass the hell out of her, like her next oldest brother.

It also meant he was going to be pissed that she hadn't told him about Max and Jesse.

She swiped a kiss on his stubbled cheek as he leaned over the bar to hug her. And when he pulled back and crossed his arms over his chest, she figured she should probably get comfortable. This was why she'd arrived fifteen minutes before she was scheduled to meet Kat and Jules.

"So."

He didn't say anything else. He didn't need to.

"I guess you heard from Jason."

"If you mean did Jason bend my ear for ten minutes about how he was gonna make life a living hell for the *guys* you were *dating*, then yeah, I heard."

She restrained herself from sticking her tongue out at him. "Then I guess you'll be glad to hear that we're not *dating* anymore."

He didn't say anything right away and she stared into this blue-green eyes, trying to read his mind. Tommy had never done the protective older-brother thing with her, which was why she'd always felt she could talk to him.

Why did it seem so hard now?

Tommy raised an eyebrow at her. "Are you're glad you're not dating them anymore?"

"Honestly?" She shook her head. "No."

"Then why would I be glad?"

Surprise made her eyebrows rise. "So you're not freaked out that I was dating two guys at the same time?"

His expression never changed. "So dating is the word we're using?"

Okay, fine. "Would you rather I say sleeping with?"

He shrugged, his expression slightly mocking. "If you can't talk the talk, chickie, how're you gonna walk the walk?"

"I'm not going to be doing any walking or talking for a while." She sighed, trying not to allow tears to well up. Again. "We broke up."

"I take it that wasn't your decision."

"You would guess right."

Tommy snorted and shook his head, shaggy brownish-red waves falling around a face she'd heard women describe as dreamy. John Matthew had been rugged. Jason was classically handsome. Finn was adorable.

Tommy... When Tommy smiled, women did double takes. Problem was, he didn't smile often.

"Guess you don't really want them. How the hell'd you get wrapped up with lowlife criminals anyway?"

Her mouth dropped open as her blood began to boil. Until she caught the challenge in her brother's eyes.

Now, she did stick her tongue out at him. "You suck."

He shrugged. "Nah, I just don't treat you like a twelve-year-old in a convent."

She laughed, startled to find she could, and watched his lips curve in one of his rare smiles. Good thing there weren't any women around or she'd have to help fend them off.

"So you think I shouldn't give them up?"

"You know what I think. You should do what you want. I've always told you that. But they hurt you. I can see it in your eyes. They do it again and I'll make sure they can't walk for weeks. So, what else can I do for you?"

Tears welled in her eyes. She adored her brothers. Even when she wanted to kill them. "Love you."

He rolled his eyes. "Yeah, yeah, love you too. Now, what else do you want?"

"I'm meeting a couple of friends. We're gonna hang out in one of the booths in the back. Okay?"

"You wanna drink fruity wine all night or you gonna man up and I should get you a bottle of Jack?"

Only Tommy would ever say that to her. Her other brothers preferred to believe she had no idea what alcohol was. Or sex.

"How about we start with a pitcher of Flying Fish and we'll see how it goes from there?"

"You know where the pitchers are. Knock yourself out."

She'd just finished tapping the pitcher when the front door opened and Kat walked through with a short brunette at her side.

Kat caught sight of her and waved then headed in her direction.

After hellos and introductions, Mally led them to the small room in the back. It was empty, which Mally had been counting on.

"So, Mally." Jules smiled at her. "Welcome to the club. Hope you're ready to be more frustrated than you've ever been in your life...when you're not pissed off at them. Or blissfully happy because there's nothing like having two men at your beck and call."

Mally's lips had started to curve, and by the time Jules had finished, she wore a full-blown grin for the first time all day. Even Kat looked amused.

"Well, I'm extremely frustrated and pissed off at the same time so I guess I'm the lucky one."

"Yep, that happens a lot, too." Jules shot a quick glance at

Kat, who nodded once. "Kat tells me there are…extenuating circumstances with your relationship."

"You could say that." It was Mally's turn to exchange a glance with Kat. Mally knew Kat wouldn't have brought Jules to talk if she didn't trust her. And Kat didn't trust many people.

After a second, Mally had made up her mind. "Max and Jesse used to work for a Russian crime family. They're taking their businesses legitimate. Last night, someone broke into their home and—"

Her throat seized up as she thought about what'd happened last night. Taking a deep breath, she blinked back sudden tears. And clasped Kat's hand when the other woman reached for hers.

"Jesse was hurt. It could've been a lot worse but…it was bad. Max didn't handle it well. We had a fight. I knew he was deliberately goading me. I knew it and I still ended up walking away. I didn't feel like I had a choice. I left and I'm afraid they'll never come after me."

Jules's eyes had widened until Mally didn't think they could get any bigger.

"Wow. You're seriously dating Russian mobsters. It's like the plot of a TV show."

Mally smiled again. Couldn't help herself. "Former mobsters, actually. And only Max is Russian. Jesse's parents were multi-ethnic. But he and Max are dedicated to each other. Have been since they were kids."

"Ah." Jules's grin was bittersweet. "And you're worried they don't really need you in their lives. That you aren't as important to them as they are to each other."

Mally blinked. "Holy crap. Did you just read my mind?"

Jules and Kat exchanged a look as Mally shook her head.

"Actually," Kat spoke this time, "it's a pretty common worry for people in our situation."

"So how do you deal with it?"

"That's not the question you should be asking." Jules leaned forward, a wicked gleam in her eyes. "The question you should be asking is, how do you make them realize how wrong they are?"

By Wednesday morning, Jesse was driving Max crazy.

Max had suggested Jesse take a few more days to recuperate before throwing himself back into work, but Jesse had told him to go fuck himself.

"I'm fucking sick of lying in this damn bed, thinking of all the things I could be doing. If we're ever— I just need to get back to work."

Max knew exactly what Jesse had left unsaid. They hadn't mentioned her name since Sunday, but Mally was between them everywhere. And they couldn't do a damn thing to get her back until they knew she'd be safe with them.

The problem was, neither of them knew exactly how to do that.

So Jesse was going to Ivy Brown's, where he planned to examine surveillance footage. They needed to beef up security at all of their properties and, since that was Jesse's domain, he planned to make damn sure no one could fuck with them again.

"I'll be sitting on my ass all day anyway," Jesse continued

when Max didn't say anything. "Might as well do something constructive."

Max had tried to keep his mouth shut. Jesse was a grown man who could make his own decisions. But when Jesse had said he planned to check out the other two clubs as well, and go to the brewery, Max couldn't help himself.

"Don't you think you're going to overdo it?"

Jesse had glared at him until Max had had to look away or be forced to growl at him in frustration.

"I'll see you tonight." Jesse had grabbed his jacket and headed for the door. "You have those meetings today, right? The ones with the city council members? Let me know how they go."

Then he'd left, making sure the door shut firmly behind him.

Yes, Max had meetings scheduled with city councilmen and their staff. He'd been maneuvering to get them set up for months and had considered it a huge victory when he'd finally gotten them nailed down.

Now, he couldn't give a shit about them.

His head wasn't in the game and it needed to be if he was going to show these assholes, several of whom were worse criminals than the men Max and Jesse had worked for, that he and Jesse were a force to be reckoned with.

Max figured he'd come up against a few pricks. But, damn it, the Wharton School of Business master's degree he'd worked so fucking hard to get had to be good for something. At the very least, it'd confuse the old bastards who expected him to be brainless street scum.

Christ, he hoped Jesse was okay. And goddamn it all to

hell, he wanted to call Mally. Wanted to make sure no one had— What? Contacted her? Called her? Touched her?

Adam and Tristan wouldn't let anyone near her.

But it's not the same, is it?

Not even close.

By eight o'clock that night, Max wanted to crawl inside a bottle and not come out until the next morning.

His meetings had left him feeling like he needed a chemical bath and possibly a lobotomy. Hell, he'd underestimated the politicians. They could teach the damn criminals a thing or two. Max had known most of them had business dealings with the city crime organizations. He just hadn't realized how deep those ties went. And how ingrained they were.

Luckily for him, that would work in his favor if he needed to do things off the books.

But he wanted out of the underworld. Wanted to leave that behind so he and Jesse wouldn't have to constantly look over their shoulders. Wanted Mally back in their lives.

But first, they needed to make sure she'd be safe.

So now he sat in the office at Shivers, going over the books. Again.

They needed to unload the third club and sink the money from the sale into Shivers and Ivy Brown's. They needed the brewery to start pulling its weight. They needed—

A knock at the door made his head pop up. "Come."

The backdoor guard, a six-foot-five mountain of dark skin and bulging muscles, stuck his head inside. His expression showed a curious mix of apology and appreciation.

Max frowned at him. "What's wrong, Dwayne?"

"Someone here to see you. Says she's a friend."

And that was probably the source of Dwayne's confusion. Max didn't have friends except for Jesse.

"Did she give you a name?"

The guy actually winced. "Said if you asked to tell you you should know who it is."

Mally.

He tried not to let the rush of excitement make him stupid. He had no idea why she was here. He'd been brutal to her the other night and he hadn't been able to stop replaying the scene in his head since. He should've done it differently. Should've done *something* differently.

But now she was here.

Probably just wanted to check on Jesse.

Then why hadn't she called Jesse?

"You want me to send her away?"

Fuck no. "Send her back. Thank you."

Dwayne nodded and disappeared. And Max leaned back into his chair, trying to squash the instinct to grab her the second she walked into his office.

What the hell was she doing here?

The door opened and his gaze snapped up, latching on to her. Christ, he'd missed her. It'd only been a couple of days since he'd seen her but he was starved for her.

And damn, she looked amazing. Short black skirt. Sleeveless emerald-green top that clung to her curves. High-heeled ankle boots that made her legs look a mile long. Her hair hung in long waves around her face in a way that reminded him of her waking up in their bed between him and Jesse.

Fuck.

"Hello, Max."

He stood, trying not to devour her with his eyes. Even though that's exactly what he wanted to do.

"Mary Alice. Are you okay? Is something wrong?"

"I'm fine." She strolled over to the chair in front of his desk and sat down. "I was in the area and I wanted to know how Jesse's doing. Since no one took the time to call me."

His jaw locked against his immediate response—that he was sorry. That they should've called. That they'd been wrong to send her away.

Instead, he sat behind his desk, more to hide his body's immediate reaction to her than anything else. What the fuck was wrong with him that he got an erection just by being in the same room with her?

"We did call."

She rolled her eyes. "You took the coward's way out and called my office phone when you knew I wouldn't be there."

Max refused to blush, even though she was absolutely right.

"I thought it'd be better for you if you didn't have to speak to me."

Her short laugh held no amusement. "Okay, sure, Max. You can tell yourself that if it makes you feel better."

Damn her, it didn't make him feel better. And he hated that she'd called him on his bullshit.

Christ almighty, she was turning him on.

You really are a prick.

"What do you want, Mally? Did something happen? Did someone contact you?"

He'd kill whoever thought they could hurt her.

Then why did you send her away?

She shrugged, her expression totally dismissive of the

menace she heard in his voice. "No one's contacted me. Adam and Tristan have been glued to my side at work. One of them probably followed me here tonight. And if I find out they did, I'm going to ream them. But you asked them to keep an eye on me, didn't you?"

He didn't respond. She knew the answer anyway.

"What are you doing here?"

He had to get her out of here. Because if she stayed much longer, he was going to break the vow he'd made to himself. The one not to touch her until he and Jesse had made their life safe for her. And he would. He just had to keep his hands off her until then.

But here she was, looking so damn beautiful. He wanted to shove that skirt up around her hips, tear off her panties, and fuck her on the desk.

"I told you. I came to find out how Jesse's doing."

"Then why didn't you call Jesse?"

She snagged his gaze with hers and refused to release him. "I did. He didn't answer. And when I went by the house earlier, no one was there."

She'd tried to track them down. That shouldn't make him harder than he already was.

"Jesse's healing well. He decided he was going back to work today."

Her lips actually softened into a sweet smile. "He was probably bored out of his mind doing nothing for three whole days."

Max's smile surprised him. "You could say that."

"And no one's tried to kill you since I left?"

He sighed. "You would've been told if you were in danger."

"Do you honestly think that's the only reason I'm here?"

From her raised eyebrow, he'd probably be safe in saying the answer to that question was no.

"Why are you here, Mally?"

Her right shoulder lifted and fell and his gaze followed it the entire way. "I guess if you need to ask that question, you really don't have a clue, do you?"

No, he didn't. "A clue about what?"

With a sigh, she rose and walked around his desk until she stood right next to him. Close enough to touch. Close enough to smell the scented lotion she used on her soft skin. A scent that drove his blood pressure sky-high.

She stared into his eyes and he saw heat there. Even after the way he'd sent her home Sunday, she still wanted him.

The rush of emotion that blew through him stole his breath. Made his heart pound out a furious rhythm.

And when she cocked her hip against the side of his desk and crossed her arms under her breasts, pushing them practically out of her shirt, he thought he might actually need to suck in air before he went light-headed.

"How can you be so smart and still be so clueless?"

He figured that question didn't need an answer so he kept his mouth shut. Or maybe he kept his mouth shut because he wasn't sure what would come out if he didn't.

The lust firing through his body made him believe he had to touch her. Just the stroke of his finger down her cheek. Or his hands sliding up her naked thighs.

His cock thrusting inside her tight body.

Fuck.

"Why don't you enlighten me?" Max said.

The way she rolled her eyes made his lips quirk but he fought to hide it.

Nothing's changed, asshole.

But right now, he didn't care. He only wanted her to follow through on the promise he saw in her eyes.

She leaned down, close enough that he felt her breath against his lips, yet still far enough away that he could see her eyes clearly.

"I guess I'll have to, won't I? Are you sure you want—"

He reached up and cupped her face in his hands, yanked her close and kissed her. He tasted his own desperation and kissed her harder, sliding his tongue between her lips to tangle with hers. She didn't play hard to get and he had a second to wonder if this was exactly what she'd wanted.

Then it didn't matter. He didn't care. All he cared about was that she was in his arms. After the way he'd treated her, he'd wondered if he'd ever have her here again.

And then all that mattered was making her burn as much as he was.

He ate at her lips like he couldn't get enough of her. Turned her head so he could kiss her deeper, harder.

She let him. Braced her hands on his shoulders so she didn't fall too far forward but let him control the kiss. It wasn't enough. He needed more. Was afraid he'd always need more of her.

Lust gripped him hard, an obsession he couldn't kick. Didn't want to kick.

He wanted her and she'd offered herself up on a plate. No way would he pass up her offer because, well...why the hell would he?

Standing, he grabbed her hips and sat her on top of his

desk. She gasped into his mouth but he didn't break the seal of their kiss. Instead, he pressed their lips together even harder and let his hands slide from her hips to her breasts. Molding them in his palms, he squeezed, rubbing his thumbs over her tight nipples, poking through the thin material of her shirt.

Jesus, was she even wearing a bra? And she'd walked into his club looking like this?

The thought that another man might put his hands on her made his blood boil. She was theirs. His and Jesse's.

You were the one who told her to walk, asshole. Is she supposed to wait for you to make up your goddamn mind?

Yes. Goddammit, that's exactly what he wanted. And he'd show her exactly why she should.

He cupped the back of her head. The instinct to hold her in place made him grip her tighter. He realized what he was doing almost immediately and tried to relax, but then she wrapped her arms around his shoulders and drew him even closer.

The need to have her hit him like a two-by-four across the back of his head. His cock went from half-hard to rock-solid in seconds. He wanted her so badly, he hurt all the way to his bones.

Hell, they both had way too many clothes on for what he wanted to do. What he *needed* to do.

Then she opened her legs so he could get closer. He pressed his hips into her soft mound and drank down the sweet moan she made when he rubbed his erection against her clit.

Dropping both hands to her hips, he yanked her skirt

higher, felt her squirm to help him. Her thighs felt like silk under his palms but he couldn't linger.

He reached for her underwear—

And found nothing. She wasn't wearing any.

Holy fuck.

"Goddammit, Mally. What the—"

He ended with a groan as she put one of her hands directly over his cock and squeezed.

"Condom, Max. Just—"

He kissed her again before she could say another word and possibly make him come in his pants.

That's not the way he wanted this to end. He wanted to be buried deep inside her when he came, pumping into her willing body.

But he couldn't go bare.

"Wallet. Desk drawer."

He barely understood himself, his voice rough, but she turned her head and used her free hand to open the drawer and retrieve his wallet. Her other hand remained on his cock, teasing him. Making him crazy. Making him want to slow down, take his time. Hell, he wasn't even sure the damn door to his office was locked.

Nothing mattered but having Mally in his arms and getting inside her body.

Her fingers found the button on his pants and undid it with a dexterity bordering on magical. Then she pulled the tab on his zipper and finally got her hand around his cock.

Slipping his fingers between her legs, he found her labia slick and hot. And when he slid two fingers into her sex, she practically melted around him.

With his other hand, he reached for his wallet and found

the condom without too much fumbling. All while kissing her like he needed her to breathe. Which he did.

Why had he ever thought he wouldn't?

When she pulled away, he followed her and she let him kiss her for another few seconds until she twisted and leaned farther away.

"Condom."

She held out her hand for the foil packet and he put it in her palm without thinking. She had him covered in seconds, her heavy breathing mirroring his as he stepped as close as he could then grabbed her hips. With one hand, he angled his cock and, with the other, he pulled her forward.

He thrust hard, sank deep. Felt her gasp, her arms wrapping around his shoulders and squeezing tight.

Her hips tilted at just the right angle to take him even deeper, her breathy voice urging him for "more" and "deeper."

He gave her what she wanted and took what he needed.

Jesus, he'd fucking missed her. And missed fucking her. Being inside her, her arms wrapped around him and her body gripping his cock tight. Taking everything he gave her and soaking in every bit of her he could.

Her breath on his skin made him shiver and his name on her lips made his heart double in speed. Putting his mouth against her neck, he kissed his way to her ear, where he nipped on the lobe and felt her shiver around him.

He tried to keep his pace slow, not a furious frenzy. But she released every single one of his inhibitions. He'd never have thought he'd be having sex on his damn desk in his office at the club.

But with Mally, he didn't care where he had her, just that he did. That she was his and she knew it.

Her soft moans inflamed his lust but he wanted to hear her say his name again. Needed it.

He nipped at her ear again, his fingers digging into her hips, holding her steady for his thrusts.

As if she'd read his mind, she turned her face into his neck and kissed him, nipped him. "God, Max, I've missed you."

His desire kicked into another gear. He wrapped her even more tightly against him while he slid one hand between them to rub her clit. He wasn't going to last much longer and he had to make her come. Had to feel her gripping him tight while he came.

He worked her relentlessly until she practically sobbed in his ear. His cock felt stiff as iron but he continued to thrust until she finally cried out and rippled around him, squeezing him like a fist until he couldn't take it and pulsed out his orgasm.

For several seconds, they just stood there, wrapped around each other, trying to catch their breath.

When he felt himself slipping out of her, he knew he had to move or make a mess.

Already made enough of a mess, haven't you?

As he pulled away, he bent to give her a hard kiss. "I'll be right back. Don't go."

He headed for the small bathroom attached to the office, discarding the condom.

When he returned, she still sat on his desk, legs crossed. She met his gaze and held it as he walked forward. He felt her eyes on him as she slid off his desk and pull her skirt back down her legs.

Then she leaned back against his desk again.

"I've missed you."

She sounded resolute, her gaze steady, almost challenging.

"Mally—"

"Is it worth it, Max?"

He didn't have to ask her what she was referring to. But he couldn't answer her question, either. Because he didn't know what the hell he would say.

Being without her wasn't worth it. Risking her life wasn't worth it. Her life meant more to him than anything.

When he didn't respond, she shrugged but he saw her disappointment in the curve of her mouth. And he saw pain in the wetness in her eyes.

Turning, she headed for the door. He followed her but stopped himself at the last moment from reaching for her arm to make her stay. Jesus, he'd just made love to her on his desk and she was going to walk out the door. Didn't she deserve better? Didn't she expect better from him?

"Mally."

She stopped, pausing for a second before turning to face him. She met his eyes with a level stare.

"Are you going to ask me to stay?"

"Not now. I can't."

"Then I guess we're done."

Then she walked out.

20

"And you're sure this is going to work?"

"No, I'm not sure of anything. I only know I have to try."

Izzy gave Mally the raised-eyebrow side glance Friday afternoon after work. "Well, having sex on the desk in his office in the back of his club sounds hot but are you sure it's not just giving him what he wants without having to commit?"

"It was more like getting what I wanted. And you didn't see his face when I walked out. He didn't want me to go. Hell, *I* didn't want to go but I can't cave now. Tonight, I work on Jesse."

"Is he really back at work already? Shouldn't he be taking it easy?"

Mally had told Izzy a sanitized version of what had happened last Saturday night. "I think so, yeah, but guys think they're immortal. I'm going to show him what he should be living for."

Izzy held her hand up for a high five. "You go, babe. Make 'em show some respect for your feminine wiles."

Wincing, she frowned at Izzy. "I'm playing games, I know. But they're not playing fair. They think they need to keep me away."

"And aren't they right? I mean, Jesus, Mally. Someone tried to kill them. You could've been hurt."

"And some disgruntled asshole with a gun could walk into the office and shoot me trying to get to Adam or Tristan. Or I could step off the sidewalk and get hit by a bus. I can't put my life on hold waiting for them to believe I'm never going to be in danger. There's always going to be danger. I know the life they lived. I knew what I was getting into with them. What they don't get is that I'm willing to stand beside them. And they have to realize that I'm not willing to stand by while they try not to get killed."

Izzy started to shake her head then couldn't seem to stop. "Did you ever think your life would become a freakin' soap opera?"

Mally snorted. "The better question is, did I ever think my love life would include two guys. At the same time."

Izzy's brows popped up and her head changed direction as she started to nod. "Well, yeah, there is that." Then she sighed. "Damn, Mal, are you really sure this is what you want? I mean, you only just met these guys a few months ago. Don't get me wrong, I'm not telling you how to live your life. And, if I'm gonna be honest, I have to admit I'm a little jealous. Two hot guys who want you and aren't jealous of each other? That's, like, every woman's fantasy."

"Until you lose both of them at the same time."

Wincing, Izzy grimaced. "Oh, sweetie. Yeah, that sucks

twice. But you haven't lost them. Not yet. I mean, it wasn't like he threw you out of his office, right?"

"No, but I kinda didn't give him a choice."

"Oh, please." Izzy rolled her eyes. "If he didn't want you there, he could've called his bodyguards to throw you out."

"He doesn't have bodyguards. He has bouncers."

Izzy smirked. "See? So there! He could've had you tossed but he didn't."

"Because he was getting laid."

"And do you really think that's the reason he didn't have you tossed? Because he was gonna get some?"

Mally made a face. "No."

"Then stop overthinking this. Now, where are you going to ambush Jesse? And when do I get to meet these guys, anyway?"

"I'm planning to get him alone at the house tonight. I know Max has an event at the club so he'll be there until at least eleven. I'm hoping Jesse will be home by nine. That gives me two hours to—"

"Make him see the error of his ways?"

Mally wrinkled her nose at Izzy's lopsided grin then sighed. "Yeah. I guess. Shit, maybe I'm going about this completely wrong. What if Jesse finds out I seduced Max? What if he thinks I'm only into Max? What if he doesn't—"

"Whoa, whoa, whoa." Izzy waved her hands in front of her. "Seriously, Mal, just slow the hell down. And think about this. These two want you so badly they're willing to share you. And they're so worried about you, they're willing to give you up to make sure nothing happens to you. And you think they don't care about you?"

Izzy paused to stare at Mally with wide eyes, her expression full of "hell no."

"Now," Izzy continued, "I may not be as good as my cousin Janey when it comes to reading people." Janey worked for her family's private investigation firm, which Tristan and Adam occasionally employed. "But I grew up with three brothers and ten male cousins. I know how to read guys. Hell, I can even read guys I've never met. And if you weren't so stuck on these two, you'd be able to see it, too. They have it so bad for you, they don't know which way is up. And the sooner you get over the fact that your life is going to be a little less normal than everyone else's, which isn't a bad thing, the sooner you'll stop freaking out and get out there and make your men see that they can't live without you."

Mally was shaking her head and laughing by the time Izzy had finished. "You're a nut case, you know that?"

"Hey, I'm not the one dating two guys." Izzy wiggled her eyebrows. "So, what are you wearing tonight that's easily removable?"

***

Jesse had spent most of the day staring at a monitor in the office at Ivy Brown's, looking for the holes in their security that had allowed someone to sabotage their buildings.

He'd found a couple that made him pissed as hell. He was supposed to be good at this security shit. And then he'd found one that, after he fixed it, locked up their security tighter than Fort fucking Knox.

He wanted to beat his chest and wrestle a gorilla. He wanted to call Max and clue him in.

But he had to admit, if only to himself, that what he really wanted was a bottle of water and the chance to close his eyes for a few minutes. His side had throbbed all day, which was an improvement over the past four days, when it'd hurt like a motherfucker if he didn't take the painkillers.

And he fucking hated taking the damn pills. They made him woozy but mostly they reminded him of his mom, who'd loved being high more than she'd loved her son. Which made it more ridiculous that he'd spent so damn many years working for a man who'd controlled the sale of illegal drugs in much of Philly.

With a muttered curse, he pushed away from the desk and stood. Slowly. He wanted to stretch out his back but couldn't because of the stitches.

God damn, he hated being an invalid and he knew he'd been pushing himself too hard these last few days and now he was going to pay for it.

But he hadn't wanted to let up until he'd found these damn holes.

Christ, he fucking *ached*. And not just his side. His entire body. And he was tired all the damn time.

When the hell did I turn into an old man? I'm barely twenty-eight.

And he'd been stabbed five days ago.

Good thing he hadn't seen Max since yesterday. Max would've known just by looking at him how much pain he was in.

So he took half a pill and drove home. He needed some food, some water, and a night on the couch.

And he really wanted Mally beside him, below him, on top of him.

Not happening.

Now in loose gym shorts and a ratty old t-shirt, his stomach full of pasta, he considered ignoring the front door bell. He didn't want to talk to anyone. But he checked the surveillance anyway.

And nearly tripped over his damn feet to get to the door.

What the hell is she doing here? And do you really fucking care why she's here?

No. He really fucking didn't.

He'd wanted to call her every day since he'd seen her walk out of their home Sunday morning. But Max had a point. A shitty point but still... Someone had gotten to them and they couldn't allow Mally to be in danger. They had to make their lives safe for her to be with them.

And if you can't?

He shoved that thought away. She was here now and he wasn't going to pass up the chance to see her. Talk to her.

Nothing else.

Because Max wasn't here.

Which didn't mean a damn thing. If Max had been the only one home tonight, he'd be all over her. And Jesse wouldn't care. Hell, he'd understand. Because even though Max had been the first to realize how perfect she was for the two of them, Jesse had to be the one to make sure they didn't lose her.

"Hey. Everything okay?"

Mally's beautiful mouth twisted in a wry grin. "Hello to you, too." Then her gaze dipped to slide up and down his body and when she met his gaze again, her eyes held a question as she stepped over the threshold. "Are *you* okay? Do you need to sit down?"

Since that would get her in the house, he didn't argue with her. And his side *did* hurt.

"Yeah. Come on. We can talk in the living room."

Stepping up to his side, she now looked uncertain. "Maybe you should be in bed, Jesse. I should go and let you—"

"No." No fucking way was he letting her leave. "I want you to stay. What do you need?"

A faint hint of a blush colored her cheeks and he couldn't help but hope she needed the same thing he did.

"I just wanted to check and see how you are."

"I'm fine. Not much pain." That might be pushing it a little but it wasn't an outright lie. "A little achy but Dorrie says I'm fine. No sign of infection and no internal bleeding."

She smiled up at him as he led her into the living room, then sat on the couch and pulled her down beside him.

"I'm so glad to hear that." She looked a little less worried than she had when she first saw him.

"I'm sorry you were worried but I'm healing. I'll be back to full strength in no time."

"Are you taking it easy? You won't get better if you don't."

"I'm taking it slow." Again, not an outright lie.

Her smile turned bittersweet. "Yeah, right. You need to take it *easy*, Jesse. Rest. I worry about you."

It was a strange feeling, having someone other than Max worry about him. Strange but satisfying, coming from her. "Have you had any trouble since the other night? Anything at all?"

She shook her head. "No, but then I haven't done anything but work since the last time I saw you. Except for Wednesday night. I went out."

Why did that sound like she'd been out with someone?

Sucking her bottom lip between her teeth, she made his cock hard. "Actually, I went to Shivers."

What the hell? "Did you see Max?"

She paused then nodded. "Didn't he say anything?"

Damn it, no, he hadn't. Why the fuck hadn't Max told him?

Probably because he knew you'd react like a madman.

"I haven't seen him or spoken to him since Wednesday."

Her eyes widened. "What? Why?"

He shrugged, trying not to wince when it pulled sore muscles. "We've been busy."

Apparently Max had been even busier than Jesse had known.

"Are you angry?"

Her voice had softened and lowered and he couldn't help but respond even more.

"No. Not at all."

He was jealous. Kind of. He wasn't jealous of Max. He was jealous of the time Max had spent with her. But right now, he didn't give a fuck because she was here with him.

"You look mad."

He met her beautiful, wary blue eyes. "Sweetheart, how can I be when you're here?"

He'd reached for her before he realized he was going to do it. She was close enough that all he had to do was lean forward a few inches, pull her forward a few inches, and their lips met with a rush of passion.

Heat spread through him like lava, rushed through his body, and lit every cell on fire until he knew the only way to quench it was to get enough of her. Which he wasn't sure was possible in a night. Or a day. Or a week or…ever.

His mother had been addicted to the high. He was addicted to her.

Pulling back, her face still cupped in his hands, he looked into her eyes. Her hands rested on his shoulders, gripping him tight.

"Do you really feel okay?"

"Best I have in days. I'm gonna feel even better in a few minutes."

Her nose crinkled as she frowned. "What happens in a few minutes?"

"You come over here and kiss me again."

Her short dress looked like a long t-shirt, cinched in at the waist by a thin leather belt. It clung to her curves, but the stretchy material should give her enough room to maneuver. But when he tugged her closer, she resisted.

"I don't want to hurt you," she said. "And I'm afraid if I get much closer I will."

"You're not going to hurt me unless you pull away. We'll be careful."

She shook her head but moved a few inches closer. "This isn't why I came here tonight. I just wanted to make sure you were okay."

Ah, but the heat in her eyes contradicted her words.

"I'm more than okay. Trust me, not having you right now will hurt much worse than anything you could do to my wound."

"There's no way we're having sex."

"Then you shouldn't be here. Especially not wearing a dress that gives me such easy access."

Her mouth dropped open, probably because he'd just sounded like a huge prick, but it was the god's honest truth. If she hadn't shown up, he would've continued to miss her like hell but he wouldn't have gone after her. He'd have stayed away because he knew it was for the best.

But now... No fucking way.

"If you don't want this, if you don't want *me*, leave now. No harm, no foul. But, Mally, I am fully capable of sitting on this couch and letting you ride me."

The flush in her cheeks told him she was just as turned on as he was. "I didn't come here for sex. I came to see how you're feeling. I've been worried about you."

He leaned forward and captured her lips for a quick, blistering kiss. "You don't have to worry about me. I'm much tougher than anyone you've ever met."

"Doesn't mean I don't worry."

"I get that." He wove his fingers through her hair, cupping her head and holding her steady so he could stare into her eyes. "But I'm not going anywhere."

He saw the instant she made the decision to trust him. Her lips and her gaze softened and he couldn't wait any longer. He drew her back for another kiss and, this time, he devoured her.

He'd been starving for her for days. Slowly driving himself insane with need and the fear that he'd never see her again. That their lives would never be safe enough for her and they'd lose her.

Right now, he didn't feel like he was losing.

She kissed him back with the same fevered intensity, her fingers combing through his hair to tug him closer. He went willingly, crushing their lips together to get even more of her.

Heat and need consumed him, damn near overwhelmed him to the point that he couldn't think. Couldn't do anything but kiss her and try to get her closer.

Wrapping an arm around her waist, he urged her forward. She let him get only so far but then she resisted.

"Mally. You're not gonna hurt me. Trust me. The only way you will hurt me is if you don't trust me."

She blinked at him. "I trust you."

"Then trust me not to let you hurt me."

Her gaze narrowed. "Are you sure you're not a lawyer?"

"I will be anything you want."

"I only want you."

"I'm right here. Take me."

She paused, their gazes locked for several seconds before she finally straddled his lap, carefully making sure she didn't come into contact with his wound.

That didn't hurt at all. All his pain was centered in his groin. And it would only get worse if she didn't touch him.

But her hands remained on his shoulders so he touched her. Let his hands roam over her body, molding every curve in his palm, soaking in the softness of her skin as his lips explored the sensitive spots behind her ear.

Her breathy groans made his cock throb against the thin covering of his shorts. If they'd been tighter, he swore he would've busted the seams.

And still she clung to his shoulders.

"Mally, honey, touch me."

"I am." She turned her head and nuzzled her nose against his throat.

"No, you're not. Put your hands on me. I swear you're not gonna hurt me."

"Jesse."

"Do you trust me?"

She pulled back to look at him, gaze steady. "Yes."

"Do you want me?"

A nod.

"Then take me, babe. I will sit here and let you do all the work. I swear."

The heat in her eyes finally drowned out the caution and her hands slowly slid from his shoulders to his nipples. She stopped to rub them between her fingers for several seconds, making his lungs struggle to draw in air. Then they stopped working completely as she trailed her fingers over his abs, keeping far away from his wounded side.

Until finally, she traced the outline of his erection through his shorts.

"This looks painful."

He heard a hint of playfulness in her voice now. And a promise.

"It is," he agreed. "But you can make it better."

"Then don't move."

That might hurt worse than anything but Jesse would follow her instructions to the letter. Leaning back into the cushions, he let his hands rest on her hips, trying not to grip her too tightly as she scooted back a few inches so she could have unrestricted access.

She barely touched him at first, trailing her fingers along the waistband of his shorts and raising goosebumps along his skin. His gaze locked on to her breasts, rising and falling at an ever-increasing pace. His hands curled into fists, trying not to reach for her and interfere with her exploration.

He'd let her have whatever she wanted. Do whatever she wanted. Anything at all. As long as she didn't leave.

She took her own sweet time, letting her fingers slide under his shirt to brush against the dark hair on his stomach. She did that for several long seconds before finally slipping her fingers under the waistband and tapping against the tip of his cock.

He responded with a groan, his eyes squeezing shut as she finally wrapped her hand around his cock and squeezed.

"Fuck, Mally."

"Don't. Move."

It took everything he had but he managed to keep still. Or at least he kept still enough for her to continue. She stroked him with a too-soft hold that infuriated and inflamed him. He wanted to thrust into her palm but didn't want her to pull away.

He heard his own breathing, felt his lungs straining for air. When she finally tightened her hand around him, squeezing harder, he groaned.

But he didn't want to spill in her hand.

"Mally."

She lifted her head and stared into his eyes. "Tell me if I hurt you."

"Take me."

"Lift my skirt."

She was wearing a thong that couldn't be more than a few square inches of fabric. "Holy fuck."

Leaning forward, she kissed the words off his lips, rising up slightly and rolling her hips forward to brush her mound against his shaft. "Rip them off."

Hell yes. "We need a condom."

"Side pocket."

She'd come prepared. Thank fuck.

He used one hand to retrieve the condom and, with the other, gripped the tiny string at her hips and tugged. It didn't take much force to do away with the last barrier. He dropped the now-useless scrap on the floor and handed over the condom that she ripped open and rolled onto his shaft in seconds. He barely had time to react to her touch before she shifted her hips and sank down onto his cock.

Her head fell forward as he filled her, her forehead pressed against his. The tight grip of her sex around his cock made every muscle in his body seize, which made his side throb. The pain added another dimension to the sex. One he embraced.

Their breath mingled, her lips so close he swore he felt their imprint on his without contact.

The rhythm she set challenged him at every turn. She challenged him to remain still, challenged him not to grab for her and force her to go faster. Challenged him not to take over.

His cock swelled but he physically reined in his first response. Her expression held so much fierce concentration, he focused on her, determined to let her lead.

Their heavy breathing was the only sound in the room, an erotic soundtrack that included the faint slap of flesh on flesh as she rose up on her knees then dropped back down. The friction threw sparks that lit every nerve ending in his body.

Her slow pace finally got to him and he couldn't not move. He thrust up, sinking deep, and groaned as she fell forward, wrapping her arms around his shoulders.

"God, that feels amazing."

He'd make it even better. He worked one hand between them and used two fingers to work her clit. The sound she made as he played with her made his cock respond with a jerk.

He wasn't going to last much longer. He couldn't.

"Mally. Come, baby. Now."

He felt her pause, felt her suck in a breath. And then she moaned as her sheath clutched at him, drawing his orgasm out of him with a power he couldn't ignore.

It took at least a minute before he could open his eyes again and even longer until Mally's breathing finally returned to normal and she started to stir.

"Did I—"

"I'm fine," Jesse cut her off before she could ask if she'd hurt him. "Everything's fine."

"No, it's not."

"Mal—"

"Don't. Okay? Just don't." She pulled back to look at him, her blue eyes intense. "I know what's going on. I know what you and Max are trying to do and I know why. I just think you're wrong."

Weaving his fingers through her hair, he pulled it away from her face. "Wrong to want you to be safe? Wrong to get our shit in order before—"

He stopped, not sure he wanted to go there. At least, not yet. Not until Max worked through the shit in his head.

"Before what?"

Jesse had no idea how to answer that question.

Max had walked into the house through the garage a little after eight-thirty and headed straight to the liquor cabinet.

He'd thought the frustration and the fear would ease after they'd gotten reassurances from the rest of David Oleksy's former associates that they fully intended to honor their agreement and not interfere with or attack his and Jesse's business interests.

Hell, they should be celebrating. Instead, Max swore his stress level had increased.

Jesse was healing fine. They'd fixed all traces of sabotage. Business was steady and he thought he might have finally found a buyer for the third club. He shouldn't be so tightly wound the slightest thing could set him off.

But he was.

So he went in search of Jesse, who he knew was already home. And found him on the couch with Mally.

His first instinct was to join them. Then the voice in his head started up again.

What the hell is she doing here? We agreed not to see her. Is that why you didn't tell Jesse about last night?

Fuck.

Which was exactly what they were doing. Slowly. Almost carefully, as if Mally didn't want to hurt him. Which of course she didn't. But obviously she wanted Jesse just as much as she'd wanted Max Wednesday night and hadn't been willing to wait any longer to see him.

Should he walk away? Or did he stay and watch? Was he intruding?

No. He knew they wouldn't think that. He knew if he walked in, she'd hold out her hand and he'd wind up with her under or over him, his cock buried deep inside her.

He wanted that. Holy fuck, did he want that.

And then... Tension flared and grabbed him by the throat, making it almost impossible for him to breathe without gasping for air.

Jesse must've heard him because he turned to look in Max's direction.

And when Mally realized that Jesse's attention had shifted, she turned as well.

"Max."

Much like Wednesday night, when she'd ambushed him in his office, she remained fully dressed. If he hadn't caught them in the act, he might've believed she was simply sitting on Jesse's lap.

But he would've been deluding himself.

He was tempted to walk away because he knew if walked into that room, they were going to have to deal with...everything. With the fact that he and Mally had had sex Wednesday and that she and Jesse had had sex today. That they still had issues between them that didn't have resolutions yet.

That basically nothing had changed since they'd sent her away.

"Max, we need to talk."

"This changes nothing. Wednesday night changes nothing."

He shot Jesse a quick look but Jesse's steady expression showed he already knew what'd happened Wednesday night. *Shit.*

Max turned and headed for his office.

"Max, wait!"

No. They had nothing more to discuss. If she and Jesse

wanted to fool around, he couldn't stop them. But Max couldn't—

"Max, goddammit," Jesse yelled from just behind him. "Stop."

Max turned at the bottom of the stairs. Almost exactly where Jesse had been stabbed the other night. The blood had been cleaned from the carpet, but Max didn't need to see it to know exactly where it'd been.

Jesse stood behind, practically right on top of the stain, looking furious.

"Don't."

"We've been through this. I thought we were in agreement."

"We were." Jesse's mouth flattened. "We are. But—"

"I'm not going to wait forever," she said. "I can't."

Max looked over Jesse's shoulder at Mally, standing behind, her hair tousled from Jesse's hands, her lips swollen and her dress falling off one shoulder. Sexy as hell.

And resolute.

"I understand that you're scared, Max. Don't you think I am, too? Don't you think I won't worry every time you're late? Every time you say you're going to call and don't? Don't you think I'm not invested in this relationship at all? Don't you get that I'm putting myself on the line here, too? And I'm twice as likely to get my heart broken. And yet, here I am, waiting for you to see what you're missing. To see that I'm willing to take the chance. What does it say about you that you're not?"

"Mally—"

She held up one hand and cut off Jesse's strangled growl.

"No. I want to hear what Max has to say. I need to hear him say it."

"We already had this conversation." God damn, he sounded cold. "I laid out the situation and you walked out the door."

"Oh, you do not get to lay that on me." Her hands went to her hips. "You practically had your foot on my ass shoving me through that door. Hell, I even understand why. But you've got to let go of the fear that you're going to get me or Jesse hurt. Because if you don't, we can't fix this. And I want to fix this, Max. I'm willing to deal with all the shit that comes from dating two guys. The looks, the whispers, the rude innuendo. Because I'm the one who's going to deal with that shit. Not you and Jesse. You two have to deal with me. But you obviously can't. So you're right. I need to leave and not come back."

No. Just fucking no. That's not what he wanted. And yet he couldn't make his mouth say the right words because he could still see Jesse lying on the floor bleeding. Even though he stood right in front of him now, he couldn't unsee what had happened the other night.

"So...what? You're telling me to put up or shut up?'

"I'm trying to give you *me*."

She didn't shout the words but Max felt like she'd hammered him over the head with them.

She huffed out an unamused laugh. "But I guess I'm not what you want."

"Mally. Stop."

Jesse turned to grab her hand before she could move but she shook her head. "You're a package deal. I knew that from the start. I just wanted to be part of the package."

Then she turned and walked away.

When they finally heard the front door close, Jesse turned to him. Max braced for his fury. What he got was something he'd never seen from Jesse.

Division.

"Get the fuck over yourself, Max. And do it fast. Because if you don't, I'm not going to stand by and watch you throw her away."

"I didn't. But maybe it's for the best. What if Antonoff decides to go after us again and decides the way to do that is through her? We can't keep her locked in the goddamn bedroom. No, you were right from the beginning. We should've never gone after her. She's safer without us."

"That's the coward's way out and you know it."

Jesse's barb struck him dead center and he realized they were faced off like opponents. For as long as he could remember, they'd stood side by side or back to back.

And now there was space between them. A divide he wasn't sure how to close.

How had one small female managed to do so much damage in so short a time?

"It would've happened anyway. You know that. She wouldn't have walked away after six months. That was the arrangement."

Jesse grimaced then shook his head. "You don't have a clue, Max. You're letting history fuck with your head. Your mom—"

"Doesn't have a damn thing to do about this. Mally is nothing like my mother."

Jesse continued to hold his stare. "I know that. But I

don't think you do. And until you figure that out, you've screwed us both."

21

"Mary Alice Dabrowski?"

Mally looked up from her computer, pasting a smile on her face. Didn't want to scare the clients like she'd been scaring everyone else lately.

"Yes? Can I help you?"

"I'm not sure."

The woman standing on the other side of the reception desk didn't return her smile. Actually, the cool blonde had one of those faces. The kind that looked even more beautiful without a smile. Haughty, cool, and total man-bait.

"Well, why don't you tell me why you're here and we'll figure out what you need. Mr. Donovan and Mr. Oleksy aren't—"

"I'm not here to see them." The blonde dismissed the idea with a slight roll of her eyes. "I'm here to see you."

Mally's brow furrowed before she managed to blink away the frown. "I'm sorry. Have we met?"

"No. But we have mutual...acquaintances."

Max and Jesse. Had to be. Just thinking about them made

her heart hurt. They hadn't come after her. The past week had been hell. Getting out of bed was a monumental task for which she deserved a medal.

She'd been dealing but instead of getting better every day, the void in her chest expanded, became a little colder.

She'd forbidden her roommates, her bosses, and her family from mentioning their names. No one knew how to deal with her like this. She felt...lifeless.

She thought she'd been covering it well but she'd noticed, just in the past few days, that she was never alone. Today was the exception. Tristan and Adam had a meeting that required both of them. She was surprised one of her brothers or friends hadn't just "dropped by" for lunch or that her mom hadn't called just to "chat." Even Kat had made it a point to stop by the office three times this week.

And now this woman. Who didn't look at all like she wanted to cheer Mally up.

"That doesn't tell me what I can do for you, Miss..."

"Larisa Antonoff."

Mally's brows rose before she could stop them.

"I see you know who I am."

"I recognize the name, yes. You're Karel Antonoff's daughter."

Larisa's perfect lips curled slightly at the corners. "I am. And you're the woman Jesse and Max tried so hard to be good for."

The disdain in Larisa's voice nearly forced Mally to her feet so she was on the same level as the other woman. But she could never hope to compete with the woman's air of utter cool. And all she'd had to do was mention Jesse and Max to make Mally go from walking dead to furiously alive.

And that *so* wasn't fair.

"I don't know what you're talking about."

"Yes, you do. I also know you don't have the backbone to hold on to them."

Mally saw red as she shot to her feet. "You don't have a clue what you're talking about."

Larisa shrugged. "Yeah, I pretty much do. Max is one of my closest friends. I probably know him better than anyone except Jesse. And I know you're not good for them."

The unrelenting need to scratch out the other woman's eyes was almost impossible for Mally to ignore. "Where do you get off—"

"And I hope you're not so stupid to believe that they're going to come crawling back to you. Because if they do, their former business associates will believe they've gone soft. And that will be so much more detrimental to their interests than you could ever imagine."

"Lady, where the fuck do you get off believing you can talk to me like that?"

Mally shocked herself at the anger that spewed out of her mouth, but she couldn't hold it back anymore. Larisa Antonoff was an entitled bitch who had absolutely no right to stick her nose into Mally's business. Especially not Mally's business with Jesse and Max. Of course, Mally couldn't ignore the fact that Larisa had known the guys for longer than she had and knew them better.

Which just made her that much more pissed off. And upset.

That big black hole in her chest began to fill with pain. Her eyes welled with tears she refused to shed in Larisa's presence. She wanted to go back to her apartment and crawl into bed and cry herself to sleep.

She wanted to be done with them. With this situation. With everyone looking at her like she was fragile.

"Well, look at that. She does get angry. Good to know."

"Lady, you do not want to see me pissed off."

"Am I interrupting something?"

Mally swung her head toward the door and found her brother Jason standing there. Dressed in his uniform, he looked imposing. Larisa gave him a once-over and immediately dismissed him.

"No, I was just leaving." Larisa gave Mally a slight smile. "Have a good day, Mary Alice."

Then she left, as if she hadn't just blown apart the safe little bubble Mally had been living in for the past week.

Damn her. She'd had no right—

"Mal."

Jason's voice snapped her out of her head. He'd used his cop voice on her and that pissed her off even more.

"What?"

Her tone held a sharp edge that made Jason's gaze narrow.

"Are you okay?"

"Yeah. I am. And I'm sick of everyone asking me if I'm okay."

"Then act like it."

She sucked in a breath to tell him to go to hell... And realized he was right. Not that she had to tell him that.

"What are you doing here? Is something wrong?"

"I'm checking up on you. And before you have a conniption, be glad it's me and not Dad. But you can't keep putting

Mom and Dad off or they will show up on your doorstep. Now, tell me what the hell happened before I find an excuse to throw those two assholes in jail."

"You won't lay a hand on either of them." She shook her finger at her brother. "I've decided I'm over them." Well, not really but she was done having her life disrupted by them. Just...done. "Time to move on. And I know exactly how to do that."

His gaze narrowed. "Why don't I like the sound of that?"

She gave Jase a look that made his eyebrows rise.

"Because you're male and you should be afraid."

***

Max woke with a shout strangled in his throat.

"Fuck."

Throwing his feet over the edge of the couch, where he'd fallen asleep, he set his elbows on his knees and tried to steady his breathing.

Damn, he hadn't had that one in a while.

"You okay?"

His head shot up and he saw Jesse sitting on the recliner across from him.

"Why aren't you in bed?"

Jesse shrugged. "Because I know when you wake up like this, you hate being alone. Nightmare?"

He didn't bother lying. Jesse knew him too well.

"Old one. Don't know why—"

"Bullshit." Jesse cut him off with one quiet word.

Max wanted to be pissed. Knew he couldn't because Jesse was right.

"It was about that night."

"I'm assuming it was the nightmare where you don't get there in time."

"Yeah."

"You know why you're having that dream, right?"

Max gave Jesse the finger. "So now you're a psychiatrist?"

Jesse didn't respond to his dig. "You know you need to talk to her, right?"

Yeah, it'd been too damn long. And surprisingly, he wanted to.

Jesse didn't wait for him to answer. "So get a shower and we'll drive over."

"I should call first."

"You know you don't have to. And you know you should talk to her face-to-face. Come on, Max. Let's just go."

An hour later, Max stood at a familiar door, waiting for it to open to his knock.

And when it did, the shock on the woman's face nearly made him turn and leave.

But then she grinned and she looked so happy to see him, Max wanted to kick himself.

"Max! It's so good to see you." Then she frowned. "Is everything okay?" She looked him over from head to toe before her gaze darted back to his face. "Are you okay? Is Jesse—"

"I'm fine. We're fine." He pointed over his shoulder, where Jesse waited a few feet behind him. "I just...need to talk to you, Mom."

Slightly overweight and several inches shorter than Max, Miranda Kurowski threw open the door of the house Max had bought for her years ago.

"Come on in." Then she smiled over his shoulder. "Jesse, how are you?"

"I'm fine, Miri, thanks."

"Good. Come on into the kitchen. Have you eaten breakfast yet? Do you want something?"

"We're fine, Mom."

"I made scones yesterday. I know Jesse likes my scones. Come have some coffee."

As his mother bustled around the kitchen of her two-story Cape Cod in Bryn Mawr and Jesse kept up a steady stream of small talk, Max tried to get his jumbled thoughts into order.

And finally he couldn't help but simply blurt out his question.

"Was I right, Mom? Did I do the right thing for you? Or was I a judgmental asshole for not even talking to you about the situation before I took over?"

Jesse and his mom exchanged a look but she quickly turned her attention to Max as she reached across the counter to take his hand.

"We never really talked much about that day, did we? We just let it...go. That was a mistake I didn't know how to fix."

"I'm not sure I could have back then. I wasn't exactly rational after what'd happened."

"You mean after Jimmy nearly beat me to death." Her smile held so much sadness, and Max could've kicked himself for dredging up this old pain again. "You were eighteen, Max. You went to work for a Russian mobster so you'd have the money to get us out. Did you think I didn't know that back then? Even as screwed up as I was, I knew what you were doing. And I was terrified. Of Jimmy. Of losing you.

And I still stayed with him. So, am I mad at you for dragging me out of that house, kicking and screaming, away from the man who'd abused us for years? No, baby. Not even a little. I just wish I'd been strong enough to walk away by myself."

"He would've killed you, Mom."

She nodded. "Eventually. I know that now. But I was ashamed of myself. Ashamed that you had to save me when I should've been doing everything in my power to make sure you were safe. I've never been ashamed of you, Max. I couldn't be."

"I could've handled it differently. I took away your choice, Mom. I forced you—"

"Away from a man who would've ended up killing both of us. And my only excuse is that I thought I loved him and that he loved me and that ''til death do us part' shit in the marriage vows doesn't actually mean he gets to beat you to death. You were never the bad guy in that nightmare. You were the hero."

Max nodded, feeling an old knot in his chest slowly unraveling. His mom tapped her fingers on his clenched fist, narrowing his focus back to her again.

"Now...what's going on?" His mom looked from him to Jesse and back again. "Did something happen?"

What the hell did he say? That their past had turned him into a jackass who'd pushed away the one woman perfect for him and Jesse?

He exchanged a glance with Jesse, who raised his eyebrows as he stuffed another scone in his mouth.

Then he took a deep breath. "So we met this girl..."

22

"Well, damn. Is that like a giant goddamn sign or what?"

Jesse stopped beside Max, standing with his arms crossed, staring at the bank of surveillance monitors in Shivers' security room.

"She's here with friends."

"They could've gone to another club." Jesse rested his hands on his hips, feeling no pain from his wound. He hadn't for the past couple of days. "And yet here they are."

"Maybe she wants us to see she's moved on."

"Or maybe fate is handing her to us on a plate."

Jesse had never believed in fate. Life was what you made it. You had to go after what you wanted. Jesse wanted Mally. Max wanted Mally.

And after Max had spoken to his mom, Jesse had thought they were back on track.

But another two days had passed and Max had avoided the discussion. Now, there was no way Jesse was letting him avoid it anymore.

But Max was right. She hadn't asked for them and she looked completely focused on having a good time with her friends. Dancing, laughing, drinking... Though Jesse was pretty sure that was soda in her glass.

"I'm done waiting," Jesse said.

Max stiffened beside him, sucking in a rough breath. "I know."

"So...do we do this together or are you seriously going to give up the one woman who's made for us?"

Max looked at him, but the anger Jesse expected from him wasn't there. Instead, he saw heat in Max's eyes.

"You think we should just walk out there and throw her over my shoulder? And expect her not to put up a fight or call the cops or her brothers on us?"

"I think we should walk out there and beg her to take us back because I'm pretty sure the caveman routine will send her running for the doors."

"And if she tells us to fuck off?"

Jesse shrugged that off. "Then tomorrow we try something different. And the next day and the next until we wear her down. Hell, I'm ready to beg if it comes to it."

Max's mouth quirked into a grin that made Jesse want to breathe a sigh of relief. "Then I guess we better prepare to grovel and do it with a smile because she's not going to let us off the hook that easily."

"We've had to fight for everything else." Jesse grinned back. "Why would our woman would be any different?"

Mally had almost begged her friends not to come to Shivers tonight.

They'd been talking about where they wanted to go on the rare night they all had off and Bethann had kept raving about this place. Of course, everyone had wanted to come here.

No one but Izzy knew that Max and Jesse owned this place or about Mally's connection to the men.

They only knew she'd been seeing someone and she'd walked away and she'd been telling them for a week that she was over them. She almost had herself convinced. And then the little voice in the back of her head laughed hysterically.

Luckily her friends had bought her story and she couldn't say no when they'd told her she had to come out with them.

"Stop thinking so much, Mally," Izzy yelled at her over the throbbing house music. "We're here to have fun, unwind. The least you could do is try."

Mally, Izzy, Damaris, Bethann, and Bethann's older twin stepsisters, who looked like freaking fashion models, had commandeered a small table away from the crowded dance floor. Mally had been trying not to bring everyone's mood down. But really, all she wanted to do was sit and sulk in the corner and keep an eye out for the two men she wanted to magically appear and whisk her into the back office where they'd tell her they couldn't live without her and they'd been pricks to let her go.

And again, that little voice laughed.

"I'm not thinking." At least, she wasn't trying to. "The music's kinda loud and I'm getting a headache."

"Oh no you're not." Then Izzy grimaced and leaned closer. "I'm sorry. This place was a bad idea. It's just that when Bethann suggested it, she was so gung-ho and then Damaris jumped on and they know I've been here a few times and really loved it so I was worried if I tried to talk them out of it, I'd have to explain why and I wasn't sure if you'd want me to."

All of which made sense. She hadn't told any of her other friends about Max and Jesse. Hadn't quite known how. Bethann might've put two and two together about her fiancé's gambling issue and then it would've become a thing.

"I'm fine. Seriously." Mally had to lean close for Izzy to hear her while the others were out on the dance floor. "Maybe it's a little soon after…everything happened. And yeah, it's kinda hard not to think about them while I'm here."

"Then maybe you should go find a guy out on the floor and have a little fun and forget them!"

The idea was so repugnant, she shook her head before she could stop herself.

"No way. I'm not ready."

Izzy's gaze drifted over her shoulder toward the dance floor for a second before darting back, brows raised. "So I guess I should tell the two men approaching the table to back off?"

Mally rolled her eyes and deliberately didn't look over her shoulder. "God, I do *not* want to deal with more testosterone today. Men are totally off-limits."

A lull in the music meant her voice sounded a little louder than she'd meant and she groaned. But if it meant these men would leave her alone, she didn't really care.

"Ms. Dabrowski. We'd like to have a word."

Mally blinked. Was that…

She sat up a little straighter, shooting Izzy a glare that

her friend answered with an apologetic shrug and a hopeful light in her eyes. Her heart began to pound out a faster rhythm than the current song, and she froze for several seconds before taking a deep breath and turning.

Max and Jesse stood only inches away. They were dressed for business, both in dark suits and white shirts. Max wore a tie that he'd loosened. Jesse had no tie. Both of them looked good enough to eat.

Mally blinked back sudden tears. It *so* wasn't fair. She wanted to be angry with them, wanted to send them away with a pissy comment or even just ignore them. She couldn't do it.

"I don't think we have anything left to say."

"We do." Max held out his hand. "Come back to our office and hear us out."

Her heart actually hurt but she knew if she went with them and all they wanted was to find out how she was feeling... That would make everything so much worse.

Jesse and Max exchanged a glance then Jesse stepped forward, holding out his hand as well.

"What are you doing?" Her voice sounded like a squeaky toy and she couldn't believe they heard her over the music.

"We're staking our claim," Max said.

She swore her heart stopped beating for several seconds before resuming at heart-attack speed. "And what's changed since the last time we saw each other?"

Jesse and Max exchanged a quick glance before Max took a deep breath. "Nothing. Except for the fact that I don't want to live without you."

Mally felt like Max had hit her over the head with a silly stick, but they'd hurt her so badly, she wasn't sure she knew how to respond. She wanted to take their hands, wanted to let them stake their claim. But...

"Did something happen?" Oh god, had someone tried to hurt them again? She jumped off the low couch she'd been sitting on and took a good look at them. "Were you hurt?"

"We're fine, Mally."

Jesse took another step closer and put his hands on her forearms. The heat of his skin seeped into hers and made her want so much more skin-on-skin contact.

Then Max closed the rest of the distance between them and put his hand on her shoulder.

"Come into the back with us. We need to talk."

Hope made her turn to grab her purse, which Izzy helpfully held out with a smile before she gave a private thumbs-up.

Then she allowed them to lead her into the back. She didn't stop to tell her other friends, though she caught sight of Damaris staring at her with wide eyes from across the dance floor. Izzy would take care of that.

With the noise from the club dampened as soon as they stepped into the office area, she turned to face them...and nearly smacked face first into Max's chest.

Looking up in to his eyes, she saw heat and desire and yearning. It was the yearning that made her weak in the knees.

And when he grabbed her shoulders to hold her steady, she felt Jesse put his hands on her hips and step closer until his chest was flat against her back.

Caught between them, she couldn't think of anywhere else she'd rather be.

"I think we should take this somewhere more private."

Max's low voice stoked her desire even higher. She wanted to say yes and please and now.

But first...

"If you're not going to tell me you've changed your mind then I'm not going any farther. You can't just keep—"

She cut off as Max dropped his mouth on hers and kissed her so hard and so deep, she couldn't think straight much less push him away.

Her brain tried to count all the implications in that kiss but only came up with one that mattered.

"We intend to keep you, Mally. Right here." Max drew back just far enough to be able to look her in the eyes. "Come home with us and I will get on my knees and beg for forgiveness. And while I'm down there, I will lick you until you come so damn hard, you can't leave. And when I'm done, Jesse and I will fuck you until you won't ever think of leaving."

She swallowed so hard, she swore they could hear her out in the club. "Not fair."

Max nodded. "You're absolutely right. I didn't treat you fairly. I let all the shit in my head get between us. I let you down and Jesse nearly lost you, too."

"And, babe." Jesse spoke directly into her ear from behind, making her shiver. "I don't plan to lose you again so you can be damn sure I will keep him in line."

Could she trust them? Or would they break her heart again? She didn't know if her heart would survive another break if they didn't come through this time.

But did she really have a choice?

Yes, she did. But when it came to these two, she knew any choice she made would always include them.

"Let's go home."

—

Max barely had the door shut behind them when Mally stopped in the front room and turned to him with that look on her face. The one that let him know she wanted to talk.

"So are you— Oh!"

Jesse grabbed her by the hips, lifted her against him and kissed her. Mally's purse dropped to the floor as she wrapped her arms around Jesse's shoulders and stepped into his body.

Max smiled because he would've done the same thing if he'd been closer. He didn't want to talk. He wanted to show her.

As Jesse steered her toward the bedroom, Max locked up and set the alarms, triple checking them to be sure. He'd probably never have enough security to keep her safe, but he'd come to terms with the fact that there were just some things he couldn't control.

Having Mally in their life was one thing he could.

In the bedroom, he found Jesse and Mally already on the bed. Jesse had stripped her and her beautiful body gleamed against the dark sheets, hair already a messy fan across the pillows.

Jesse had his mouth on her breasts, kissing his way between each tip before he latched on to one, making her back bow and her hands sink into his hair.

Leaning back against the doorframe, Max watched as Jesse made her moan, made her writhe beneath him. Jesse had only gotten his shirt off before he'd started on her. The bandage on his side was a stark reminder that he wasn't completely healed yet.

And he still wore his pants, which made the scene that much more erotic. Max couldn't blame Jesse for wanting to hurry. But Max didn't want to rush. He planned on having a hell of a long time with her.

But first he had to make sure she understood.

He walked to the bed, saw her eyes open as Jesse trailed his lips down the center of her body, kissing each rib as he passed.

Her gaze caught his as he began to strip, dropping pieces of clothing along the floor as he made his way to her. She reached for him, fingers outstretched. He dropped his boxers and twined their fingers together.

Jesse moved farther down her body, his mouth moving to her hip and nipping.

"Max."

"I need you to listen, Mally. And hear me."

She swallowed hard and nodded, her beautiful breasts quivering as her lungs worked overtime.

"I'm sorry. I was an ass and I let my own shit get between us. I hurt you and that's unacceptable."

Jesse moved his mouth from her hip to her mound before pulling back and sliding his hands under her hips, making her suck in a deep breath. Her eyelids fluttered as she waited for Jesse to move. But Jesse was waiting for Max.

"I want you to forgive me. But I want to make it up to you first. *We* want to make it up to you."

"Although I gotta say, it's mostly his fault."

Jesse's dry comment made her huff out a soft laugh but it didn't do anything to release the tension in her body.

"He's right. It is."

Max leaned forward to kiss her, letting his free hand play with her breasts. She met his lips eagerly, opened her mouth to him, and let his tongue tangle with hers. Her fingers tightened around his, tugging him even closer.

"I forgive you."

"Thank you, sweetheart. I can't promise that I won't ever hurt you again. I'm gonna screw up again."

"So will I," Jesse added. "And we know it's gonna be tough for you, being with both of us. But we'll try to keep you so satisfied, you won't remember you're mad at us."

Then Jesse dipped his head and put his mouth over her sex and proceeded to make her cry out.

Max watched Jesse pleasure her, working her higher then easing her down then ramping up again. His cock throbbed, his balls tight as he waited, watched. Saw her body tighten and the flush that went from her cheeks down to her thighs as she came around Jessie's tongue.

Before she came down, he rolled on a condom then slid onto the bed beside her, rolling her on top of him. He urged her legs to spread across his thighs, making her moan and squirm, trying to get his cock where she needed it.

He was so hard, he had to help her, angling his cock up so she could slide down onto him. Damn, she was wet. And tight. So damn tight. With breathy sighs that made desire heat every cell of his body, she rolled her hips and took him deep. Pushing up with her hands by his shoulders, she started a jerky but totally erotic rhythm that put him closer to the edge than he wanted to be.

"Slow down, sweetheart." Jesse grabbed her hips,

slowing her down as he maneuvered between her legs. "I want to join you."

"Then hurry up."

Max barely heard her but Jesse obviously had because he groaned as he dribbled lube between her ass cheeks then slowly began to ease inside.

Mally's head fell forward as Max tried to stay still until Jesse was all the way in.

"Max."

"Hang on, baby."

"Jesse, please."

"Fuck." Jesse's low growl made every muscle in Max's body tense, and his cock pulsed in anticipation. "God damn, move. Now."

Max released his self-imposed restraints and started a wicked rhythm. He and Jesse made sure everything they did added to her pleasure, made her shiver and shake and cry out.

They held on long enough to make her break again. Max felt her moan as her orgasm shook her body, clamping around them and pulling them along with her.

Jesse fell to the side, breathing so loud Max could hear him over his own ragged breathing.

"Mally."

Jesse curled around her from behind, pulling her into the curve of his body and shoving her forward until she pressed against Max's side and laid her arm across his waist.

"Hmm."

"I love you. I think I have since the moment I saw you."

Before she could say anything, Jesse wove his fingers

through her hair and pulled her head back so he could kiss her throat.

"Ditto, babe. Love you."

She breathed against his chest in uneven bursts, her fingers digging into his shoulder.

"I never thought…" She stopped then reached behind her to clutch at Jesse's shoulder and then to tug Max even closer. "I have no idea how this is supposed to work. I never thought I'd be in love with two men but I am. And I'm not giving you up. You both need to realize that."

"I never plan to." Jesse looked over her shoulder at Max, a promise in his eyes. "We won't."

"Agreed." Max grabbed her hand and pressed a kiss to her palm. "We're in this together. Forever."

But wait! There's more. Check out Dorrie's story in An Indecent Longing

ALSO BY STEPHANIE JULIAN

WICKED & CHARMING

Seducing Whitney

Claiming Ellie

Sharing Brianna

INDECENT

An Indecent Proposition

An Indecent Affair

An Indecent Arrangement

An Indecent Longing

An Indecent Desire

SALON GAMES

Invite Me In

Reserve My Nights

Expose My Desire

Keep My Secrets

Rock My Heart

FAST ICE

Bylines & Blue Lines

Hard Lines & Goal Lines

Deadlines & Red Lines

REDTAILS HOCKEY

The Brick Wall

The Grinder

The Enforcer

The Instigator

The Playboy

The D-Man

The Machine

LOVERS UNDERCOVER

Lovers & Lies

Sinners & Secrets

Beauty & Brains

Thieves & Thrills

FORGOTTEN GODDESSES

What A Goddess Wants

How to Worship A Goddess

When A Goddess Falls

Where A Goddess Belongs

DARKLY ENCHANTED

Spell Bound

Moon Bound

MAGICAL SEDUCTION

Seduced by Magic

Seduced in Shadow

Seduced & Ensnared

Seduced & Enchanted

Seduced by Chaos

Seduced by Danger

Moonlight Seduction

LUCANI LOVERS

Kiss of Moonlight

Visions of Moonlight

Edge of Moonlight

Temptation in Moonlight

Grace in Moonlight

Shades of Moonlight

ABOUT THE AUTHOR

Stephanie Julian is a USA Today and New York Times best-selling author of contemporary romance and romantasy.